MW00628833

# Three Dumb

Wheelin' & Dealin'

Book Three in the Val Fremden Midlife Mystery Series

Margaret Lashley

# Copyright 2017 Margaret Lashley

For more information, write to: Zazzy Ideas, Inc. P.O. Box 1113, St. Petersburg, FL 33731

# What Readers are Saying about Three Dumb:

"The action, and the emotion, in this story start on the first page, and it just builds and builds."

"An intelligent whirlwind of girlfriend talk and crisis management from a motley crew who live off the beaten track."

"A laugh riot all the way through."

"Perfect to pop into your beach bag when you need something light and humorous to read while keeping your brain cells still powered on."

"If you like absolutely off-the-wall characters and situations mixed with a good dose of really sound life advice wrapped up in a cozy mystery (without one dead body so far) this is the series for you."

"This series has a way of making you take a look at your own life, friends and family. It's hard not to relate to Val and the people in her life."

"A middle-aged woman finds truths that we all have had to find, and she does it with humor and grace. The book is filled with the best one liners and I found myself highlighting several profound insights."

"If you are looking for entertaining adventures, a story filled with colorful characters, and a book you cannot stop reading, get this book. Its "true to life" wisdom is touching and will make you see yourself in a new way."

# More Val Fremden Midlife Mysteries

by Margaret Lashley

Absolute Zero
Glad One
Two Crazy
Three Dumb
What Four
Five Oh
Six Tricks
Seven Daze
Figure Eight
Cloud Nine

*"They say three's the charm. But charming isn't my style."*

Val Fremden

# Chapter One

"How could you do it, Tom?"

I stared into the sea-green eyes of Lieutenant Thomas Foreman, my cop boyfriend. He was in the kitchen drying dishes, as happy as a clam on Prozac. He'd just pulled off a surprise 49th birthday party for me right under my nose, and was swaggering in self-pride about it.

The festivities had ended just a moment ago, when Laverne, my next-door neighbor and former Vegas showgirl, finally took the hint and wobbled back over to her place on those stork legs of hers. It hadn't been easy to convince her it was time to go. I'd changed into my pajamas, tidied the couch cushions around her, took the wineglass from her hand, and, when all that failed, resorted to yawning in her face. Laverne never was one for subtlety.

Tom raised a blond eyebrow on his smug, unforgivably handsome face. "Val, with you on my case, keeping the party under wraps was no piece of cake."

He winked and grabbed a glass from the kitchen drain board. His lip curled into a satisfied smile as he wiped the glass dry with a dishcloth, oblivious to my growing rage. I crossed my arms and planted my feet. My mind was made up. I had a right to be pissed, and no one was going to take that away from me.

"I would hope not, Tom," I hissed, "as it probably involved forgery on your part."

Tom blanched and looked up, surprised at my anger. "Wait a second. You're not talking about *the party?*"

"No! I'm talking about selling my mother's RV—*without even asking me!*"

"Oh...*that*."

Tom grinned at his own cleverness. He obviously didn't realize how close he was to being strangled to death with that darn dishtowel.

"Well, that *was* the tricky part, Val. And you almost caught me. I had to rifle through your silly shoebox filing system to find the title to it. It was still registered in Glad's name, but I signed it over. Seeing as she's dead, I didn't think she'd mind."

"Arrgh! Tom, I didn't mean, '*How did you do it logistically*.' I meant, 'How could you do it *at all?*' The Minnie Winnie was *mine*. My mother's. It was...."

Tom dropped the cloth on the counter and folded his arms over his chest, mirroring mine.

"It was a piece of junk, Val. I traded it for the tiki hut. I don't know why you're so angry. If you ask me, you got the better half of the deal."

I raised my hands in frustration. "You still don't get it. It was *all I had left* of Glad besides the piggybank with her ashes. And Tom, the piggybank was *inside the RV*."

Tom's face drooped. His arms fell limp to his sides. "Oh. I...I didn't know."

"Well, now you *do*. Why couldn't you have just asked me first?"

Tom bit his lower lip and scrunched his nose. "I don't know. It sounds lame *now*, Val. But it would have spoiled the surprise."

"And *avoided* this one."

Hot, angry tears rimmed my eyes. Tom winced sympathetically and put his arms around me.

"I'm sorry, Val. But how in the world did Glad's piggybank end up in the RV anyhow?"

I thought back to the drunken night a week and a half ago, when my imagination and half a bottle of gin had convinced me that Tom and my best friend Milly were having an affair. I'd spent a lost night in the old RV, commiserating with my mother's spirit as she'd stared back at me, wise and all-knowing, through a plastic, holographic monocle....

My face flushed. I jerked away from Tom's arms.

"Look. I don't have to explain myself to you, Tom. What I *need now* is to know where I can find the RV and get Glad back."

Tom took a step backward and showed me his open palms. "Okay! Take it easy! A buddy at work gave me the name of a junk dealer out in Pinellas Park. I've got his card around here somewhere."

Tom's eyes scanned the kitchen counter for the card, then his face registered a thought. He reached toward his right butt cheek and pulled his wallet out of the back pocket of his jeans.

"Tom, I know you meant well. I don't mean to sound ungrateful. I mean, what you did with the backyard...the makeover...it's beautiful. But I'm so mad at you right now I have half a mind to charge you with grand theft."

Tom's tan, clean-shaven face lost the remainder of its usually good-natured, boyish charm.

"So that's the thanks I get. Nice one, Val. You know, I put up with a lot from you, but tonight takes the cake. I tell you 'I love you,' and you return the favor by telling me you're going to have me arrested. Not an even swap."

A pang of remorse hurtled toward my heart. I knocked it away with a baseball bat.

"Well, neither was you're swapping my mother's RV for a blasted tiki hut!"

Tom pulled a business card from his wallet and tossed it on the kitchen counter. "I guess it's true what they say. No good deed goes unpunished."

Tom glared at me and pursed his lips. He shook his head and marched out the front door, slamming it behind him. I waited until I heard the engine start and his SUV drive away before I picked up the card. Maybe I should have felt guilty. After all, Tom truly *had* meant well. But not a single speck of slithering guilt dared crawl near enough to be scalded by my boiling anger. Not *this* time. I was tired of always paying the tab for others good-intentioned misdeeds.

*Why did everything nice have to come with a crap-smeared string attached?*

I looked down at the business card. It read, "Lefty's Hauling: We make your troubles disappear!" The bitter irony forced a puff of jaded air through my pinched lips. It was 11 p.m. on a Saturday night. I took a chance and called the number. No one answered. The card stated the business was closed on Sundays. It seemed I was going to have to wait.

Something I was definitely no good at.

# Chapter Two

I idled away Sunday morning swinging in my new hammock, going back and forth as to whether I should call Tom and apologize or call Tom and rip him a new one. I should have been ecstatic. Tom had just told me he loved me for the very first time. I'd been contemplating whether to say it back to him when I'd been blindsided by the news he'd gone and traded away my mother for a thatched-roof shack.

*How could the man have been so insensitive?*

I scowled and looked across the freshly landscaped backyard. It was so gorgeous I nearly forgave Tom again. The comfy, macramé hammock I was swaying in was tied between two palm trees, offering a beautiful view of the sparkling Intracoastal Waterway. A set of six floral-cushioned lawn chairs formed a ring around a circular fire pit made of terracotta-hued pavers. Even the traitorous tiki hut was charming, with its shaggy, conical roof of woven palm fronds.

It was all so beautiful—and in need of a lifetime of constant maintenance.

By 9 a.m., the newly installed plants had already begun to wither in the tropical heat of the sixth day of May. I got out my old garden hose and spent the second half of the morning watering the freshly planted lantana bushes, canna lilies, pygmy date palms and St. Augustine grass. To save work, I took a quick trip to the little Ace Hardware store on Boca Ciega and bought a sprinkler to irrigate the neat swath of newly lain lawn.

In the backyard back home, an itchy irritability began to crawl across my brain. Sweat dripped off my chin as I stood in the glaring sun and fiddled with the new sprinkler. I adjusted the angle to 45 degrees and turned on the tap.

Before I could say, “Oh crap!” the hose swelled up like a pregnant snake and blew the sprinkler off the end like a bottle rocket. It slammed into my shin, prompting me to scream my entire repertoire of cuss words and dance the one-legged hip-hop. While I was performing my one-woman show, the garden hose, like a heckler in the audience, curled itself upward, and, with deadly accuracy, shot a stream of cold water into my obscenity-hurling face. Given the horrid heat, it should have cooled me off. But the cold blast only managed to refresh my seething anger at Tom.

*This new landscaping is the gift that keeps on giving. As in giving me more ways to sweat my freaking butt off! Thanks a* lot, *Tom!*

Soaked to the skin, I gave up and lay back down in the hammock. My clothes were just beginning to dry and my temper to cool when that freaking jerk Guilty Conscience showed up and tried to convince me that maybe *I* had been the insensitive one.

*Had I been wrong to grouse about Tom's beautiful and probably darn-expensive birthday gift?*

I gave my unwanted visitor an angry glare and a couple of Tanqueray and tonics. The second TNT, along with a Southern dollop of self-righteousness, had just begun to loosen guilt's whiny stranglehold on me when I heard a familiar voice call my name.

“Val?”

*So much for enjoying the tranquility of my new backyard....*

*Oh geez! Maybe I really* am *being an ungrateful sourpuss!*

I took a tentative peek out of the hammock at the nosey, long-legged, horse-faced old woman in a gold bikini.

“Hi, Laverne.”

Those two little words transformed Laverne's hesitant stare into a big grin. She waved at me with ridiculous, child-like enthusiasm.

"Hiya, sugar! Wasn't sure if that was you or a hobo. That was a nice party last night. Were you surprised?"

I sat up in the hammock and smiled despite my lousy mood. Laverne had been cutting roses in her backyard. She had a handful of blooms in one hand, a clipper in the other. Her strawberry blonde curls peeked out from under a floppy white hat tied with a gold ribbon. Her boobs hung halfway to her navel, supported by two small, triangular patches of gold fabric attached to a pair of dangerously thin strings that didn't look up to the task.

*This is the side of Florida no one warns you about.*

"Yes, I actually *was* surprised," I said.

Laverne shot me a sly grin. "So...looks like Tom wasn't boinkin' Milly after all."

I studied Laverne's face with new intensity. She wasn't as dumb as she looked.

"No. You were right. But you knew all along, didn't you?"

Laverne winked and showed me her perfect, pearly dentures. "Like I've said before, growing up in Vegas, I learned how to keep a secret. Have you had any lunch yet, sugar?"

I held up my empty glass. "Does Tanqueray count?"

"Only in Vegas. How about joining me for a Skinny Dip?"

The thought made me lose my appetite. "Uh...no thanks."

"Come on. I've got chicken cacciatore and veggie lasagna. Only 300 calories each. I hate to eat alone."

"Oh. Um...okay."

"Good girl! I'll break out the microwave!"

I crawled out of the hammock, walked past the fire pit and straddled the low picket fence separating Laverne's and my backyards. With a liver-spotted hand spiked with long, red gel nails, Laverne ushered me into her home-sweet-home-away-from-Vegas. I looked up at the red acrylic clock made of dice mounted on the wall above her white Formica kitchen cabinets. It was already half-past the white cube with a one on it.

"I didn't realize it was so late," I said.

"I got used to eating lunch late, in-between show times," Laverne replied. "Funny, it's been thirty years since I last kicked a leg up on stage. Seems like not more than three or four decades ago."

In the short time I'd known her, I'd learned better than to try to improve Laverne's math skills. I shrugged in agreement, took a seat on a barstool and watched as she fished around in the freezer and pulled out two small, rectangular cartons.

"Yeah. Time flies, Laverne."

"It sure does. Pick your poison."

Laverne held up two blue-and-white boxes labeled Skinny Dip Cuisine. One had a picture of chicken cacciatore, complete with mint sprig. The image of a gooey, delicious-looking hunk of lasagna was displayed on the other.

"I'll have the lasagna, thanks."

"One lasagna, coming up!"

Laverne popped the whole, unopened carton into the microwave and set the timer for five minutes. I kept my mouth shut as the oven hummed. The off-centered box circled around lopsided, catching corners and shifting around haphazardly like a drunken sailor on a merry-go-round.

"Speaking of time, sugar, what are you going to do with yourself now that you're all settled into your house?"

"I don't know. Water my new lawn, I guess."

"Gosh, it sure is pretty. Tea?"

"Sure. Thanks."

I looked over and grimaced. Unwittingly, I'd chosen a front-row seat to the shriveled-butt-cheeks show, starring Laverne Cowens. She bent over in front of me and pulled a pitcher out of the fridge. *They really should put an age limit on thong bikinis.*

The microwave dinged. Laverne sprang into action like a trained chimp. She flung open a drawer and grabbed a lime-green oven mitt with a clown's face on it, probably lifted from Circus-Circus. She shoved it onto her right hand, then reached into the microwave and yanked the swollen, slightly charred carton of lasagna out onto the counter. A second later, she placed the luckless box of chicken cacciatore in the oven, clicked the door shut and pushed the button, setting off the next carousel ride of the doomed.

"You should take a class down at the college, like I do."

Laverne yanked off the oven mitt and poured tea into two tall, thin glasses. Each had the words "El Cortez Casino" etched in red above a fan of colorful playing cards.

"Really? What classes have you taken?"

She handed me a glass of tea. I took a sip.

Laverne straightened her shoulders proudly. "Well, I don't mean to brag, but I just finished a cooking course on international cuisine."

Brown liquid invaded my lungs, making it impossible to breathe. I tried to cough up the tea with my mouth closed. My effort resulted in a deep, rattling howl reminiscent of an asthmatic dog trapped in a well.

"Oh my goodness, honey! Are you all right?"

"Yes, just...drank...wrong."

The bell on the microwave tolled, announcing the death of another Skinny Dip. Laverne turned her attention to the seared carton. She pulled it from the microwave, stabbed through one end of it with a knife and cussed like a sailor when steam shot out and turned her index finger as pink as bubblegum. I smirked, despite my close brush with a Lipton-inspired death. Laverne sucked her index finger as she sawed open one end of each carton with a knife, then dumped the two cardboard meal trays onto the counter.

A disconcerting shiver went up my spine at the delighted gleam in Laverne's eye as she wielded the knife like Norman Bates in a shower and popped the bulging, clear-plastic blisters covering the paper trays. Satisfied with her work, Laverne plopped the meal that was supposed to be lasagna on the counter in front of me. It appeared to have been pre-chewed for my dining convenience.

"Can you believe it? Only 300 calories!" Laverne exclaimed.

She sidled onto the stool next to me, still wearing nothing but that gold thong bikini. One glance at her dinner made me grateful I'd opted for the lasagna. The chicken cacciatore looked as if it had been scooped up from a local vomitorium. Thankfully, the portions were miniscule. I took a bite of lasagna. It tasted better than it looked, but that wasn't saying much.

"This isn't bad," I said. "But really, there must be like, *two tablespoons* of food here, Laverne. For 300 calories, you could eat two tablespoons of *anything*."

Laverne grinned, wide-eyed and goofy as a child. "I know, right? Isn't it amazing?"

My first prick hadn't burst Laverne's bubble. I decided to not be a prick by taking another poke. Instead, I took the second, and final bite of my lasagna. *Crap. I could have eaten a Mounds bar for 300 calories.* I sighed. Then I lied.

"That was delicious Laverne. Thanks."

Laverne studied my face, her head cocked sideways like a confused Rhesus monkey. A square-ish piece of carrot from her cacciatore clung to her long chin like Picasso's interpretation of a witch's wart. Despite the appearance of lacking sophisticated cognitive faculties, Laverne had picked up on my lack of enthusiasm.

"What's wrong, sugar? I thought you'd be happier about your party and your birthday surprise."

My shoulders drooped. "Oh. I'm sorry, Laverne. Does it show?"

Laverne's drawn-on eyebrows arched. "Like a black bra through a wet T-shirt."

I slumped on my stool. "Crap. I don't mean to be ungrateful, but that new backyard is going to take a lot of maintenance. That's work *I'm* stuck doing. And did you know? Tom sold my RV without asking me."

Laverne shrugged. "Yeah. So?"

"The Mr. Peanut bank...*it was in the RV*, Laverne. I've lost Glad. Again."

Laverne's smile wilted. "Oh. I'm so sorry, honey."

"And somehow Tom made me feel like this was all *my* fault. I mean, isn't some of it *his* fault? I *know* I should be happy about the yard...about the party. But I'm not, Laverne. I'm just...*pissed.*"

"But what are you winning?"

I shot Laverne an angry glare. *Was she even listening?*

"What do you mean?" I groused.

"In Vegas, we had this saying. What are you winning?"

Laverne smiled at me sweetly, like a mother donkey. She'd chosen to ignore my rudeness, and part of me was grateful. But it wasn't fair. Laverne had Lady Luck on her side. She'd hit the sweet spot with intelligence. She was smart enough to function in society, but dumb enough to always be in a good mood. High IQs were definitely overrated. I didn't watch TV or read the papers, hoping to benefit from the old adage, *ignorance is bliss*. But the tantalizing idea that Laverne didn't even *know* that she was missing out on anything made me want to bite through a car tire with envy.

"I don't get what you mean," I muttered.

"So, what are you winning by being pissed?"

*Dang. Her dumb question was actually pretty smart.*

"I don't know. My self-respect? My right to be...*right?*"

"Maybe. But that ain't hitting the jackpot."

"What? What's the jackpot?"

Laverne's horsey face registered the innocent, dumbfounded concern of a worried puppy.

"Why, *happiness*, honey. Don't you know that?"

Laverne's kind, simplistic answer ignited a blaze of rage inside my chest. I scrambled off the stool, too angry to remain seated.

"But why should *I* have to pay for others' mistakes, Laverne?" I screeched. "Why does happiness always come at a cost?"

Laverne, unfazed by my anger, didn't miss a beat. She smiled at me sweetly.

"Well, that's easy honey. Can't nobody win the jackpot without playing. And it always costs something to play."

# Chapter Three

I'd spent Sunday evening alone, cooling down slowly, like the nuclear reactor at Chernobyl. I'd avoided a critical meltdown, and when I woke up Monday morning, I'd found myself on the verge of no longer being a lethal danger to other life forms.

After a cappuccino and a long, cool shower, at 8 a.m. I called Lefty's Hauling again. It rang fifteen times, unanswered. This was, of course, totally unacceptable. It was time for Plan B.

I slipped on a sundress and sandals, put my hair in a ponytail and climbed into the red pleather driver's seat of Maggie, my 1963 Ford Falcon Sprint convertible. With a little encouragement in the form of smashing her gas pedal to the floor, Maggie carried me north along Gulf Boulevard. The four-lane road, lined with two- and three-story beach resorts, skirted the Gulf of Mexico like stiches in a hem.

Year round, tourists flocked to the quaint mom-and-pop motels and sugar-white beaches. I couldn't blame them. All-in-all, St. Pete Beach was a great place to be.

I turned east on 107$^{th}$ Avenue. Immediately, the salt air and kitsch beach shops disappeared, replaced with anywhere-USA strip malls. At 66$^{th}$ Street, I turned north in the direction of good-old Pinellas Park.

Every major metropolitan area had a section designated especially for rednecks. How they found each other, I didn't know. Maybe they were all related, or there was some special redneck hotline I wasn't privy to. At any rate, in Pinellas County, the mecca for country bumpkins and politically incorrect-and-proud-of-it folks was definitely Pinellas Park.

If it weren't for Florida's history of hurricanes and tropical storms, Pinellas Park would have choked to death on doublewide trailers decades ago. But in 1993, a freak storm took out all but the very highest quality manufactured homes. It had been dubbed the "1993 Storm of the Century" by some, the "'93 Super Storm" by others, and the "Great Blizzard of 1993" by the Yankees up north. But we locals simply called it the "No-Name Storm," because it had come up so quickly and unexpectedly not even the weather forecasters had had time to register it with an official moniker.

It had begun on March 12$^{th}$ as a cyclonic storm in the Gulf of Mexico, then quickly grew into a beast that stretched from Cuba to Canada. It moved into Florida around midnight, catching us unaware with winds over 100 mph. It spawned 11 tornadoes and a storm surge in St. Pete that topped out at seven feet. For folks along the coast, bay and rivers, it had been devastating. It wiped out or damaged over 18,000 homes in the Sunshine State and killed 47 of our citizens, more than Hugo and Andrew combined. Suffice it to say, it was not a good time to be living in a tin can on wheels.

Florida's seasonal tropical storms like No-Name and the annual seven months of relentless heat and humidity were like cancer and the plague to anything made of metal. Even so, every year, seniors and other derelicts from up north took their chances in RVs and mobile homes. They came down to Florida by the millions right after Thanksgiving and left the day after Easter in hordes like migrating wildebeest, after carefully placing tinfoil in the windows of their metallic abodes to protect them from space aliens, I guess.

It was the first week of May, so the snowbirds had already flown the coop. In their stead had come the hard-faced, barrel-chested, androgynous Europeans in speedos and industrial-strength two-piece suits. Insulated with blubber and Nordic genes, they thought any ocean water above freezing was warm enough to swim in. Bless their hearts.

On 66th, I drove past the endless rows of uninspired strip centers anchored by monotonous chain stores. These were the same kind of soulless shopping centers that had popped up all over the country like mushrooms after a rain, and threatened to turn St. Pete into another generic city. I scowled and took a left onto a side road called Lewis Lane.

A few blocks in, I was surprised to find commercial buildings give way to open, grassy acreage big enough for horses to roam. I followed a double-rut, white-sand road wedged between horse pastures to a chain-link fence that marked the end of the line. A hand-painted sign on the right side of the twelve-foot-wide gate read, "Lefty's is Right Here." Next to the sign was a three-foot wide butt of someone bent over in a pair of dirty blue overalls. At the sound of Maggie's glasspack muffler, the overalls straightened up and turned around, revealing a white male occupant with a cue-ball shaped head, a trace of eyebrows, and not a single front tooth.

"Woo hoo! That's a beaut!" the ruddy-faced man said in a spot-on impression of my redneck friend Winky. He hobbled up to the car, limping as if he might have recently injured or lost part of his lower left limb.

"Thank you. This is Maggie."

The man reached over to shake my hand with fingers as big and round as already plumped Ball Park franks. Thankfully, he didn't have to prove his manhood by squeezing my fingers to the bone. Instead, he put a thick thumb in my palm and daintily shook the ends of my fingers as if they were made of fine porcelain.

"Nice to meet you, Maggie. I'm Lefty. What can I do you for?"

"No, I'm..." I thought about explaining that I was Val Fremden...that Maggie was my car's name...but I figured there was no real point. "I came to get back an RV you hauled away on Saturday. Down in St. Pete Beach?"

Lefty showed me his toothless grin. "Oh yeah. Cute little thang."

"So, what do I need to pay you to get it back?"

"Oh. Nothing, Maggie. 'Fraid you're a little late. A girl come by yesterday and bought her."

A needle of pain dug a sharp, deep stitch in my chest. "But...I thought you were closed yesterday."

Lefty laughed and scratched the top of his head. "Yeah. Don't nobody pay no attention to that around here. And this here girl, she was a mighty persistent little spitfire. Seen that RV and wasn't nothin' gonna stop her having it. Paid cash. I like me some cash, you know."

"Selling the RV. It was...a mistake. I need it back. Can't you help me? I have cash too."

"Sorry, little lady. Wish I could help, but the man who swapped it give me clear title. Then this girl come up Saturday with cash. I hadn't even had no time to re-register the title yet. She said she'd take care of it. I mean, what's a feller to do?"

"Can you tell me her name?"

"Uh, yeah. Let's see...Baloney?"

"Baloney? Is that a joke?"

Lefty scratched his head. "Um...no. That ain't it. Dang it! I can't rightly recollect at the moment."

"Well, where's the RV? Did you haul it to her place?"

Lefty's face broke out into a proud, toothless grin that made me think of the Gerber Baby—if he were forty years old and chewed tobacco.

"Ha ha. That's the beauty part, Maggie. I hauled the RV here and old Nick, our mechanic, cleaned the sparkplugs and changed the oil and air filter and that little RV hummed right back to life. Good old American-made engines. Don't build 'em like they used to. Doubled the value in an hour's work. Good old Nick. He can fix anything. So you see, I didn't have to haul it nowheres. That girl drove it right on out of here."

As he spoke, the needle of pain in my heart got busy sewing a quilt. *Crap.*

"Did she leave something with her address? Fill out some paperwork?"

"Paperwork?" The idea sent Lefty into fits of laughter. "Do I look like the kind of guy who'd bother myself with paperwork, little lady? Hell, I don't even have a bank account. Those fat-cat bankers ain't gonna steal my money away."

"Well, in case she comes back, would you have her call me?"

"Why shore, Maggie. Be glad to."

I handed Lefty my card. He slipped it into the back pocket of his overalls without looking at it. As I drove away, I had the sinking feeling that, for all the good it had done, I may as well have used the card to wipe my own butt.

ON THE DRIVE HOME, I passed Ming Ming's sushi place on Central and saw Milly's red Beemer parked out front. It wasn't until I was a block past her that I remembered I was supposed to meet her there for lunch. *Crap on a cracker!* I hit the brakes and pulled a one-eighty on Central Avenue, causing a jaywalker to kick it up a notch to jay-sprinting. I checked the time on my cellphone as he waved an angry fist at me. It was two minutes until noon. *Sweet!* I wasn't even going to be late. I pulled into the lot and made my way inside the restaurant.

One look at Milly's face and I knew she was chomping at the bit with some juicy news of her own.

"Hey, Valiant," she said playfully as I walked in the door.

"Hey, Millicent," I said back.

After we'd insulted each other with the despised names given to us by our parents, it was time to get down to business. For Milly, that always meant men.

It wasn't her fault completely. Milly had always been a man magnet. She was blonde and had a button nose and a body that, on several occasions, even made me think about giving up chocolate. Her looks had always garnered lots of flirty attention from the opposite sex. But when it came to actually *dating*, she'd proven as finicky as a blue-ribbon show cat. Over the dozen or so years I'd know her, she'd endured so many bad dates she could've easily been listed in *Ripley's Believe it or Not*. But to her credit, Milly had always taken it all in stride. In fact, she'd turned her penchant for shooting down men's proposals into an all-season sport.

I wasn't in the mood to hear about her latest shenanigans. But I needed some cheering up. Her horrific tales of dating made me appreciate my own pathetic life.

"So, spill it, Milly. Who, what, where, when."

Milly's eyes sparkled with delight. "Good old, direct Val. You're the poster child for keeping it real. Have I told you lately that I love you?"

I grinned back. "No. But it seems to be going around."

Milly eyed me curiously, then her eyes flew open like a kicked-in door. "Wait. What? Did Tom—"

I smirked. "Yes. Saturday. At the party."

"Oh my word! What did you say?"

My smirk switched to a grimace. "Oh. Uh...'Thanks.'"

Milly flinched. "Ouch!"

I shook my head. "That's not the half of it."

"What else hap—"

Milly's voice faded as the waiter came to the table to take our order.

"Sea dragon roll and an iced tea for me, please," I said, looking up at the waiter.

"The same for me," Milly rattled off absently, then dismissed the waiter with a flick of her hand. Her eyes remained locked on me. I got the feeling she'd have replied "the same" if I'd ordered a deep-fried cow patty. She leaned over the table and whispered.

"So what's the other half?"

I raised my left shoulder to my ear and let it drop again. "We had a fight. I haven't spoken to him since."

"What?! After all he did?"

I leaned in and glared at Milly. "Before you go taking sides, hear me out. He sold my RV without asking me. The piggybank with mom's cremains was in the RV."

Milly's judgmental expression crumpled. "Crap, Val!"

"Hold on. It gets worse. I just came from the junkyard that hauled it away. They've already sold it to somebody else for cash. No paperwork. No name. No nothing. Milly, Glad is gone for good. I don't have a clue where to even begin looking."

"Aww! Double crap, Val. I'm sorry!"

The waiter set two glasses of tea in front of us, along with a pair of straws. We both smiled up at him courteously, as if he existed in some other dimension, then shifted back to glowering at each other as soon as he left.

"What are you going to do now?"

"There's nothing I *can* do but hope that 'Lefty' gives me a call."

"Lefty?"

I shook my head and blew out a breath. "Don't ask."

Milly studied me for a moment and played with her straw. "I'm sorry about your mom's cremains, Val. But you know, you have to let go of her sometime. I mean, now that the house is finished, you need something to do. You have too much time on your hands."

"That's weird. That's exactly what Laverne told me yesterday. She said I should take an adult education class at the college. She's starting a ceramics class next week."

"Ceramics? Are you crazy? You don't need a *hobby*, Val. You need a *job*." Milly cocked her head coyly. "Did I mention we have an opening?"

I raised my eyebrows dubiously. "No. No you didn't."

"Would you be interested?"

I curled my upper lip. "I'm not broke by any means. But according to my bank account and the average mortality charts, it's probably a good idea."

Milly smirked. "A word of advice, Val. Don't use that line in the interview."

I jerked to attention. "Interview? *What* interview?"

"I set one up for you. Tomorrow at ten. It's for a junior office assistant."

I stared at Milly like a kid who'd just been grounded for a month.

"Come on, Val. It'll be good for you. You need to get out and do something...*normal*."

"Normal?"

"You know what I mean."

The scary thing was, I actually *did* know what she meant.

"You'd be a natural, Val."

"As far as I can tell, I'm unemployable, Milly. Thanks to my seven missing years abroad, I can't even get a job as a waitress. Who'd hire me?"

"I would."

"Is the hiring at your decision?"

"No. But let's just say I can pull some strings."

I blew out a sigh. "Do I have a choice?"

Milly shot me a wry smile. "Now *that's* the spirit!"

The waiter arrived with our sea creature rolls. I suddenly realized I hadn't eaten anything since yesterday's Skinny Dip debacle. I was starved. I looked over at my good friend Milly. I figured I might as well have a show with my dinner, so I repeated her favorite prompt.

"Okay, so...where were we? Who, what, where and when?"

Milly grinned and took her cue like a professional thespian. She straightened her shoulders, rolled them a few times for good measure, and launched into her bad-date monologue.

"Well, the who is a six-foot tall piece of crap named Dexter Ponds. The what? A MatchMate date, of course."

Our heads nodded in unison. "Of course."

"Where? This dump on Central. When? Yesterday at 7 p.m. You didn't ask, but the why? I don't know. You tell me. Why do I keep doing this to myself, Val? Do I hate myself that much?"

"Why? What happened *this* time?"

"What *always* happens. The guy shows up and he's ten years older and thirty pounds heavier than his profile picture. He eats like he was raised in a laundromat, and he automatically thinks he can do better than me."

"Why do you say that? You're beautiful."

"Not according to *Poindexter*, master of the insult disguised as a compliment. My favorite was when he told me I was plump, but still 'kind of' pretty. Val, am I losing my looks?"

"What? No! The guy's a jerk!"

Milly pouted with insecurity. "Are you just telling me a nice lie?"

"No. I think you're the prettiest woman I know. So shut up and eat your dragon roll."

Milly smiled, only half convinced. "There ought to be a law against free-roaming dumbells like him."

I raised an eyebrow. "Free-roaming dumbbells? That doesn't sound like you."

Milly laughed softly. "That's because it's not. I mean, I can't take credit for it, anyway. I almost forgot...this was where the date got good. Val, in the middle of Dexter's insulting monologue, a woman came up from out of nowhere and told him to piss off!"

I blanched and sat back in my chair. "What?"

"I know. Val, it was so...*unexpected*. One minute I'm sitting there trying to figure out how to get out of the whole Dexter disaster, and the next minute this woman with a rainbow Mohawk and fifty face piercings slides into the booth right next to me. She puts her tattooed arm around my shoulder and says she couldn't believe I was cheating on her with *a man*, and a fat ugly one to boot!"

My eyebrows flew up an inch. "No way!"

"Yes way! She told Dexter to get lost. I can't remember word-for-word what she said, but it was something along the lines that she 'didn't have time to waste on cotton-candy, unicorns or free-roaming dumbbells like him.' I'm telling you, Val, that guy nearly crapped his pants! He couldn't have gotten out of that restaurant faster if he'd been strapped onto a rocket!"

"Whoa!" I shook my head in disbelief. "Milly, when you think about it, what she did, it's pretty ingenious, actually. Did you get her name?"

"She told me her friends called her Cold Cuts. Weird, right?"

"I dunno. Sounds pretty spot-on to me."

# Chapter Four

It was Taco Tuesday, my official date night with Tom. We still hadn't spoken to each other since our fight Saturday night. For me, it had been a matter of principle. I still hadn't made up my mind about who'd been more right and who'd been more wrong. But there was one thing I knew for sure. The contents of my refrigerator couldn't keep a cricket alive one more night.

I'd finished off the last of the birthday party leftovers—two dried-up chicken wings and five hard-cornered cubes of cheddar cheese—with my cappuccino this morning. Unless I wanted my lunch to be a Dijon mustard sandwich with dill pickle slices for bread, I was going to have to go buy some food.

I hated grocery shopping. I wasn't sure why. Maybe it was because there was way too many options to choose from nowadays. I mean, fifty different kinds of peanut butter? What happened to the good old days, when there was simply "crunchy" or "smooth?" Or that "exotic" one with swirls of grape jelly? It was all just too much. I always left the store feeling like I'd picked the wrong things. But this morning, my habit of procrastination left me no choice. It was go shopping or starve.

As I slipped into shorts and a tank top, I thought about calling Tom. I missed him. And my traitorous stomach, like clockwork, had begun craving its weekly taco delivery. I picked up my cellphone and almost clicked #7, speed dial for Tom. But I couldn't think of what to say beyond 'hello,' so I slipped the phone back in my purse and headed out the door.

CARBON BLEW OUT IN thin, black puffs from Maggie's muffler as I cruised south on Gulf Boulevard toward the Publix on Treasure Island. Even though it was part of a chain, this particular Publix was a small, neighborhood store that catered to hard-core locals and transient, semi-sober beachgoers. I found a spot in the parking lot and laid my hat on the passenger seat. A split-second later, my shoulders began to roast in the glaring sun. My sandals clung like sticky-notes to the semi-molten asphalt as I trotted across the lot. It was quarter to nine and already a scorcher.

Stacked along both sides of Publix's glass entry doors were cheap, folding beach chairs and colorful pool floats. I skirted past a goofy-eyed inflatable dragon and stepped inside the cool, welcoming air. The aroma of fresh-baked bread set my mouth to salivating. It forced me, against my will, to pick up a sesame-seed baguette. Avocados from Mexico lay stacked in small pyramids by the front door, irresistible at the bargain price of two for a dollar. I yanked a clear plastic bag from the roller thingy. After finally getting the flimsy bag peeled apart, I slipped a pair of avocados inside.

*Guacamole and...what else? Tortilla chips.*

I left my shopping cart next to a stack of Styrofoam coolers and wandered over to the summer display of chips, soft drinks, burger buns and barbeque sauce. That's when I saw it. The hideous banner cheerfully announcing; "Mother's Day is May 13$^{th}$!"

*Crap. Already?* In less than two weeks, I'd have the pleasure of being reduced to rubble over the phone by Lucille Jolly-Short, my adopted mother, evil-genius, and master of the back-handed compliment. Her only saving grace was she'd agreed to adopt me after her husband found me on the side of the road. That, and she'd saved the other half of the dragonfly pin my real mother had fastened to my diaper.

*Maybe if I sent her a card, I wouldn't have to call her.*

I sauntered over to the small rack of greeting cards and sifted through the cheesy offerings. Every last one of them were pink and plastered with hearts—doting and happy and *way* too sappy. *Where were the other cards? The ones that said, "Thanks mom, for setting me up for a lifetime of slowly recovering my self-esteem."*

I couldn't have been the only one. In fact, I was certain Hallmark was missing the marketing opportunity of a lifetime.

*Crap on a cracker. I guess I'll have to call her.*

I shuffled back to my grocery cart. In the top basket, next to my avocadoes and baguette, someone had slipped in a box of reservoir-tipped Trojans. I picked up the carton and looked around.

"There you are."

I turned in the direction of the voice and tried not to blanch. Standing less than two feet away from me was a man in his late fifties who hadn't seen a razor or a shower since sometime last month.

Cheap, black-plastic shower shoes revealed he hadn't had a pedicure lately, either. His canary-yellow T-shirt was stained with lord-only-knows-what. It featured armholes that hung halfway down his sides, flashing innocent victims with unwanted views of his hairy armpits, side-fat rolls, and an alarming assortment of suspicious moles. His plaid shorts were baggy enough to support a small family of trolls. And, of course, he sported my favorite hairdo—a greasy, grey, ratty ponytail. If this guy had been in a contest to turn women off, he would have gotten my vote, hands down.

"I'm sorry?" I replied.

He took the condoms from my hand. I stared, dumbfounded. I couldn't believe this guy ever actually got laid.

"You put your stuff in my cart."

I started to protest, but glanced into the cart and changed my mind. It was filled with a jumble of bachelor survival goods; hot dogs, TV dinners, two cases of beer, hemorrhoid cream and a family-sized container of Tums. Either he'd commandeered my cart, or someone else had. Then they'd dumped my stuff in *his* cart.

"Oh. Sorry about that."

I grabbed the bag of avocadoes and the baguette and tried to make a getaway, but the guy side-stepped and trapped me between the coolers and the wall. He motioned with his eyes downward, toward the bag of avocados in my hand.

"Fruit. I like fruit, too, you know. My favorite is *melons* and *peaches*. Get it?"

He wagged his unkempt eyebrows at me as his grotesque, greyish tongue darted between his lips like an anemic slug.

*Illiterate, disgusting and incapable of subtlety. What's not to like?*

"Thanks, but I'm not interested."

The man looked surprised. "Then why the signal?

"*Signal?*"

The man pointed at my crotch. My eyes darted down. To my horror, the baguette and bag of avocados I was holding had unwittingly arranged themselves to mimic a huge, albino penis and a low-hanging, gangrenous scrotum. My face flushed with heat. In motions too fast to be seen by the naked eye, I shoved the baguette under my arm and swung the avocados to my side. I fumbled for words.

"Look...um...this was purely uninten—"

"Why Sally Harper! If that don't beat a goat a gobblin'! How have you been, honey?"

The man's eyes shifted to the left and locked onto a busty, big-haired blonde. She was squeezed into purple spandex pants and a T-shirt spattered in an explosion of rhinestones. She grinned at me from behind a pair of cheap, white, heart-shaped sunglasses. Tiny, plastic starfish adorned the glasses in a tacky salute to Florida kitsch.

Fruit man's interest in me dropped like a frog hopping off a cliff. I guess gentlemen really *did* prefer blondes.

"Hey there, pretty lady."

The woman ignored him and punched me on the arm.

"Girl, it's me. Sherry Perry. From high school. Pompom princesses! You and me!"

Sherry wriggled her body with cheerleader enthusiasm. I stood and stared at her, as speechless and stone-still as a statue of the class dork.

"Hey, Sherry. I like your *pompoms*," the hideous man said.

I watched, still frozen with awe, as Sherry sidled up to captain condom and whispered something into his ear. The guy withered and shrunk. I could almost *feel* his testicles recede inside his plaid-tent shorts. He shot me a disgusted glance, commandeered his cart and made a hasty getaway.

Sherry turned to me and grinned. She folded her arms at shoulder level and nodded her head once, quick and bouncy, like Barbara Eden in *I Dream of Jeannie*.

"Poof! Man be gone!"

I couldn't help but be impressed. Her powers truly did seem magical.

I grinned back at her. "What did you say to him?"

Sherry laughed. "I told him you and I were incurable hermaphobiatics."

"Gross! Is that a real thing?"

"No. I just made it up."

"Why? I mean...why did you...help me?"

"Let's just say I have 'creep phobia.' I hate to see a good woman bothered by a creep like that."

I smiled in gratitude. "That's pretty cool. Thanks, Sherry."

"You're welcome." Sherry took off her sunglasses and studied me for a moment with eyes as brown as dark chocolate. "Hey, have you got time to have a coffee with me? They just opened a Starbucks in this Publix and I'm dying to try it."

"I don't know, Sherry. I think I've got—"

Sherry popped her sunglasses back on. "Hey don't sweat it. Just so you know, my name's not Sherry. That was just for getting into character. My real name is...well...my friends call me Cold Cuts. See you around."

As she turned to go, something churned in my mind. *Cold Cuts? But wait...this woman didn't look anything like Milly had described her. Could it be...?*

"Hold up, Cold Cuts," I said.

The busty blonde stopped and pivoted on her purple high-heels.

She smiled and I said, "You know what? I think I'll have that cup of coffee after all."

# Chapter Five

Cold Cuts took a sip of her skinny cinnamon double mocha latte. It was hard to be sure, but underneath that big blonde wig and all that makeup, she looked to be in her late twenties or early thirties at the most.

"So what's with the costume?" I asked, then immediately blushed with regret. Maybe this wasn't a costume. Maybe this was how the *real* Cold Cuts normally dressed.

"Oh. Yeah." She laughed and pulled at her rhinestone shirt. "I'm in costume so often, I have to look in the mirror sometimes to remember who I am."

"You know, I think you may have helped out a friend of mine the other day. Not as Sherry Perry, though. Milly said the woman had a rainbow Mohawk and face piercings. And tattoos?"

"Oh, sure. That's Scary Kerry. She's one of my favorites."

"Really? How many of these 'characters' do you have?"

Cold Cuts shrugged. "There's no real number. I make them up as I go along."

"Oh." I leaned across the table toward her. "I'm curious. Why do you do this?"

Cold Cuts cocked her head to one side. "I dunno. I guess the idea of having to be the same old person my entire life would be a horrific bore. Who says you can't try out new roles? Be a different person when you feel like it?"

I sat back in the booth. "I never thought about it. But that's brilliant. You're pretty young to be so wise."

"I know, right? I credit my parents."

"I *blame* mine."

Cold Cuts laughed. "Yeah, most people do. But I got lucky. I was raised by people who, I guess you could say, didn't care anything about being 'normal.' They were always trying out new things. Living off the grid. Organic farming. Different religions. They kept what they liked and tossed the rest. Still do."

"Wow. That sounds pretty cool, actually."

Cold Cuts tapped a fake purple nail on the table. "I know, right? My folks let me do anything I wanted. Let me be whoever I wanted. My dad always told me I could create my own life however I wanted. My mom thought I could do no wrong."

An image of Lucille Jolly-Short flashed in my mind. "I can't even imagine that."

Cold Cuts studied me and laughed. "From the look on your face, I guess you can't. But let me tell you, it was total freedom. I didn't realize what a gift they'd given me until I watched my friends spend their teens and twenties hacking up their parents unwanted beliefs like nasty hairballs. It was easier for me. I got to be my own person from the get-go. I didn't have to sort through the mess later with drunk, hysterical games of, 'Whose belief *is* that, anyway?'"

"I don't think I've ever been so jealous in my life."

Cold Cuts grinned. "How so?"

"I grew up totally different. Southern Baptist."

"And?"

"Well, that was my mother's religion. In hindsight, I know that she wasn't typical. Her favorite saying was, 'God's going to get you for that.'"

Cold Cuts looked at her coffee and crinkled her nose. "That must have been tough."

"You have no idea. When I was a kid, my mother taught Sunday school to me and my friends. That woman single-handedly destroyed more self-esteem in the 1970s than all the Toni home permanents combined."

Cold Cuts' brow crinkled quizzically. "Home permanents?"

"Oh. Well, yeah. Back in...oh, forget it. You're too young to understand."

"I understand a lot. It sounds to me like you picked a Mount Everest life."

"What? What do you mean?"

"Basically, you wanted a challenge. A big one."

"I don't get it."

"Most people don't. But just suppose, for one minute, that you actually *chose* everything that's happened in your life—including your parents."

My eyebrows shot up along with my temper. "Are you *kidding* me?"

Cold Cuts flinched. "I know. You want to punch me in the face."

I relaxed a notch. "So you're a mind reader, as well."

Cold Cuts grinned. "Hey, I've got my challenges, too. But now I choose to look at everything not as *good or bad*, but as *information*. Contrast. You know?"

"*Really?* Being lied to and stolen from and abandoned are *good?* They're *information?* This I've got to hear."

Cold Cuts took a deep breath and exhaled. I tried to do the same, but my chest was tighter than my Aunt Pansy's girdle.

"Well, think back to where *you* were. Right *before* this lying, thieving, dirtbag of a guy abandoned you."

I locked stern eyes on Cold Cuts. "I didn't say it was a guy."

Cold Cuts cocked her head and raised her eyebrows.

I looked down sheepishly. "Okay. It was a guy. Friedrich Fremden. And before he did all that? To be honest, I wasn't sure I wanted to be with him anymore."

"Would you have stayed if he hadn't lied?"

I looked up at Cold Cuts again, my anger giving way to shame. "I *did* stay. For *years*. Even *after* I'd caught him lying."

"Uh-huh. What came next? The thieving, right?"

Something in Cold Cuts' calm, non-judging demeanor made me want to come clean with her...with *myself.*

I nodded. "Yeah."

"Did you leave then?"

"No...not right away."

"Why not?"

"I...I.... When I found out the money was missing, I thought it was just a mistake. A misunderstanding. I thought I could...*fix things*. That he didn't mean what he did."

"Did that turn out to be the case?"

My gut dropped into my lap. "No. Just the opposite. I think it was intentional."

"Yet you stayed."

"Yes. But if I'm honest, my heart wasn't in it anymore. I already had one foot out the door when he told me he never wanted to speak to me again."

"So, his abandoning you got your other foot out the door. Be grateful for it."

I shot Cold Cuts a suspicious, venomous look. "Grateful that Friedrich *abandoned me? In a foreign country?* Are you serious?"

She deflected my poisonous stare with a soft smile. "Yes, I'm serious. Think about it. His leaving you to fend for yourself gave you the 'information' you needed to finally follow your heart."

I looked into Cold Cuts' clear, unflinching eyes and saw the reflection of my own confused expression.

"But I didn't *know* what I wanted," I said. "I...I only knew I couldn't stay with him any longer. That I didn't want to *be* with *him* any longer."

Cold Cuts' eyes brightened welcomingly. "*Exactly*. That's the *information you needed*. The *clarity*. The whack upside the head, if you want, that got your butt moving away from what you *didn't* want and toward something you *did* want."

Something clicked inside my brain. My chest loosened slightly. "Oh. I get it. Sort of."

Cold Cuts smiled. "Tell me, do you still want to kiss this guy?"

I flinched. "Friedrich? *No way*."

"Do you want to kill him?"

I eyed her dubiously. "Could I get away with it Scott free?"

Cold Cuts laughed playfully. "So, you're not over him yet."

I frowned in disappointment. "What do you mean? It's been nearly *two years*."

"Time means nothing to the heart. If you still want to kiss him or kill him, you're not done yet. Your feelings are still...*in turmoil*."

I wanted to deny it, but it seemed pointless to try to hide from this girl. She seemed capable of seeing right through me.

*Maybe this was the reason I couldn't commit to Tom. To* anyone.

I frowned. "Crap. So, how *do* I get over Friedrich, then?"

Cold Cuts shrugged. "The fastest way? By being grateful for him."

I nearly choked. "*Grateful?* Now I *know* you've got to be kidding!"

"No. I'm not. Look. You said that in your heart-of-hearts, you didn't want to be with him. But you didn't want to leave him, or hurt him. So he stepped up to the plate and kept swinging the bat until he hit the zinger you'd been waiting for. Your chance for a homerun. Or should I say, a *run home*. In other words, if he hadn't been a total jerk, you'd still be there, living a half-life of misery you never even actually wanted."

Her words stunned me. I sat and stared at the woman who spoke like a sage and looked like a bimbo.

"Dang," I said finally. "You're right. I would've gone on forever trying to 'make it work' for *us*, but not for *me*."

Cold Cuts grinned. "*Exactly.*"

"Wow. I never thought I'd say this, but here goes. Thank you, Friedrich, for being such a jerk."

Cold Cuts' blonde eyebrows flew halfway up her forehead. A second later, she burst out laughing.

"Ha ha! That's the best line of gratitude I've ever heard!"

I smiled sarcastically. "Thanks."

Something buzzed. Cold Cuts glanced down at her phone. Her clear, open face switched to serious in a split second. "Listen...oops! I don't even know your name!"

"Val Fremden."

"Hey, listen Val. I've got to run. See you around?" Cold Cuts started to stand up.

"Sure," I said. "I've still got to pick up a few groceries. I'm sure we'll run into each other around here again sometime. Thanks for the free psychotherapy session."

She stood and shook my hand. "My pleasure."

I watched from my hard, plastic Starbucks seat as Cold Cuts disappeared out the front door of Publix. I sighed, wiped the table with a napkin and threw our cups into the trash. I picked up the baguette and avocadoes, and, careful to avoid another pornographic display, wandered over to the snack isle and grabbed a bag of tortilla chips. I got in line to pay behind a frizzy-haired woman about my age. I noticed she was buying a lawn chair, a six-pack of Bud, a cucumber, and a douche.

I forced myself not to think about her plans for the evening.

I thought about Tom instead. The conversation with Cold Cuts had loosened me up. I felt a lot...*lighter* about Tom and me.

*Maybe there was a reason we were together. Maybe there was even a good reason for the fight we were having.*

I smiled to myself and dug a hand into my purse. My fingers wrapped around my cellphone. I pulled it out and punched #7. Tom answered on the third ring, just as my turn came up in line. I ended up having a double dialogue between him and the cashier.

"Hi Tom. Huh? Oh, yes, that's all."

"Val? What's all?"

"No, I don't have any coupons. Tom, I just wanted to say..."

"Coupons? Val, have you been drinking?"

"No. That's on sale."

I wedged the phone between my shoulder and ear and handed the cashier a twenty.

"What's going on, Val?"

Tom sounded annoyed. I grabbed the grocery bag and my change. "I'm sorry, I just wanted to tell you...."

"Tell me what?"

I dumped the change in my wallet, then looked up. My mouth fell open, but no words came out. Through the glass storefront, I watched an old RV pass by. The Minnie Winnie's backend was plastered in dragonfly stickers. My heart skipped a beat.

"Tom, I'm gonna have to call you back."

I clicked off the phone and ran out the door. Fifty feet to the left, the RV had come to a stop in the parking lot. It idled roughly as two sunburned tourists in flip-flops ambled lazily in front of it. Through the side-view mirror, I made out the image of a blonde woman in heart-shaped sunglasses.

*Cold Cuts!*

I took a lunging step toward the old Minnie Winnie, but tripped on the curb. I lost my balance and let go of the grocery bag. The avocadoes hit the pavement and rolled into my path like little green land mines. My right heel found one. My leg flew out from under me like an ice skater on an oil slick. A second later, my butt met the asphalt with a dull thud.

I blinked hard at the stars dancing around my head like little meteors. As they cleared, I found myself sprawled in the middle of the road—my legs stuck straight-out in front of me like a Barbie doll. I heard the rumble of an engine and pulled my knees in toward me just in time to see a rat-tailed guy on a Harley run over my tortilla chips. The bag burst like a New Year's popper, spewing shards of toasted-corn confetti all over me like salty, greasy rain. I rubbed the chip dust from my eyes and looked up. The RV skittered off, leaving behind a thin cloud of grey smoke.

*Crap!* I lifted my left butt cheek and pulled out the flattened baguette. As I hauled myself up on one knee, my phone rang. I wheezed into the speaker. "What?"

"What *my butt hole*, Val," Milly said. "Where are you? You had an interview today!"

*Aww, crap!*

"I'm sorry, Milly. I forgot."

A horn honked. A man with a bloated face as red as his rented convertible yelled at me. "Lady, you gonna get your fat butt out of my way or what?"

I gestured obscenely at him with my mangled baguette and hobbled off toward my car.

"What's going on, Val?"

"Milly, I'm sorry. But I promise, I've got a good excuse."

"I'm sure you do." Milly said sourly. "I can't wait to hear all about it."

"No. I'm serious, Milly. I ran into that woman you told me about. Cold Cuts."

"What?" Milly gasped. "Are you serious?"

"Yes. And I think she's the one who bought my RV."

# Chapter Six

My mention of running into Cold Cuts softened Milly up a bit. That, along with some Academy-award-worthy groveling and the promise of a free lunch. My best friend forgave me and rescheduled another interview for the following morning at 9:30 a.m. After the interview, I was to meet her for lunch and fill her in on all the juicy details of my chance meeting with the odd young lady who'd made a habit of rescuing women like me and Milly from ourselves.

When I got home from Publix, I wrote a reminder note about the interview and went to tape it on the bathroom mirror. That's when I noticed the picture of Glad I kept on the mirror was missing. I looked around on the floor and in the drawers, but couldn't find it. My heart registered a twinge of panic. Had I lost that, too?

I limped into the kitchen, ripped off a hunk of road-killed baguette and crammed it into my ravenous maw. I was doing an impression of Alvin the gluttonous chipmunk when the phone rang. It was Tom. I'd forgotten to call him back.

*Geez.*

"Hi, Tom," I said, trying to sound cheerful despite the gummy wad of bread clogging my mouth.

Tom's voice conveyed the tension of our unresolved stalemate. "Val, what's going on with you? Are you drinking? It's only 11 a.m., for crying out loud."

"No!" I yelled. My sudden intake of breath vacuum-suctioned the slimy dough ball halfway down my throat. I choked and hacked like a tuberculosis-ridden wino.

Tom's voice softened. "You sound terrible. Have you got the flu?"

"No," I wheezed. "Just...choked. Need...water."

I grabbed my throat, turned on the kitchen tap and filled a glass as Tom spoke.

"What's going on with you, Val? You hung up on me."

"I was trying to—*cough*—catch the RV."

"Catch it? Was Lefty throwing it?" Tom said, then snickered at his own joke.

I knew he was trying to break the ice, but his lame attempt at humor left me cold. I took a sip of water and slammed the glass down on the counter.

"No, Tom. I went—*hack*—by the scrapyard yesterday. They'd already—*wheeze*—re-sold the RV. And this guy...Lefty...couldn't even tell me who to."

Tom's tone went soft and serious. "Oh. Crap, Val. I'm really sorry."

Finally, an apology. The words I'd longed to hear from Tom warmed my cold shoulder like a woolen shawl.

*So why was it so hard for me to return the favor?*

"To be honest, Tom, I've been so *pissed* at you. I was mortified when I found out you sold Mom's RV."

"I know," Tom said softly. "I feel like a heel. I had no idea the old piece of...the *RV* meant that much to you. I wanted to apologize earlier. But to be honest with *you*, coming near you when you're on the warpath isn't safe for my *cajones*, if you know what I mean."

I did.

"But I had a right to be mad," I said. "Didn't I?"

"Yes. You did. But I didn't mean to—"

"I know," I said, cutting him off. "But it still hurt. I thought I'd never find the RV...that I'd never see my mom again. Then, this morning at Publix? When I was talking to you on the phone? It went rolling by the window. I'm *sure* it was Glad's RV. I tried to run after it. That's why I hung up on you. But I couldn't catch it."

"Well, that's *kind* of good news, isn't it?" Tom said. "At least you know now it's still in the neighborhood. Did you get the tag number?"

*Dang it!*

I frowned. "No. I didn't think to look."

"Hmmm. Maybe I could get a buddy at the DMV to search the database for all the new tags being issued for RVs. It would be worth a shot."

Tom's idea perked me up a bit. "Yes! That would be great. Thanks, Tom. Maybe she...uh...I mean, whoever bought the RV would go in for one of those special 'classic' license plates."

"Good thinking. I'll mention it. So, *she?*"

I never could hide much from Tom. But at that moment, I didn't feel like getting into the whole story about Cold Cuts. "I think the person I saw driving it was a woman."

"Oh."

The line grew silent. Finally, Tom spoke. "You doing okay...otherwise?"

"Yeah."

"Does that mean you might be up for Taco Tuesday tonight?"

I rubbed the bruise spreading over my right butt cheek and allowed myself to smile, albeit begrudgingly. "Sure."

Given that my dinner options were between tacos with Tom or a mustard-and-pickle sandwich alone, it wasn't a hard choice.

I SHOVED THE REST OF the baguette in the freezer. The poor tortilla chips and avocados had never made it home alive. As I closed the fridge door, out of the corner of my eye, I caught a glimpse of something flash by the window in the backyard. I hobbled over to the sliding glass door and peeked outside.

*Weird.*

It hadn't rained, but the freshly laid grass was soaking wet. I glanced over at the faucet. The old hose had been patched and the nozzle replaced. The psycho-killer sprinkler had also been reattached to the hose. It glistened at me in the sunlight like Jack Nicholson's eyes in *The Shining*. Who was the trespassing good Samaritan?

*Maybe Laverne did this. She's always trying to fix things around here.*

But maybe she didn't. I snuck outside and glanced around the tiki hut. Nothing. I poked around the hammock. All clear. I tiptoed along the back wall of the house and stuck my head around the corner to take a peek. I found myself nose-to-nose with a raggedy, sweaty, half-naked man. A scream flew out of my mouth.

"Aaaahh!"

"Whoa!" Winky hollered. "Gaul dang it, Val, you nearly scared the bejeesus freak outta me!"

"*I* scared *you*?" I hissed. "What are you doing here?"

I stared into the pink, freckled face of my ginger-haired, redneck friend. He was sweating worse than a politician at the Pearly Gates. He wiped his brow with an old T-shirt and spit a chunk of chewing tobacco into the cypress mulch surrounding the lantana bushes. He pulled the sweat-rag T-shirt on over his head and adjusted it with tugs and pulls to ensconce his impressive beer belly.

"Well, Winnie's got herself a job at Davie's Donuts just down the street from you. I rode with her this morning. Figured I'd walk down and see you, but you wasn't home. These poor plants was just about to kick the bucket, so I got to waterin' 'em. Hate to see 'em bite the dust. Plantin' 'em was hard work."

"Oh. Well...thanks."

"Didn't mean to get your haunches up, Miss Scaredy Cat."

Winky grinned at me in a way that made me feel foolish.

"I...I just wasn't expecting to find anybody out here."

"Yeah. I wasn't 'specting Water Loo's to burn up, neither. Life's full of surprises, Val. Winnie done lost her job and we couldn't pay the rent. I got to find me somethin' to do. That van's worse'n sleepin' on good ol' Mother Earth."

"You two are living in the van?"

"Yep."

"Oh. Sorry to hear that. What about your job...fixing engines and stuff?"

Winky shrugged. "It's kinda sporatical."

Part of me wanted to help Winky. Part of me regretted I'd ever met him. In other words, he was just like every other man I'd ever known. I bit my lip and forced kind words out of my mouth like bitter pills.

"Oh. Is there anything I can do?"

Winky shot me a sideways look.

"I never took nothin' from nobody, Val. Not about to start now. But if you don't mind it, could we park the Dodge in your driveway tonight? Ever'body but Walmarts has been running us off."

"Uh. Sure. It's just temporary, right?"

I tried to look hopeful instead of panicked. My charade must have worked. Winky beamed with gratitude.

"Yep! I promise. 'Preciate it, Val Pal."

Winky patted me on the back and walked toward the backyard. I smiled. I was a sucker for gratitude. Besides, I'd already gone and said, 'yes.' There was no turning back now.

"You know, Winky, I think I might know of some work for you."

Winky whipped around and studied me with a face as carefree and open as a three-year-old boy's. "Oh yeah? What 'cha got?"

"I don't want to say just yet. I have to run it by someone first."

Winky spit brown goo in the grass, winked and shot me a mock salute.

"Sure thing, Val Pal. You're the boss."

WINKY WAS IN THE BACKYARD, drinking a beer and straddling one of the barstools at the tiki hut. I walked out and handed him a mustard sandwich. (He'd informed me he didn't care for pickles.)

"What happened to this here bread? It's flatter'n a sunken chest."

"It's a Panini," I lied. "A fancy Italian baguette."

"Oo la la." Winky raised his eyebrows and both pudgy pinkies—then took a bite big enough to choke a Billy goat.

I heard Tom's 4-Runner pull into the driveway.

"I gotta go. Enjoy yourself."

"You, too, Val Pal." Winky raised his voice three octaves. "Give Tommy boy my love!"

I jeered playfully back at him, then walked around the side yard and waved at Tom. I trotted over and climbed onto the passenger seat of his silver Toyota before he had time to turn off the engine.

"Hi. What...I'm not allowed inside anymore?" he asked, only half joking.

"Huh? Oh."

I reached over and touched his arm. "It's not that, Tom. I have...a *houseguest*. Or maybe I should say, a *hut* guest. Winky and Winnie are homeless again. Living in the van. Winky's in the backyard right now. I told him they could park the Dodge in the driveway for a few days, but between you and me, I'm worried about them staying here. Is that wrong?"

Tom shrugged. "Not wrong, per se. But I thought you cared about them."

His reply did nothing to bolster my opinion of myself. "I *do* care, Tom. I care about a lot of things. That doesn't necessarily mean I want to make a *lifetime commitment* to them."

Tom's eyes darkened.

*Crap! He must have thought I was talking about him!* I backpedaled.

"It's just that...I guess...well, I just don't want my backyard to become the new hangout for all the Water Loo's orphans of the world."

Tom's eyes lightened again. He nodded.

"I understand. I mean, I get it. The guys can be a handful, even for me. But I think you'll be able to survive for a couple of days. You're a pretty tough cookie...emphasis on the *pretty*."

Tom took my hand and squeezed it. I smiled and blushed at his cornball compliment. A woman my age. Can you imagine?

"Thanks, Tom."

He smiled tentatively. "So...you're enjoying your birthday gift?"

"The yard? Yes!" I said a bit too loudly, grateful for the change of topic. "Very much so. It's beautiful."

I leaned over the bucket seat to kiss Tom.

He met me halfway.

THE EVENING SKY THREATENED rain, so instead of taking our usual walk along the waterfront, Tom found a parking spot off 1st Avenue and 3rd Street. The ice between us melted quickly as we ambled along the tiny patch of urban jungle known as downtown St. Petersburg. The city was still in the fits and starts of a reluctant renaissance. Tom took my hand as we passed scabby little bars and thrift shops trying desperately to survive among the slick, new bistros and high-end boutiques. I realized for the first time how much St. Petersburg reminded me of my relationship with Tom. We were both struggling to let go of the past and trust in a brighter future.

Red Mesa, our favorite Mexican restaurant, was one of the first businesses to take a chance on St. Pete's rebirth. Now it was enjoying the rewards of its smart decision. It was crowded almost every week night, and impossibly so on the weekends. Tom and I strolled arm-in-arm up to the low, red-brick wall that formed the restaurant's outdoor courtyard. Arranged within its walls were clusters of wrought-iron tables and chairs, separated by terracotta pots planted with cascading flowers and small bay trees. Lanterns strung on wires overhead glowed golden in the slate-blue sky and gave the whole place a cozy, garden-party atmosphere.

I preferred sitting in the outdoor courtyard, even in the oppressive summer heat. I enjoyed the tropical ambiance, and the relative quiet. Red Mesa's inside dining area was nice, but one try had been enough for me. The concrete floors and glass walls made the place an echo chamber. I'd found myself shouting just to be heard above the din. No thanks. I'd already gotten too old for that crap.

Tom found us a table for two in the courtyard next to a planter box full of fragrant, pink petunias. I ordered a black-bean burrito and a glass of white sangria. Tom got soft tacos and a beer. Good old, Tom. He always ordered the same thing. I smiled at the handsome blond man with the crisp white shirt rolled up at the sleeves. I watched him as he chatted with the waiter and placed his order. Unlike me, Tom was a study in unfaltering confidence and cordiality. In fact, Tom was boringly reliable in all the right ways. And deliciously *unpredictable* in all the right ways, as well.

*And he loved me.* The thought made me catch my breath.

Tom put down the menu and took my hand. His warm touch sent tingly electric shocks racing to some of my most private places.

"What are you thinking about?" he asked.

"Oh. Just wondering how your work is going," I lied.

If I'd told him the truth, we'd have never made it through dinner.

ON THE DRIVE HOME, Tom seemed far away. At my prompting, he groused a little about work, but didn't say anything specific. I asked about the tag search for my mom's RV, but he hadn't had anything to report yet. I considered telling him about the idea I had brewing in my head—my plan to catch Cold Cuts—but decided against it. Tom hadn't been too thrilled when he'd found out about my last scheme involving Goober, a dog stroller and a bottle of Jack. So, I decided to keep my mouth shut and enjoy the ride in silence.

I guess, like Tom, I got lost in my own thoughts. I was taken by surprise when he pulled up in my driveway.

"Oh. We're home already," I said absently.

"Well, *you're* home, at least," Tom joked.

I looked around. "And no van, either. Not yet, anyway."

Tom took my hand. "Look, Val. I'm sorry I've been distracted lately. Stuff at work. Nothing to do with you. And I want to apologize again...about the RV...and Glad. If you think of anything else I can do to help, just let me know. I promise, I'll be on it."

His earnest face melted the last shard of ice I'd been holding onto. "Thanks, Tom."

He squeezed my hand again, then employed an index finger to gently dawdle a line on my inner arm from my wrist to my elbow. "Too bad I have to work tomorrow," he said huskily.

His comment jarred me to attention. "Oh! Work! I forgot to mention it! Tom, I'm thinking about taking a job at Milly's office. I have an interview tomorrow."

"You're kidding." Tom's sexy voice took on a playful, curious tone. "I thought you wanted to be a *detective*."

"Ha ha. I can't even solve the mystery of how to get out of my own way."

Tom looked into my eyes, but he didn't say a word. I pushed him with my shoulder.

"This is where you're supposed to laugh Tom, and tell me, 'That's not true.'"

Again, Tom grinned, but uttered not a syllable. I frowned and punched him in the arm.

"Jerk!"

Tom laughed and pulled me close to his chest.

"A job, huh? It might be just what you need to keep yourself out of trouble."

"Very funny. But, I guess I could use the money."

"Who couldn't?"

I pulled away enough to look Tom in the face. "Yeah. Plus, if I had a job, I'd have a good excuse for not going up to visit my mother on Mother's Day. Is that wrong, too?"

Tom looked me up and down skeptically. "Possibly."

I pouted. "Well, if it is, then I don't want to be right."

Tom flashed his sexy, devilish smile. "Well, as long as you're in the mood to be wrong...."

He took my chin in his hand and kissed me hard on the mouth. *Dang it!* That man was a good kisser. I wanted him. Badly. But part of me was having second thoughts. I pulled away and frowned.

"Are you okay?" he asked.

"Yes..."

I tried to explain, but Tom started nibbling my neck and my mind went blank. He whispered in my ear.

"Val, can I spend the night?"

"No," I whispered back. "Winky and Winnie will be here soon."

Tom returned to nibbling until he broke down my resistance.

"Okay. You can come in for a nightcap."

I took Tom by the hand and led into the house and back to the bedroom, unbuttoning my blouse along the way with my free hand. I peeled off my skirt and lay on the bed in my bra and panties and watched Tom undress. His white shirt glowed in the dim light against his tan, muscular chest. As he lay down next to me and kissed my ear, my back arched all on its own. His fingers, like hot silk, caressed my skin....

I wanted Tom to stay the night. Part of me wanted him to stay forever.

But it was not to be. Not right now. Tonight, we would both have to settle for a quickie.

Tom wasn't to blame. Neither were Winnie and Winky. It was that blasted burrito I'd eaten for dinner. Experience had taught me I had about an hour before those dastardly black beans would work their magic in my colon. In sixty or so odd minutes, those little ebony legumes would generate enough methane to propel me halfway to the moon.

I didn't want Tom around to witness my unscheduled lunar blastoff.

# Chapter Seven

I woke up feeling like Paul Bunyan had kicked me in the butt with his giant logging boot. I swung my legs over the right side of the bed. Wrong move. My eyebrows met my hairline. My teeth clamped together. My body froze in pain.

I took a deep breath, held it for a second, and blew it out. This time, I scooted slowly to the edge of the bed, moving cautiously through the aching soreness. I put one foot, then the other onto the floor, testing each joint as if it were a rusty hinge that might lock up or, worse yet, break completely off. I stood, then staggered and lurched like a robot on stilts. By the time I got to the bathroom, either the pain had faded or I'd gotten used to it.

The mirror on the back of the bathroom door revealed the reason for my rude awakening. I lifted my T-shirt and pulled down my panties. Overnight, a nightmarish watercolor of yellow, black, purple and green had covered my right buttock like a macabre canvas. *Ouch!* My mind flashed back to the parking lot...to that poor bag of tortilla chips. I frowned sourly.

*Well, at least I don't have tread marks.*

I pulled up my big-girl panties and made a slow, geriatric amble toward the coffee maker. Surely this was nothing a cappuccino with a shot of Bailey's couldn't cure. I upped my dosage when I hit my hip on the corner of the kitchen counter.

*Ooww! Make that* two *shots....*

The coffee maker was humming along nicely when I noticed Winnie's old, grey-blue Dodge van in the driveway. It backfired, belched smoke and backed slowly out of the drive. In its place, Winky stood there, staring at me wide-eyed, like a stagehand caught unaware at an unexpected curtain opening. Our eyes met. I waved. He waved once, dropped his gaze downward and disappeared behind the garage. *Weird.*

Then I remembered I was in my underwear.

*Crap!* I poured two shots of Bailey's in my cappuccino and drank it down in a couple of quick gulps. It was going to be a long, strange day. I made another cappuccino and sipped it as I stared out the window at my beautiful backyard. The tiki hut and hammock looked even better now that Tom and I had kissed and made up. I smiled to myself and hobbled to the bathroom. A note on the mirror kicked my fledgling good mood in the teeth.

*Aw, nuts! Milly's interview!* I shuffled like a crippled crab back to the kitchen and looked at the clock on the stove. It was already 8:45. I had...let's see...*fifteen seconds* to get ready *Crap on a cracker!*

There was no time to shower. I ransacked my closet for something appropriate to wear. Zilch. All I had was shorts, T-shirts, sundresses, jeans...and one little black dress that was way too short for the occasion. I had a cute skirt that would do, but I'd splotched mustard on it when I made Winky's sandwich yesterday. Out of options, I squeezed into the black dress and put a white, button-up blouse over it to dress it down.

I dumped my underwear drawer on the bed and rifled through the jumbled pile, searching desperately for the lone pair of pantyhose I kept around for weddings, bad dates and funerals. *Voila!* When I tried to pull them on, they tore apart in my hands. *Dry rot. What a perfect analogy for my career.* I tugged a pair of black high-heels onto my bare feet. When I took a step, a red-hot flash of pain shot from my right hip to my brain. I flung the shoes off and slipped on a pair of old-maid flats.

Okay. All I had left to do was prepare my head for public presentation.

I took a look in the vanity mirror. My hair was a frizzy mess. I tied it in a ponytail. Somehow, it looked even worse. *How was that possible?* Panic kicked in. Sweat trickled down my back. I let my hair down and fluffed it up with what was left of the can of Aqua Net that Laverne had used on me right before my infamous chicken fill-it disaster. I tinted my cheeks with blush, slapped some eyeliner under my eyes and smeared on some lipstick. It would have to do. I was out of time.

I grabbed my purse, took a step toward the door and the room went a bit wonky. The Bailey's had kicked in.

*Oh, crap! I...I might be too drunk to drive!*

What was I going to do? There wasn't even time for a sobering piece of toast and butter. I shut my eyes in utter disbelief. *What else could go wrong?*

That's when I heard it. A rapping sound from the living room. I doddered down the hall and peeked into the living room. Winky was standing at the sliding glass door, his hands folded together at his waist like a naughty schoolboy. *Now what?* I slid the door open a crack.

"What's going on?"

"Hate to ask, Val, but nature's bangin' at my backdoor with a sledgehammer."

"What?"

"Can I use your *facilities?*"

Unsavory images tried to worm their way into my mind. I batted them away. "Uh...okay. But make it quick. I've got a job interview to get to ASAP."

I stepped back out of his way and winced.

"You look all stove up, Val Pal. Rough night?"

"Something like that."

I hobbled over to the couch.

"You don't look like yore in no condition to drive."

I wasn't. In more ways than one. I shrugged.

"How 'bout this. I'll do my business, then drive you where you gots to go. Just give me two shakes of a lamb's tail."

An image of Winky shaking something else came in for a landing before I could swat it away. I closed my eyes and winced. But it was desperate times. I couldn't fail Milly again. And there was no time to call a cab....

"Okay."

WINKY TURNED THE IGNITION on Maggie and grinned as she rumbled to life. His eyes lit up like a full moon over a hayseed's hayfield.

"Woo hoo! I always been wantin' to drive yore car, Val!"

"Have you got a license, Winky?"

"Somewheres."

I sighed, forced a smile, and resigned myself to my fate.

"Okay then. Let's roll."

Winky backed Maggie down the driveway, shifted into gear and hit the gas with his big, lead foot. I nearly got whiplash.

"Geez, Winky. Take it easy!"

"You in a hurry *or not?*"

"Yeah."

"Well, all right then. Hold on!"

Winky mashed the gas again. I rubbed my neck and looked on the bright side. Maybe the open air would sober me up. I took a deep breath, then caught my reflection in the side-view mirror and gasped. My blown-up hair, crude makeup and too-short skirt made me look like a televangelist's mistress. All I needed was some shoulder pads and I could have starred in an '80's sitcom as a skanky lush.

*Awesome sauce.*

"So. Job interview, huh? What you applyin' for?"

"Some kind of accounting assistant." I took my eyes off the side mirror and stared at the road ahead. I prayed we'd get stuck in traffic.

"Sounds fancy."

"I dunno. I probably won't get it. My résumé is...Oh crap! *I forgot my freaking résumé!*"

"Want me to turn around?"

"No. No time. Geez! I am so freaking...*unemployable!*"

"Aw, come on, now Val. Don't be so hard on yourself. There's all kind a jobs out there. You'd be surprised. I found me plenty a opportunities. Things you'd never think about."

I raised a skeptical eyebrow at Winky. "Like what?"

Winky flew past a bread truck and spit a hunk of chewing tobacco out the window.

"Well, one time I got paid 50 dollars to leave a weddin'. That there kicked off a whole new income stream for me. For the next couple a years, I crashed ever weddin', anniversary and hootenanny I heard tell of around Hawksville. Got myself so well knowed, people'd drive up to my place and hand me a twenty note just so I wouldn't show up at their shindig. Heck, them was good times. Didn't even have to leave the trailer."

Winky beamed at me proudly, then jerked the steering wheel to the left. He took the corner so hard I had to grab the door handle to keep from ending up in his lap.

"So why'd you quit? I mean, if the money was good, why'd you come down to Florida?"

Winky shot me a serious look. "Val, they's some things you don't ask a man. That's one of 'em."

"Oh. Sorry."

"Not a problem. You know, Goober said up in New York City, you can make good money just standing in line for people. Rich people don't like to wait."

"They don't like their parties crashed, either."

"Ha ha! That's right. Hey, speakin' a right. Wasn't you a writer?"

"I was. I tried to go back to writing last year. But I couldn't find a job at an ad agency. I *did* have a couple of ideas for some books, though."

"Oh yeah? What kind a books?"

"Books like, *How to be Happy in a Cardboard Box*. Or, maybe *The Art of Dumpster Diving*."

"Well, sounds like good information to me. *I'd* read 'em."

I shot Winky a smile. "Thanks. Pull in there. That's the place."

Winky skittered into a slot and slammed on the brakes. I glanced in the side view mirror again. The wind had whipped my hair into cotton candy. It was officially big enough to come in handy as an air bag. I sighed, unlocked my seatbelt and groaned out loud as I lifted my trashy-looking butt out of the car.

"What's wrong with you? Sounds like the world done whipped your butt and it ain't barely nine o'clock."

I turned around and shrugged. "There's some things you don't ask a woman, Winky. That's one of 'em."

Winky's smile was tinged with concern. "Fair enough. I'll be here waitin' for ya when ya get done. Break a leg."

I didn't half to. I already almost had.

THE INTERVIEW STARTED at 9:30 a.m. It was over at 9:33.

I hobbled, half drunk, up to the reception desk at Griffith & Maas, CPAs. An exhausted looking woman in dire need of a root touch-up glanced up at me through her smudged bifocals. Her pained expression exactly mirrored how I felt inside. I forced a smile.

"Hi. I'm Val Fremden."

She gave me a quick once-over. "Look, lady. We don't take solicitations."

"Oh. No. I'm here for an interview with...uh...." *Crap! What was that guy's name?* "I'm here about the accounting assistant position?"

"Oh." The woman's left eyebrow ticked up a notch. The rest of her pinched, haggard face remained motionless. "Yes. Ms. *Fremden*, did you say? I'm Mrs. Barnes. I'll ring Mr. Maas in his office. Please take a seat."

While I was trying to decide whether it was worth the pain of attempting to settle my bruised butt in a chair, a man came out of an office down at the end of the hallway. He was thin, balding, and just might have come over on the Mayflower. Dressed in an unremarkable blue suit, he reminded me of Mr. Burns on *The Simpsons*. When he reached the end of the hallway, he looked me over with eyes that hadn't expected much, and were therefore not disappointed.

"This way, Ms. Fremden," he said tiredly, without making eye contact.

The old man herded me down the hallway with a wave of his mummified hand. I tried my best not to limp or groan as he led me to an office with a gold placard on the door. It read, "J. W. Maas, Senior VP."

"Have a seat."

The office was large, but felt claustrophobic due to six-foot tall stacks of files piled up along the walls. His desk and credenza were buried under a foot-deep layer of papers. Only Mr. Maas' desk chair and a plush leather chair reserved for clients were free of clutter. I bit my lip, stifled a groan and lowered myself down onto the cushioned seat. I tugged at the hem of my dress in a vain attempt to cover my thighs. When I looked up, Mr. Maas was staring at me.

"Your résumé?"

*So much for making a good first impression.* "Uh. I forgot it. I was...."

And then it happened. I *farted. Out loud.* A long, whiny fart, like a balloon slowly losing a quart of air.

I froze for a split second, mortified. I scrambled for something to say, and raised my voice a decibel, hoping by some miracle my voice might override—no, *blot out*—my flatulent dissonance.

*Blasted burrito!*

"I was in a bit of a hurry this morning and..." I practically shouted at the old man.

Oddly, Mr. Maas hadn't even so much as flinched. I noticed he was wearing a hearing aid. *Geez! Could it be? He didn't hear it?* I lowered my voice a bit.

"...well, sir, I meant to bring it. I really..."

Mr. Maas cleared his throat and looked at me with the most played-out, bone-weary eyes I'd ever seen. "Ms. Fremden, I have to say...."

I shut my eyes and cringed. I took a deep breath and plotted my painful, humiliating getaway.

"You're hired."

I opened my eyes and did a double take. "What? You're kidding!"

"I am not," he said, with a face like a knackered Basset hound.

"But...?"

"The last person who applied bit her toenails...*during the interview*."

"Oh."

"And you did come recommended. By Ms. Halbert."

"Um. Yes. I did." I rallied a smidge from the shock and smiled. "Thank you, Mr. Maas. You won't be sorry."

Mr. Maas' droopy face shifted ever so slightly, as if he'd amused himself with a thought.

"To be honest, Ms. Fremden, I'm too tired to look for anyone else. We just finished tax season. My fifty-fourth. I'm worn out. But I can't leave for vacation until I've hired someone to help Ms. Barnes clean up the files. So I just did. This is your lucky day."

Mr. Maas pulled open a drawer and took out a manila envelope. "Take this. It has all the forms you'll need to fill out. Give it to Ms. Barnes when you're done. You start Monday."

"Wow. Thank you, Mr. Maas!"

"Don't thank me. Thank exhaustion. And, Ms. Fremden?"

"Yes?"

"Here's a tip. On the house. Try Beano."

"Beano?"

"For the...um...flatulence."

AFTER A LONG WALK OF shame down the short hallway back to Mrs. Barnes' desk, I filled out the paperwork and fled before Mr. Maas had a chance to change his mind. When I stepped out into the parking lot, I found Winky busy fiddling with Maggie's knobs.

"How did it go?" he asked.

I opened the passenger door and eased my butt into the bucket seat.

"It was okay, I guess. But not exactly what I'd hoped for."

"Huh." Winky nodded. "Kind of like my bowel movements nowadays."

I looked over at him and blew out a jaded breath.

"Yes, Winky. Exactly like that."

# Chapter Eight

On the ride home, the realization I had to show up for work at an actual job Monday morning sobered me up like a missed period after the prom. I dropped Winky at Davie's Donuts, took the wheel and drove Maggie back to the scene of the crime to pick Milly up for lunch. On the way to Griffith & Maas, the shock of my impending employment was slowly replaced by a persistent, niggling irritation. I was hangry—a deadly combination of hungry and angry. My butt hurt. And I hadn't had a thing to eat all day except humble pie. Granted, it was a huge, gut-busting portion....

I pulled up in the lot of Griffith & Maas and texted Milly. She came out the door a moment later. One look at me and she burst out laughing.

"I thought you had an interview for an accounting assistant...not a low-budget remake of *Rocky Horror Picture Show*."

"Shut up and get in the car, Janet, before I run you over."

Milly opened the passenger door and climbed in. "Hey...why didn't you come say 'hi' to me after your interview? I was so swamped I lost track of the time."

"Oh...I didn't want to disturb you," I lied, trying not to embarrass myself all over again. "I know you're busy. And I didn't want to look like a suck-up."

Milly smiled. Her emerald eyes sparkled with excited anticipation. "So? Did you get the job?"

I turned to face her, surprised. "Mr. Maas didn't tell you?"

"No. In fact, I haven't seen him this morning. He must have taken off right after your interview."

*I bet he did.* "He did mention he was going on vacation soon."

Milly nodded impatiently. "Yes, yes. So, did you get it?"

I cringed, uncertain how I felt about the whole thing. "Yeah."

Milly raised her arms in victory. "Yes! Now I won't be the only live body on the set of *Dead Accountants Walking!*"

"SO, ARE YOU AND COLD Cuts best friends now?" Milly asked, then wiped her face with a napkin. We were chowing down on cheeseburgers at a little dive called El Cap's.

"No. I just met her the one time."

"Oh. I thought maybe she'd dressed you this morning."

"Ha ha,"

I curled my lip, but Milly was too preoccupied to notice.

"Oooo...look at him!" Milly said. Her eyes shifted to the right. I glanced over and saw a man that made Brad Pitt look like Burgess Meredith. He sauntered by our table in his tight jeans, oblivious to our wanton stares.

"Wipe your face again, Milly."

She grabbed her napkin and looked at me self-consciously. "Mustard?"

"Drool."

"Very funny." Milly's smirk drooped into a frown. "Did you see that? I don't think he even noticed us. Are we getting old, Val?"

"Yes," I answered dryly.

Milly shot me a stern look. "Speak for yourself. You're in that hideous getup. I...I'm all dressed for work. I don't have any excuse."

"Excuse? For what?"

"For not being seen. For being ignored."

"Milly, stop it. You're gorgeous. Maybe he's gay."

Milly brightened up a smidge and eyeballed the guy. "Yeah. That's probably it."

But she didn't sound convinced. Her eyes looked distant. It was time to change the topic.

"Cold Cuts has my mom's RV. I'm nearly positive."

"What?" Milly's attention came back to the conversation. "Oh. Yes. You mentioned that on the phone. You think you saw her driving away in it?"

"Yeah. I'm pretty positive. The lady was blonde, and she wore these tacky, white, heart-shaped sunglasses with starfish on them. I mean, what are the odds?"

"Like these?" Milly fished around in her purse and produced a pair of sunglasses matching those I'd just described.

"Uh. Yeah."

"On sale at Target for three bucks. They had barrels full of them."

"Oh." My heart sank a little. "But still, the blonde hair and all."

"Yeah, only me and half the other women in here."

I looked around. Milly was right. Still, my gut told me it was Cold Cuts I saw driving that RV.... It *had* to be, didn't it?

"So what did you two talk about?" Milly asked, then tucked the last bite of her cheeseburger into her mouth. "Anything profound or earth-shattering?"

"Actually, yes. Profound, I mean. She said something I can't quit thinking about."

"What?"

"She said that life is too short to play one role for a whole lifetime. Milly, I've played a lot of roles in my life, but I've never felt like the star. I guess the closest I ever felt to playing my *real self* was when I was in Italy. Before I met Friedrich. When I was totally free."

"You didn't *have* to play a role then. No one you knew was watching."

Milly's words struck a chord. "*Yes. That's it.* Why do we change how we act when we think someone's watching?"

Milly gazed wistfully at the handsome man who'd payed us no mind. "I dunno. Because we think our normal behavior isn't good enough? That what we're doing is somehow inadequate? Wrong, even?"

"Milly, you're a genius. Yes. I think that's it *exactly*. My mom—"

"Lucille or Glad?"

I grimaced. "*Lucille*. She made me feel like that my whole life. *Inadequate*. Everything I ever did was to please her or appease her. It became a...*survival mechanism*. If I learned anything from Lucille Jolly it was this: 'If mama ain't happy, ain't nobody happy.'"

Milly shook her head. "Lucille. Yes. There ought to be a law against moms like her."

I shrugged. "I mean, she wasn't Attila the Hun or anything. She was just...well, anyway, I survived. You know, she *still* makes me feel like everything I do is wrong."

"Well, it's *not*, Val. You found me. And your *real* mom, Glad. And Tom. Nothing wrong with that."

I shrugged. "True. But as they say, even a busted clock is right two times a day."

Milly's face grew stern. "Val, you're not busted. Do you hear me?"

"Well, I know I'm not quite right. Some things that look so easy for other people seem like an impossible dream to me."

"What are you talking about?"

"I don't know how to describe it exactly, Milly. I guess...it's just that...well, I got so good at stuffing myself away to please my mom, I never learned how to be true to myself, you know? I don't know how to be my real self when I'm in a relationship. I think three failed marriages proves that."

"How are those your fault?"

"I don't know. I just...compromised myself away to nothing, Milly. And it's not like they even *asked* me to. I guess I felt responsible to please them more than I did to please my own self. So I just abandoned my dreams and desires and did what they wanted. And all three times, I ended up resenting the hell out of them, just like with my mom, when it was actually my own fault all along."

"Excuse me? Those men weren't blameless! And your mother certainly isn't! Sometimes, Val, it's just time to...*let go*. That doesn't mean it was all your fault. Or that everything was bad...or wrong. Look, you can have a real relationship. You're your true self with me, aren't you?"

I thought about it for a second. "Yes."

Milly cocked her head and smiled tenderly. "So see, you're not a hopeless cause."

I smiled gratefully at my friend. "Maybe you're right. Thanks, Milly. I owe you lunch."

Milly straightened her head and winked at me. "Darn straight you do."

I grinned, then looked at her with pleading, puppy-dog eyes. "Milly, I wanted to ask a favor."

"I know. We can go shopping for work clothes this weekend."

"Huh? Oh. Yes, thanks. But—"

"That wasn't it?"

"No."

"So, what do you need?"

"I want to find Cold Cuts. I have this idea. Could you help?"

"Sure. What can I do?"

"Well, you know how she comes to the need of damsels in distress?"

"Yeah."

"I was thinking you could be the damsel."

"Huh?"

"You could go out on a bad date. As a setup. Hopefully, Cold Cuts would show up to rescue you. I'd wait in the wings and nab her."

"Oh, Val. Not another MatchMate date."

I gave her the puppy dog eyes again. She cringed. "Please, no."

"Okay, then. I do know a few guys who could be your fake dates."

Milly sat back in her chair and looked at me sideways. "You don't mean..."

I smiled devilishly.

"Oh no. Come on, Val! Are you serious?"

"They're available. They're harmless. And they work for food."

Milly pursed her lips. "Winky is off the table."

"Okay."

Milly scrunched her eyebrows. "Jorge is usually *under* the table...."

"True."

"That leaves...oh dear lord...Goober."

"He *is* the one most likely to remain coherent."

Milly rolled her eyes and sighed. "You owe me *big time* for this, Valliant."

"I knew I could count on you, Millicent."

# Chapter Nine

"Can I use your crapper? Been prairie-doggin' it for the last hour and a half. Startin' to feel like one a them there Whack-a-Mole machines."

My face grimaced involuntarily. I unlocked the sliding glass door and let Winky inside. His stray-dog act at my backdoor the past couple of days had put a distasteful glitch in my morning routine—one akin to finding a cockroach in my cornflakes.

"Come on in."

Winky sprinted down the hallway. I shuffled over to the kitchen and made a pot of coffee. I'd temporarily switched from cappuccinos. I didn't want the pleasure of sipping them to become mingled with memories of Winky's disgusting defecation analogies.

I heard the toilet flush and poured two cups of joe. *Thank goodness for Ty-D-Bol.*

Winky appeared in the living room, adjusting the waistline of his cargo shorts. "That there coffee smells like heaven in a cup."

"Here, this one's for you." I held a mug in his direction.

Winky grinned in delight. He wiped both hands on the back of his shorts then rubbed them together. "Don't mind if I do. Thanky, Val Pal!"

"Yeah. Winky, I'm curious. What does *Winnie* do? For *facilities*, I mean?"

"That woman's got a bladder like a dried-up camel. She just holds it 'til she gets to work. Speakin' a work, did you ever talk to whozee-whatzit about that job?"

"Oh. Actually, that was *me*. I wasn't sure about it when I mentioned it to you the other day. But I am now. I want to hire you as a lookout."

"A lookout?"

"For Milly. On a set-up date. I was—"

Winky's eyes lit up. "Woo hoo! Another stakeout! I'm in!"

"It's not a stakeout. It's just a...."

Winky smirked and stared at me patiently. Try as I might, I couldn't think of a better term for it. I guess it *was* a stakeout. *Dang it.*

"*Whatever*. Winky, I want you to get in touch with Goober and Jorge. I want them to meet us here tonight. At my house. To discuss the...."

"Stakeout."

"Okay. Stakeout."

"I'm on it. What time you want us here?"

"When does Winnie get off work?"

"'Bout five, usually."

"Okay. Tell them five thirty. And tell Winnie she's invited. I'll make sandwiches or something."

"Hot dog!"

"Oh, and Winky?"

Winky had his coffee cup to his mouth. He looked at me over the rim. "Yes'm?"

"Don't tell Jorge what the meeting's about. He's a bit of a blabbermouth. I don't want Tom to find out. At least, not yet. He'd probably want me to call it off."

"Well, all right. But it's yore life Val. Yore a growed woman. You don't owe Tom no explanation. You can do what you want."

"So I've heard."

"Well, lemme see. I'll tell Jorge it's a surprise. That'll give you time to get your ducks in the road."

"You mean in a row."

Winky scrunched his eyebrows together and nearly choked on a mouthful of coffee.

"Ain't that what I just said?"

NO SOONER HAD I GOTTEN rid of Winky when the next fly landed in my ointment. I answered the doorbell to find Laverne standing there holding a shiny, brown glob in her hands. It bore an uncanny resemblance to what I imagined might result if someone took a sizeable dump in an anti-gravity environment.

"Howdy, neighbor!"

I tore my morbidly mesmerized eyes away from the glob and looked up at Laverne. "Hi. What's up?"

"Just wanted to stop by and show you my work of art!"

"Work of art?"

"From the ceramics class. Sugar, you don't know what you're missing."

Laverne beamed like a first-grader with a shiny gold star. She thrust the petrified turd in my face. I flinched.

"What is it?"

"Why, it's the happy banana man! See? That's his face."

The area Laverne's red-lacquered fingernail pointed to didn't look that happy to me.

"Wow, Laverne. I've never seen anything like it."

"I know, right? The teacher says I have latent talent."

"Yes, I can see that." *Very latent.*

Laverne tried to hand me the hideous feces-inspired figurine.

"Here, I want *you* to have it."

I took a step back and put up both my palms. "Oh no, Laverne. I couldn't."

Laverne pouted. "Why not?"

"It's your very first piece, right?"

"Yes."

"You *have* to keep it. To...commemorate the beginning of your whole new...*artistic venture*."

Laverne's pout disappeared into a smile. "You're right! You're so smart, Val. I'll keep it as a memento."

"It'll go perfectly with all your Vegas stuff."

"You think so?"

"For sure." *Another useless piece of crap on the heap.* "Perfectly."

Laverne admired her sculpture anew, then looked up at me. "So, Winky tells me you went and got yourself a job. Good for you."

"Uh. Yes. When did you see Winky?"

"When did I *not* see him? He and Winnie are practically living here, aren't they?"

"It's just temporary." *I hope.*

"I can help you pick out clothes. If you want. You're gonna need a new work wardrobe."

I thought back on the last time Laverne dressed me. I'd had to free myself from the stranglehold of the red-sequined dress with a pair of scissors. "Oh. Thanks, Laverne, but Milly already volunteered."

"Oh." Laverne's shoulders slumped. "Well, I guess I should be going."

"All right."

Laverne dawdled hesitantly, then headed for the door. "I'll see you around."

I hadn't planned on getting Laverne involved in the stakeout to find Cold Cuts. But she'd been a big help last time. And she looked like she could use the company.

"Wait. Laverne, would you like to come over tonight? I'm having a meeting...uh...a little get together about—"

Laverne perked up like a puppy on Paxil. "Really? That'd be great! Can I do anything to help? Should I bring something?"

"No. Don't bother. It's not necessary."

"I tell you what, Val. I'll make us a banana cream pie."

"Great." *Just so long as Mr. Happy doesn't end up in it.*

IT WAS NEARLY 6 P.M. and the stakeout team was assembled in my living room. As I looked around at the goofy, eager faces of Laverne, Jorge, Goober, Winky and Winnie, I suddenly got the feeling I should have been dressed in white and dispensing pills in little paper cups. Milly stood by my side. She punched me on the arm.

"So, are you ready to get started?"

"Uh...*yes*. Thanks for coming everybody. As you all know, Tom sold my RV to Lefty's Scrapyard...and that Glad's ashes were in the RV."

Heads nodded around the room like bobble-head cartoon figures.

"Well, before I could get to Lefty's to recover the RV, a woman bought it. Two days ago, I think I spotted her driving it at Publix."

"Oooo, Publix," heckled Winky. "Too fancy for Winn Dixie?"

I scowled. "Anyway, I think it was her. I had a conversation with her over coffee—"

"Oooo, coff—" Winky began.

I shot him a dirty look. He stopped mid-word. Winnie shoved a peanut-butter cookie in his open mouth, then looked at me apologetically through her thick, red-framed glasses.

"The thing is, I talked with this woman before I knew she was the one who had bought the RV. Her name is...well, her *nickname* is Cold Cuts. And she makes a habit of uh...*interacting*...with bad conversations."

"Interacting?" Goober asked. He ran a thumb and index finger over his bushy moustache. "What do you mean, *interacting?*"

Milly jumped in before I could answer. "She tells awful guys who are harassing women to get lost."

"Oh," Goober nodded his peanut-shaped head. "Why didn't you just say so in the first place?"

"Sounds like a public service to me," Laverne said. Winnie nodded in agreement.

"Well, yes. So, that's where you *guys* come in."

"What do you mean?" Jorge asked.

I tried to tread lightly. "You guys are going to pretend to be men harassing women."

Milly interjected again. "And by women, Val means *us*." She pointed a thumb at herself, then at me.

"Wait a minute," I balked.

"You didn't think I was doing this *alone*, did you Val?" Milly mocked with feigned innocence. "Oh no, dear. You get to play, too."

Everyone eyed me expectantly as I tried in vain to find a way out of the corner Milly'd backed me into. *Well played, Millicent.* "Why of course not. We'll all do it together."

"A double date," Milly purred. "We'll lure Cold Cuts with twice the bait."

Goober raised his hand as if he were in school. "Wait a minute," he said. "We've gotta go out with *you* two? What do *we* get in return?"

"A free meal," I said dryly.

Goober's suspicious expression dissolved into mild approval. "Oh. Okay. Works for me."

"Me, too," Jorge agreed.

Winky raised his hand. I began to feel I was teaching a special needs class. "Yes?"

"Does that include doggy bags?" Winky asked.

"Uh...yeah, sure."

"Okay, I'm in."

"Then it's settled," I said. "All we need now is a place to set up the stakeout. Publix's coffee shop is an option, but it could have been a one-time fluke. Any ideas?"

"Oh, that's easy," Milly said. "Garvey's."

"Garvey's?"

"Sure. It's the tri-county mecca for bad dates. It's common knowledge among on-line daters. If a guy asks you to Garvey's, you can pretty much count on him being a douche."

"How do you know this?" I asked.

Milly eyed me jadedly. "You really gonna go there?"

I looked around at the ring of bobble heads and sighed.

"Okay, then. Garvey's it is."

# Chapter Ten

As usual, Laverne was the last to leave the party. She wobbled around in her gold heels and gathered up empty beer bottles while I wiped down the kitchen counter. Overall, the stakeout meeting had gone to plan. Everyone had been assigned their roles. We were to meet at 6:30 p.m. at Garvey's tomorrow night, dressed and ready for our fake dates. We were also, by Laverne's decree, to keep our fingers crossed that Cold Cuts showed. The Vegas veteran admitted it wasn't statistically helpful, but it never hurt anything, either.

Laverne added two empty beer bottles to the impressive collection at the end of the counter. "What about me?" she asked.

"What do you mean?"

"What do *I* do? For the stakeout?"

"I told you. You're on emergency call. In case we need backup."

Laverne frowned. "That's not much of a role. I know a bit part when I see one."

"Would you rather go out with Winky?"

Laverne grimaced, then laughed. "No, I guess not. But sitting at home waiting for the phone to ring is a bad habit I broke a long time ago, honey. I don't want to get the lonesome Bugaboo stirred up again."

"Bugaboo?"

"Oh. Pet name someone used to call me. Whenever he bothered to call."

"Hey, I know, Laverne. You can help me with logistics."

"Huh?"

"We need to do some reconnaissance work."

Laverne cocked her horsey head. I dumbed it down for her.

"You can help me check out Garvey's tomorrow."

"Oh!"

"So we'd better get rested up. A good night's sleep, you know?"

"Yes. Sure!" Laverne smiled at me brightly.

"In our beds."

She nodded eagerly. "Uh-huh."

"Soon." I yawned like a lazy lion.

I was about to go grab Laverne's purse and hand it to her when she beat me to it. She picked up her pocketbook and headed for the door.

"Okay, Val. See you in the morning. What time...6 a.m.?"

"Uh...I don't think they open until 11:30."

"See you at 11, then." Laverne scooted happily through the door, then turned and waved goodbye. "This is gonna be so much fun!"

*Fun? For the moment, I'd settle for non-catastrophic.*

WITH WINKY SCRATCHING at my backdoor and Laverne's imminent arrival at 11, my casual Sunday morning was shot to hell. I should have had a cappuccino in my hand and Tom in my bed. Instead, I had a pair of rubber gloves on my hands and a bathroom so revolting it made me wish I owned a hazmat suit. I tied my hair back, grabbed my bottle of Ty D Bol and set my resolve to 'annihilate.' This was not the life I'd signed up for. Something needed to give, and it needed to give *ASAP*.

Tom had called around four o'clock yesterday. He'd told me his buddy at the DMV was on vacation, so there'd been no chance to run the license plate search yet. Oddly, Tom hadn't mentioned coming over last night, so I hadn't had to lie about what I'd been up to. He had, however, asked about dinner tonight. I'd told Tom I needed to color my hair, and opted for lunch tomorrow instead. When he'd agreed without a fuss, my radar went up. Was he giving me space? Or had he just given up on me ever taking him seriously?

Just as I finished showering and dressing the doorbell rang. Laverne was right on time. I opened the door to find the six-foot tall, skinny old broad dressed in a skin-tight black body suit. She held a ski mask in her hand.

"What are you wearing?" I asked.

"Well, you said we were spying, right? I googled 'reconnaissance' when I got home last night."

*WTF?* "Yes. Sure. But...it's in the *daytime*, Laverne."

"Oh." Laverne scratched her empty head.

"Wait here," I said.

I riffled through my bedroom closet and grabbed a jean skirt.

"Just put this on over your tights. And lose the ski mask."

"You're a good spy, Val. Always ready to improvise. Like MacGyver."

"Yeah. Just give me a roll of duct tape and I can save the world."

GARVEY'S TURNED OUT to be one of those places people picked mainly because the parking lot was in the back of the building, away from prying eyes. I squeezed Maggie into a tight space next to the alley dumpster. I shoved the gear into park and looked over at Laverne. She winked at me and my wavering convictions about the whole stakeout idea took a nosedive off a short pier.

"Maybe this isn't such a good idea," I mumbled.

"Nonsense!" Laverne shoved me on the arm, then pried her black grasshopper legs out of the car. She stood up and beckoned me with a wave of her hand. "Come on, Val. Let's go!"

I followed Laverne's thin, black silhouette through the scruffy parking lot to the front door of Garvey's. The glass doors were painted black on the inside, an attempt to add to the dining mystique, I supposed. Inside the decrepit foyer was furnished with a dusty-caked fake Ficus tree and a couple of paintings I wouldn't pay a dollar for at a garage sale. Behind a hostess podium stood a crusty old woman with a swirl of bright-orange hair impressive enough to make Bozo kick a kid in a fit of jealous rage.

"Welcome to Garvey's, where we don't ask no questions. Cash only."

*How quaint.* I did a mental rundown of my wallet. I had two twenties and a five. "Okay."

The clown-haired lady led us to one of a dozen or so black vinyl booths that lined the dark paneled walls. The place reminded me of Water Loo's—minus the vagrants, sticky brown splotches and dead roaches in the corners.

"Here you go." She set two menus on the table. As we scooted into the booth, she spoke with the deadpan of a washed-up comedienne "Our special of the day is....ha ha ha! What am I saying? We don't have no special."

The woman laughed at her own joke. It wasn't funny to me, but it seemed to tickle Laverne's fancy. She giggled as the woman walked away.

"She reminds me of one of those old Vaudeville acts. Those were the days!"

"Yeah. Looks like this place has seen better days itself."

I turned my nose up at the fake red rose in the cheap glass vase next to the salt and pepper. Laverne pulled a pair of leopard-print bifocals out of her purse and ogled the menu. We were the only customers in the place, except for a pair of spritely dressed octogenarians. They were drinking dark-colored liquor out of short glasses and laughing like newlyweds. I secretly wondered if they were having an affair....

"Know what you're having?" Laverne asked.

I took a look at the menu. In a desperate, fruitless stab at sophistication, Garvey's offered a list of 'fine wines,' each of which I'd seen for under five bucks a gallon at Publix. Any polish this place might have once had was scuffed off in the 1970s. To top it off, Garvey's specialized in fondue. I hadn't eaten fondue since kitchen appliances came in avocado and harvest gold.

"You up for the cheese fondue?" I asked Laverne.

"Sure! You know, I've got a fondue set at home. The little handles are made out of—"

"Let me guess. Dice?"

Laverne's eyes goggled in astonishment. "Val, you're not just MacGyver. You're like that famous mind reader, too. What was his name?"

"I wouldn't know."

Laverne frowned. "No. That's not it."

WELL, AT LEAST I KNEW that a stakeout at Garvey's wouldn't cause much suspicion. I had the feeling I could have walked in with a gorilla and old Orange Whip wouldn't have batted an eyelash. The best thing about Garvey's, besides leaving, was the fact that it was right across the street from Chocolateers. After paying the bill and feeling the acid already rising in my throat, I had the notion that some chocolate-covered cherries might be just the ticket to nip my indigestion in the bud. I looked across at Chocolateers and smiled.

I was about to mention the idea to Laverne when my smile switched into a cringe. I hadn't been back to Jack's chocolate shop since our last stakeout, when I'd throttled his Easter bunny to death in the display window. I sighed and decided to save Chocolateers for another time.

"Have you got your outfit picked out for tomorrow?" Laverne asked.

"What do you mean?"

"For your first day on the job, sugar."

"Oh." I'd forgotten all about it. Again. "No."

The thought gave me a second reason to have heartburn.

"Well, look over there!" Laverne grinned and pointed. "There's a used clothing store. Let's stop inside."

Her suggestion made the reasons three.

IT WAS JUST AFTER 2 p.m. when I returned from Garvey's with a ninja granny, a gurgling stomach, and two sacksful of used women's apparel. As I pulled up the driveway, we were greeted by two old 'friends' of questionable intent. Winky was one. The other was that hideous, lump of a sofa and its crap-brown cushions. The upholstered hulk leered at me from the side of the curb like a drunken deviant.

"Hey there, Val Pal! Look who showed up fresh out a the hoosegow."

"What's going on, Winky?"

"Cops just dropped it off. Said they didn't need it no more, now that the case was closed."

"What case?" Laverne asked.

"The one that involved me being charged with human dismemberment, remember?"

"Huh?"

"The finger? When I found that finger in the couch? The cops hauled it away as evidence."

"Oh. Sure. That's right, honey."

Laverne and I climbed out of the car. Winky handed me a piece of paper.

"It come with this here."

The note read: "Many happy returns. Lieutenant Hans Jergen."

"What 'cha gonna do with it?" Winky asked.

I knew what I wanted to do with *the note*. The couch, on the other hand, I wasn't quite sure.

"Well, honey, I'm heading out of this heat," Laverne said. "I'm about to sweat through my leotards! Here's your skirt back."

Before I could object, Laverne shimmied out of the skirt and handed it to me.

"Uh...thanks, Laverne. For your help today."

"Loved every minute of it, sugar! Good luck tonight...and tomorrow!"

I watched Laverne slip off to her house like a geriatric cat burglar. I turned around to see Winky stretched out on the lumpy old sofa.

"What are you doing, Winky?"

"Just givin' her a test drive." He hauled his chubby butt to standing. "Here. Lemme give ya a hand with it."

"What do you mean?"

"To haul it into the house."

Bile rose in my throat. "I don't want it!"

"Well, Val, for all intensive purposes, yore stuck with it."

"Intents and purposes."

Winky stared at me blankly. "Yeah? So, what are your intents?"

"I dunno. Wait. Let's throw the piece of crap on the fire pit out back. Have a couch bonfire."

Winky grabbed his chin and gave the couch an intense once-over. "As gaul-dang fun as that sounds, Val, I got me a better idea. When Winnie gets here, let's load this bad boy into the Dodge. It's gotta sleep better than that blasted old air mattress."

# Chapter Eleven

What was wrong with my life? The things I wanted to get rid of kept coming back. The things I wanted to hold onto kept slipping away. I pondered this and the meaning of life as I dressed in someone else's cast-off clothes for a fake date with a derelict Hispanic man who hadn't been sober since the invention of cellphones. *Oh joy.*

On my reconnaissance mission with Laverne, I'd discovered that trying to park Maggie in Garvey's narrow spots was a challenge, even when the lot was empty. Therefore, I opted to ride with Winky and Winnie in the van. Their role in tonight's stakeout was to stay outside on "parking lot patrol" in case the RV showed up. Goober and Jorge were to be Milly's and my dates. They'd told Winky they'd get there "by other means of transportation." We waited in the van for them to show up.

"So what's this woman look like?" Winnie asked. She turned around in the driver's seat and peered at me through her red-frame glasses. The thick lenses magnified a pair of dark eyes that darted between narrow slits above her puffy, pink cheeks. "You never said."

"Yeah," Winky chimed in. "Who should we be on the lookout for, supposin' she don't drive up here in the RV."

"Well...," I fumbled. "She...she could be blonde. Or she could have a rainbow-colored Mohawk. Tattoos...or maybe...."

"That's quite a range," Winky taunted.

"Sorry. She dresses up. In disguises."

"That's cool," Winnie said. She fussed with her black bob hairdo in the rearview mirror. "I'd like to—"

A city bus pulled up and hissed. We all turned to the right in the direction of the noise. The bus doors flew open. Two vagrants tumbled out.

"There they are now," Winky said. He yelled out the van window, "Hey fellers! Over here!"

Goober saluted. Jorge tripped and fell face-down on the asphalt.

*Lovely. We're off to a great start.*

IT WAS SUNDAY NIGHT and Garvey's was packed to the brim with losers. We fit right in. The lady whose orange-swirl hairdo defied gravity and description didn't bat an eye of recognition at me, even though barely five hours had passed since I'd been here with Laverne. Perhaps for her, discretion was the better part of valor—or perhaps Valium? She grabbed a handful of menus from a stack on the reception desk and escorted us through the land of misfit boys to the only open booth on the poop deck.

Just as we scooched in, my phone rang. It was Milly.

"Val, I can't make it."

"What? Why not?"

"I promise, I have a good reason. I'll explain later. Gotta go."

She clicked off, leaving me to fend for myself on the merry-go-round of mayhem.

"Milly's not coming," I said.

"This place reminds me of Water Loo's," Goober said, not missing a beat. He'd worn a black T-shirt that looked like a tuxedo. *Mr. Class.*

Orange swirl lady returned and deposited three glasses of water on the table with as little care as humanly possible. The third thud caused Jorge to return to this plane of existence. He lifted his head and smiled at me sheepishly.

"Yeah, it does look a bit like Water Loo's," I agreed. I picked up a glass and studied the tiny white flakes swimming around in the liquid. "Minus the water."

"And the Loo," Jorge said.

Goober and I smiled at each other. It was rare for Jorge to say much. Booze usually robbed him of conversation skills beyond a few slurs. Goober reached across the table and shook him on the shoulder. I encouraged our shattered friend to keep going.

"So, what's new with you, Jorge?"

"My mother got remarried," he offered, then stared at the menu.

I knew Jorge had been living in his mother's garage in a makeshift "apartment" since his wife and kids were killed in a traffic accident years ago.

"Oh. So, good for her. Will you stay in the house?"

"Jes. She's giving it to me." Even though he kept his eyes on the menu, I could tell Jorge didn't seem thrilled with the news. "She's moving in with *him*."

"You're not happy for her?" I asked.

Jorge looked up at me. "What? Oh, jes. I'm happy for her. But now...I'll be...."

Jorge's attention faded before he could finish his thought. But I could guess what the problem was. He'd be in that house all alone. The poor guy had lost everyone in his family that he'd cared about except his mother. And now she was leaving him, too. I'd like to think what I said next was completely altruistic, but that would have been a lie. However, killing two birds with one stone was...an efficient way to kill two birds.

"Jorge, why don't you invite Winky and Winnie to live there with you?"

Jorge stared down at the menu. "I dunno. My mother wouldn't like it."

"Your mother won't be there. Besides, she gave you the house, right?"

He looked up. "Jes."

"When is the wedding?"

"This morning."

"What? You never...."

Goober shot me a warning look. *Tread lightly.*

"Oh. So she's gone already? The house is empty?"

"Val, it's not empty," Goober said sarcastically. "Jorge lives there. And I'm moving in tonight."

"Oh. Is there room for Winnie and Winkie, too?"

Goober and I looked at Jorge. He shrugged. Then smiled.

"Sure. Why not? We could be a fam...."

Jorge stopped dead in his tracks. He'd almost pushed his own self-destruct button—the f-word 'family.' I held my breath. Goober came to the rescue.

"Famished, right Jorge?"

Jorge gave a tiny nod.

"Me, too," I said, way too cheerfully.

"Me three," Goober said and shot me a dirty look.

The old lady came back with a notepad. "So, what'll it be?"

"The cheese fondue for three," Jorge said.

Goober and I exchanged raised eyebrows and grins.

"Sounds good to me," I said. *Very good, indeed.*

WE MADE IT ALL THE way through dinner with no Cold Cuts attack. In a way, I was glad. I'd gotten to share a special moment with the guys. One that had the potential to be a turning point for Jorge. At 8 p.m. I declared the stakeout officially over. I paid the bill and we bid Garvey's adieu.

We'd just rounded the corner to the back parking lot when we heard Winky holler from the van window.

"'Bout time, you three. Let's go!"

I walked up to the van window. Winky stared straight ahead, madder than a busted-up hornet's nest. "What's wrong with you?" I asked. He didn't answer.

"He's ticked off about something else, Val," Winnie said. "Nothing to do with you."

I looked across the van to Winnie. "Did you two have a fight?"

"No. It's just—"

Red-faced Winky turned his head toward me. "Val, we was just sittin' here, mindin' our own business, when this crazy woman came up and tried to steal Winnie away from me."

Winnie put a hand on his shoulder. "She didn't try to steal me away, Winky."

"She did, too. Asked Winnie if she needed to go back to rehab."

My jaw fell open. "What?"

"You wouldn't a believed it, Val. That gal talked a pile a horse hockey. Said she thought Winnie'd done been cured once."

"Of what?"

"Of dating...what was it?" Winky looked over to Winnie for an answer.

"Moronic hicks," she offered softly.

Goober and Jorge began laughing their butts off.

"What did she look like?" I asked over their guffaws.

"A witch!" Winky hollered. "All dressed in black. Long-ass black fingernails. I tole her to get on her broom and fly back to where-evers she come from."

"What did she say?"

"She said she would a, but her broom was busted. In the shop 'til Wednesday. Told Winnie she should drop me like a hot tamale. Can you believe that?"

I glanced at Winky's beer belly, atrocious haircut and wife-beater T-shirt.

Could I believe that? Oh, yes. I certainly could.

# Chapter Twelve

I awoke to the sound of someone rapping on my sliding glass door. I wrapped a bathrobe around me and shuffled into the living room to let the annoying stray hound in.

"There you are. Finally," Winky scolded me. "I need to pinch a loaf. Drop a deuce, you know."

"Yeah. I figured."

As Winky defiled my facilities, I made coffee and wrote a mental note; *Buy more Ty D Bol.* I awaited the royal flush and the arrival of his majesty from the throne.

"Woo doggy! That was a tough one. Hey, Val Pal. D'you ever hear the one about the constipated mathematician?

I groaned in my mind. "No."

I absently handed Winky a cup of coffee, somewhat stunned he could pronounce the word "mathematician." He grabbed the cup and wagged his ginger eyebrows at me.

"Yeah. You know, the poor old feller worked it all out with nothin' but a pencil and a piece of paper."

I groaned audibly this time. But I had to hand it to Winky. He was a miracle worker. I actually *wanted* to go to work.

I PULLED SHABBY MAGGIE into the parking lot of Griffith & Maas. Milly pulled up beside me in her shiny, red Beemer. I accosted her before her matching, shiny red pumps hit the pavement.

"Why couldn't you make it last night?"

"Milly shut the door and locked it behind her, then shot me a smug look. "I wanted to teach you a lesson, Val. In responsibility. You're a working girl now. You need to act like one."

She marched toward the front door. I scrambled to follow her.

"How is *you* not showing up last night going to teach *me* responsibility?"

Milly spoke without looking back. "Now you know how *I* felt...when you blew off your interview appointment last week."

I grabbed Milly's elbow as she reached for the door. "I didn't blow it off, Milly. Something...came up."

"Uh-huh."

"Look, you were right about Garvey's. Cold Cuts was there."

Milly's face registered surprise. "So, you caught her already?"

"Well, not exactly. She ambushed Winky in the parking lot. He didn't realize it was her."

"Oh. Too bad." Milly opened the door to the accounting firm. I followed her inside.

"Milly, we decided to do a second stakeout tonight. Can I count on you?"

Milly looked at me, then nodded toward a jumbled stack of files bigger than her Beemer.

"I dunno. Can *I* count on *you?*"

BY 11:30 THAT MORNING, I'd lost both heels and my entire sense of humor. For nearly three hours, I'd been schlepping around files nonstop for Mrs. Barnes, aka "The Little Old Sadistic Slave Driver from Pasadena." My aching feet and back made me forget all about my black-

and-blue bottom. I was about to cause an avalanche by collapsing dead onto a heap of files when the old taskmaster herself stuck her shriveled head in the file room and announced it was time for lunch.

I dropped an armful of files and peeked down the hallway. Milly was nowhere in sight. *Screw her*. Besides, I had a lunch date with Tom. I tiptoed out of the office and slipped my heels back onto my blistered feet. I hobbled out to the parking lot, turned the key in the ignition and hit the gas. I smiled smugly to myself. I'd made a clean getaway.

"MILLY HASN'T BEEN VERY friendly today," I whined.

Tom looked up from the Ming Ming's menu and shot me a silly pout.

"Poor baby. The kids at school didn't like you?"

I kicked him under the table.

"Ow! Hey! Look, maybe she doesn't like to mix business with pleasure. Lots of people don't."

"But there's no one else in the office to see her do it...except for Mrs. Barnes."

"That's funny. In high school, I had a teacher named Mrs. Barnes. She was a real ballbuster."

"I wouldn't be surprised if she was one in the same. She's already worked me to the bone this morning. And the woman's old enough to be Methuselah's grandmother."

"So, what does my favorite working girl want for lunch?"

I hadn't realized I'd developed such an appetite. But food had nothing to do with it. I looked at Tom longingly and blew out a breath. "The usual, I guess."

"You know, you're sexy when you have to work, Val. It adds to your mystique. Ms. High-Powered Career Woman. Me likey."

Tom's knee rubbed up against mine. I moved my leg to reciprocate, causing my stiff thigh muscles to grumble with pain. I'd just finished a

180-minute, complete-body workout. If I hadn't felt like I'd been run over by a steamroller, I'd have jumped Tom's bones in the parking lot.

AFTER LUNCH, TOM WALKED me to my car. He kissed me goodbye as I leaned against the driver's door of Maggie. Afterward, he lingered, holding my hand.

"What's up, Tom?"

He looked deep into my eyes. "Nothing."

"Nothing?"

"Well, to tell you the truth, I was wondering. If you'd thought much about...what I told you at the party."

"Oh, Well, now that you mention it, yes. I have."

Tom snuggled a little closer to me. "And?"

"Why *did* you get a vasectomy?"

Tom flinched and jerked his hand away.

"Oh. Well...umm...I guess I just thought it was time to give up on the whole idea of having a family."

"Oh. I see."

Tom shrugged. He took my hand again and studied it, rubbing my palm with his thumb as he spoke.

"To be honest, Val, I didn't want to end up like my cousin Karl. He got divorced a couple of years ago. Then he went and knocked up his thirty-year-old girlfriend. He married her. But the girl was *twenty years* younger than him. How did he ever think that was going to work?"

Tom looked at me as if he expected an answer. I shook my head and gave him one.

"I dunno."

"Right. Well, no surprise. They ended up getting divorced a few months after the baby was born. Now she's raising the kid alone. And he's gonna have a kid in grade school while he's pissing in his diapers in a nursing home. It's just not fair."

"What do you mean, Tom? Not fair to who?"

"To *anyone*. Karl finally got some sense and started dating women his age. But it's kind of too late. I mean, what does he expect these women to do? Marry him and take care of a two-year-old on the weekends? The man was a fool to go messing around with a woman that much younger than him."

I studied Tom with new eyes. Maybe it was the sunlight gleaming off his sandy blond hair. Maybe it was knowing he loved me, and wanted me to love him in return. But if I had to put a finger on it, I'd say it was the magical words from his lips. Tom had never been sexier. I leaned over and kissed him with a lip-lock that meant business. Forget my aches and pains!

*It was Tom's day off. We could...oh crap! No we couldn't. Dang it! This "job" stuff was turning out to be a real cock-blocker.*

I RETURNED TO THE DETENTION camp known as Griffith & Maas with the disgruntled attitude usually reserved for long-term postal employees. I could have been having my way with Tom. Instead, I was screwing around with heavy piles of useless paperwork.

"Where'd you go for lunch?" Milly asked when I stomped in the door.

"Is that a requirement of the job? To tell you my personal business?"

Milly's left eyebrow arched like a Halloween cat. "No."

I kicked off my shoes and carried them toward the file room. "Then let's just get back to work, shall we?"

"You know, that attitude isn't going to fly around here, Val. What's up your butt?"

"So *now* you want to get personal?"

"Ladies, let's cut the bull crap and get back to work," Mrs. Barnes interjected, nipping our catfight in the bud. She picked up a pack of cigarettes and walked toward the front door. "The sooner this mess is cleaned up, the sooner we can all go back to our pathetic lives."

Milly eyed me up and down, her mouth a pinched line.

"You know, Val, maybe you should come to my Ladies' Network meetup on Sunday. You might learn how to conduct yourself in an office. I'm afraid after all these years, you've gone a bit...*feral*."

Luckily for Milly, I wasn't a cat. I'd have scratched her eyes out. I turned to the old woman who'd already worked me to the bone. *Thank you, ma'am. May I have another?* I put on my prissiest business tone.

"Mrs. Barnes, what would you have me do next?"

The old woman pointed to the room heaped with files. "What else, Sherlock?"

Milly smirked and disappeared into her office.

I returned to my dungeon, beaten down, but not defeated.

*Speak for yourself, you jerks. My life isn't pathetic. Tonight I'm going to ditch a handsome man who loves me in favor of eating cheese-flavored vomit with three homeless guys in the hopes of nabbing the lunatic master of disguise who stole my mother's ashes.*

*Let's see you top that.*

WE WERE IN A BOOTH at Garvey's, waiting for our pot of cheese glop to arrive. Winnie had to work and Goober had gone AWOL. I'd been forced to take his place as one of the three stooges—Winky, Jorge and Val. I was desperate to find out if Jorge had invited Winky to live with him, but I didn't want to jinx it, or hurt anyone's feelings if the answer had been "no."

"Where's Milly tonight?" Jorge asked without slurring his words.

I eyed him suspiciously. "Don't ask."

"Okay. Then where's Tom?"

I was in a foul mood and Jorge was getting on my last nerve. Why did he have to pick tonight to sober up and resume his washed-up career as a police detective?

"Tom needs to stay out of it. And *uninformed*, Jorge. I don't want his reputation on the line. Besides, I'm not a hundred percent sure Cold Cuts is the same woman who bought the RV."

"If you're not sure, why don't you go show this Lefty guy a picture of her? Find out if Cold Cuts and this baloney woman are the same person?"

"Two reasons, Jorge. One, she wears disguises. She could have looked like anyone when she bought the RV. Second, I don't have a picture of her."

"Well, I do," Winky said.

"What?"

"Yep. Took it last night. Got her on camera, so she ain't no vampire. But she shore is a witch."

Winky pulled his cellphone out of his pocket. I jerked it out of his hand.

"Let me see that."

In the left side of the screen stood a woman in a Goth outfit. Her hair was jet black, her face ghostly white, and her eyes were encircled by thick bands of black liner. Overall, the shape of her face was right. And I thought I recognized the ring on her middle finger. She'd been caught in the act of displaying it prominently.

I handed the phone back to Winky. "It *could* be her. Hopefully, she'll show up again tonight."

But she didn't.

The only measurable result from the second stakeout attempt involved copious amounts of methane. That night, I'd had to tie my foot to the bedpost to keep from rocketing into outer space. Good thing I'd turned down Tom. He'd asked at lunch if he could come over and spend the night. The evening had been embarrassing enough. Besides, I was completely knackered. It turned out that work was...well...*work.*

# Chapter Thirteen

When I woke up the next morning, there was no desperate, red-haired mongrel at my backdoor. A tiny part of me felt empty and sad at the realization. The rest of me smiled and danced a jig. I peered out the sliding doors. Definitely no Winky! I flung off my ratty bathrobe and sang along with the imaginary bluebirds flitting around me. I brewed up a cappuccino and crawled back in bed with the warm cup of froth. *Ahhh. Life was back to normal.*

Then I remembered I had to go to work.

The bluebirds pecked me on the nose, crap all over the place and flew out the window.

I groaned and hauled myself out of bed. I searched my closet and picked out a pair of skorts and a halfway-decent T-shirt. No fancy blouse, polished pencil skirt or heels today. I tied my hair back and slipped into some flats. *Why dress for success when all you are is a grub?*

The bruise on my butt was fading. And it hurt less than my sore muscles. Looking on the bright side, I figured another week of hauling files and I could go to the beach without being reported to the Florida Fish & Game Commission. Manatees were still endangered, after all.

I climbed into Maggie and backed down the driveway. When I glanced back at the house, I nearly swallowed my gum. Sitting in the yard by the corner of the house was that dang hideous sofa that had almost landed me in jail.

"Winky!" I screamed his name like an obscenity. Of course, now that I needed him, he was nowhere to be found.

Back in Greenville, where my mom lived, it would have been considered a status symbol to have upholstered furniture in your front yard. Here, not so much. I cringed in embarrassment. My mother would've told me I'd gotten too fancy for my britches. *Why did I care what she would have said?*

I was running late. There was no time to move the couch, even if I could have on my own. I pulled onto Bimini Circle and hit the gas.

WHEN I GOT TO THE OFFICE, Milly's car wasn't there. Maggie and Mrs. Barnes' old Lincoln Town Car were the only vehicles in the lot. I breathed a sigh of relief. At least I wouldn't have to start the day off with another confrontation with Milly.

I yanked open the door to Griffith & Maas. Mrs. Barnes glanced up from her desk. A look of surprise livened up her usually tired face.

"What's up?" I asked.

"Here, this is for you."

I walked up to the desk. Mrs. Barnes handed me a jelly donut and eyed me up and down.

"Uh...thanks." I took the donut from her hand and wondered where her fingers had been.

"You earned it. You've worked harder than anyone else we've ever hired."

"Really?" I smiled with pride.

"Yeah. And you even showed up for a second day of it." She shook her head, as if she could barely believe it and muttered something indistinguishable. From the tone of it, it wasn't complimentary.

My smile faded. I was pretty sure the old lady had just insulted me. Mrs. Barnes dismissed my existence and grabbed a yellow pencil. She scratched at the inch-wide stripe of undyed gray hair running down the middle of her head, then turned her tired eyes to the light-green pages of an accounting workbook. She nodded in the direction of the file graveyard.

"Best get at it."

I trudged to the room crammed with stray files. I set my purse down and was contemplating my escape when I noticed something unusual lying on the first heap of files. It was a pink envelope and a white, lipstick-sized box. I recognized the tiny carton immediately. It was from Chocolateers. My name was on the envelope. I tore it open. The note inside read: "There ought to be a law against best friends arguing. I'm sorry. Lunch today? Nitally's. Noon. My treat."

I smiled, opened the tiny box and shoved the two chocolate covered cherries in my mouth. I poked my head out of the file room.

"Where's Milly?" I asked Mrs. Barnes, my words garbled by cherry cordial and dark chocolate.

"Off to see a client this morning."

"Oh."

"Back to work!" she barked. The powdered sugar on her upper lip made her look like an ancient, coke-addicted skunk.

"Yes ma'am."

I smirked to myself and went back to filing.

"VALLIANT!"

I let go of the door to Nitally's restaurant and waved at my old friend. She was seated at a table for two.

"Millicent!"

It felt good to be free of the tension our spat yesterday had caused. I rushed over to Milly, and leaned over and hugged her. "Thanks for the peace offering. It was delicious."

"I'm glad. Sorry I didn't support you, Val. With the stakeout, I mean. I feel like a turd. But I've been on so many bad dates, I kind of got cold feet. You know what I mean? Like going to the doctor's when you know you're going to get a big-ass shot."

"I get it. But it really wasn't that bad."

Milly appeared shocked. "No?"

"To be honest, the guys' company was better than the food."

Milly scowled. "I've eaten at Garvey's. That's not exactly a glowing endorsement."

I snorted, then grabbed Milly's hand. "Do the next stakeout with me, please?"

Milly looked unconvinced.

"I was thinking Saturday night."

Milly clicked to attention like we were in a board meeting. "No. Statistically, most bad dates happen on Wednesdays and Thursdays. Friday and Saturday are reserved for the A list."

"Where do you get all this stuff?"

Milly shot me a look of disbelief. "Date Data dot com, of course."

I hid my abject ignorance behind a feigned recollection. "Oh, yes. Of course. So...Wednesdays and Thursdays. Can you do it tomorrow?"

"No. But I could on Thursday."

"Tomorrow isn't Thursday?"

"Ha ha. Don't you *wish*."

Yes. I certainly did. I thought I'd worked at least three days by now. I sat back in the chair, disarmed by disappointment.

"You okay?"

"Yeah. So we're on for Thursday?"

"Yes. But you have to do me a favor in return."

"What? *Anything*."

"You have to come with me to my Ladies' Networking Meetup on Sunday."

"Argghh. I hate those things."

Milly shrugged. "No meetup, no date."

"Crap. Okay. Are you going back to the office this afternoon?"

"Yeah. Why? Are you afraid to be alone with Battle-Ax Barnes?"

"You know, she was actually nice to me this morning. She gave me a donut."

"And you're still alive? Lucky you. Don't let her fool you. Mrs. Barnes plays both sides of the fence."

"She's bisexual?"

Milly chewed on the thought and spit it out in disgust.

"Eww. Well, I suppose it's possible. But I was talking about her being a snitch. She reports everything back to Mr. Maas. You can best believe that."

"Oh. Whatever happened to Griffith?"

"I think he ate one too many jelly donuts."

I smirked. Milly's eyes scanned the room.

"Look at that guy, Val. There ought to be a law against fat men in biker shorts."

ON THE WAY HOME FROM work I spotted Winnie's van in the parking lot of Davie's Donuts. I hit the brakes and pulled in. I needed to find out what was going on with the couch. I hoped the reason Winky had left it in my yard this morning was because he and Winnie were moving on. Probably to Jorge's. But it didn't matter so much *where*. Just *when*. If I had to hear another euphemism for taking a dump, I was going to lose it.

I stepped inside the small shop. The aroma of coffee and vanilla made my mouth water.

"Hey, Val Pal!"

Winky greeted me from his perch on one of the twenty or so shiny chrome bar stools surrounding the 1950s-themed dining counter. For 5:30 on a Tuesday afternoon, the place was doing a respectable amount of business. The counter was full except for the stool next to Winky. On the other side of the empty seat was a fat cop eating a donut and drinking coffee. *How apropos*. I slid onto the empty stool between Winky and the portly policeman.

Winnie's slits for eyes peeked out of a porthole in the stainless steel door leading to the kitchen. She emerged a second later wearing a black shirt and skirt covered by a white apron emblazoned with Davie's Donuts, Better by the Dozen. Twelve maniacal donuts danced around the red trimmed edges of her apron. I noticed the trim perfectly matched Winnie's red glasses. Her outfit and her black bob hairdo made me think of Minnie Mouse—if she were a plump, Asian soda jerk.

Winnie smiled at me and absently plopped a plate of donuts and sandwiches in front of Winky. They were all cut into bite-sized pieces as if for a child. Winky beamed proudly.

"See there, Val? My gal treats me right."

Winnie leaned her chubby body over the counter. She cupped her hand over her mouth and whispered in my ear.

"I make 'em out a customers' leftovers. You want a plate?"

Winnie withdrew her hand. Her ample torso returned to the other side of the counter.

"No thanks, Winnie. I just ate. I'll take some coffee, though."

"Coming right up."

I turned to Winky. He'd already scarfed down half the food on the plate.

"Why'd you leave the couch in my front yard?"

Winky wiped his face with a napkin and took a dainty sip of coffee.

"Winnie and me's found ourselves other accommodations."

"Oh. That's great!" I said, trying not to sound as elated as I felt. "Chez Jorge?"

Winky looked at me like I'd lost my mind. Maybe I had.

"Jorge ain't a 'she.'"

"I meant...look. Are you moving in with Jorge?"

"Yep. Done did it last night."

I felt my stomach relax. "That's great. Good for you. But I need you to help me move that couch to the backyard."

"Sure. You gonna have that bonfire with it?"

"Uh...why not. Friday night okay with you?"

"Hot dog, yeah!"

Winnie came back with my coffee and another plate of hand-me-down hors d'oeuvres.

"What's going on?" she asked.

"We just got ourselves invited to a bonfire party," Winky beamed. He popped a chunk of donut in his mouth. I flinched internally at the trace of red lipstick on it.

"That's right," I said too loudly. "Bonfire Friday. And the next stake-out at Garvey's is Thursday night at 6:30 sharp. Can you two make it?"

"Sure!" Winnie said. "Can I bring anything to the bonfire party?"

"Oh, no." I eyed Winky's rapidly disappearing secondhand smorgasbord. "Nothing at all. Your help with the stakeout is contribution enough."

I WAS TOOLING DOWN Gulf Boulevard with the top down, humming and pleased with myself. The sun was shining and everything was going according to plan. By the end of the week I'd be rid of Winky *and* the couch, I would have found Cold Cuts, and I'd have put Glad and her Mr. Peanut piggybank back on my mantle.

I smiled and hit the gas on Maggie. Nothing happened. I mashed the pedal again. The old car sputtered and died. I coasted to the side of the road and put her in park. A second later, I saw blue lights flashing in my rearview mirror. I figured this could go either way.

A uniformed cop in a beige fedora and sunglasses climbed out of his patrol car. I watched in the side mirror as he walked up to the car.

"Ma'am, you can't park here."

"I know, officer. My car just died."

"Try to start it again."

I turned the ignition and pumped the gas. Nothing happened.

"Hmm. Could it be out of gas, Ms. Fremden?"

My head involuntarily jerked to the left. "Do I know you?"

The man answered my question by lowering his sunglasses on his nose. It was Lt. Hans Jergen, the smug son of the Chief of Police, Franz Jergen. The same jerk who'd given Tom a hard time over a misunderstanding about his sister. A misunderstanding that Tom didn't want cleared up, even though it made Tom look like a heel in Jergen's eyes.

"Oh. Lieutenant Jergen," I said stiffly. "Hello. Thanks for returning the couch to me. I was desperate to get it back. Can I have the finger, too?"

"Look, Ms. Fremden. It was nothing personal. It's standard procedure. Just returning no longer needed evidence."

"With a snarky note?"

"Interpret it however you want." Lt. Jergen fingered the rubber service baton hanging off his belt.

"You're not going to hit me with that, are you?"

Lt. Jergen took a step back. "What? With this? No. Look, have you got a gas can?"

"No."

"Then come with me."

I eyed him warily. "Am I under arrest?"

"No. I'm giving you a ride to the nearest gas station."

"Oh. Let me grab my purse."

I sat in silence in the back of Lt. Jergen's police car and looked out the window. At a traffic light, a young girl in the car beside me shook her head at me scornfully. Horrified, I tried to use gestures to explain, through the window, that I wasn't a convict. My efforts resulted in a view of her bubble-gum pink tongue. I scooted to the middle of the backseat and kept away from the windows.

Lt. Jergen pulled his cruiser into a gas station. I tried to get out, but the doors were locked...and...to my horror...had no handles. Jergen smirked at my frightened face, then opened the door. I stuck my chin up and got out. To ease the embarrassed awkwardness, I tried to strike up a conversation as he pumped gas into a red, plastic fuel can.

"You know, Tom's not a bad guy," I said.

Jergen shot me a sideways glance. "Yeah? Well, neither am I."

"If you only knew...."

"Knew what?"

He waited impatiently for words I couldn't say.

"Yeah. I thought so," he said sourly. "Look, I'm running inside for a minute."

"Okay. Here's a five for the gas."

Jergen took the money, put the fuel can in the trunk and disappeared in the store. All of a sudden, I realized I needed to pee. I left the cruiser, went inside and followed the restroom sign leading to the back left corner of the store. I yanked open the door and got the shock of my life. Standing before me was Lt. Jergen, his pants to his knees, offering me an unobstructed view of his "personal baton."

He screamed and slammed the door. But not before I got an eyeful. Or, to be more accurate, a *thimble* full.

That explained a lot about Lt. Jergen.

# Chapter Fourteen

By late morning Wednesday, the BMW-sized heap of files in my cell at Griffith & Maas had eroded to the size of a VW Beetle. As piles got sorted and filed away in cabinets, I began to unearth things that had gotten lost amid the giant mass of paperwork. So far, I'd found three writing pens, a desiccated mouse carcass, and, oddly, a dental retainer. But the most interesting discovery occurred when I reached down to pick up the last stack of files before lunch. It was the name on top that caught my eye. The file was labeled H.F. JERGEN.

*OMG! Could it be Hans Jergen's file? I've already seen his private parts. What would it hurt to take a peek at his private papers?*

I looked down the hallway to make sure no one was watching. The door to Milly's office was closed. Mrs. Barnes wasn't at her desk. The old lady was probably on one of her many cigarette breaks. That woman smoked more than the grease fire that had burned down Water Loo's.

I opened the file. It belonged to Hans Franz Jergen, all right. Hans' tax return for last year was right on top. I looked at the bottom sum. *Geez! Police work was more profitable than I thought.*

On closer inspection, I found that most of his income hadn't come from his salary, but from stockholder distributions from a company called Pet Patrol. I flipped to the second page. Besides being a cop, Jergen was the CEO of Pet Patrol, Inc.

*Funny. Jergen didn't seem like the kind of person a dog would like.*

I heard the front door open. It was Mrs. Barnes hacking up a lung on her way back to her desk. I shut the file just as her head peeked around the corner.

"Taking an early lunch, Val. Got a doctor's appointment. Milly's keeping down the fort. Should be back by two."

"Okay. Hope it's nothing serious," I said in a cheerful tone that I hoped hid my nervousness.

"Yeah. Too late for that," she said dryly and turned to leave. It was then that I noticed that Mrs. Barnes' skunk-striped hair, which was all neat and tidy in the front, was matted and flat in the back. I guess she'd forgotten to comb it after getting out of bed. I watched her disappeared from the doorframe. A minute later, the front door opened and closed again.

I couldn't help myself. I reopened Jergen's file. I wanted his address. It might come in handy if I decided to set that old couch on fire and throw it in his yard. I envisioned it my mind—the first "drive-by sofa-ing."

I placed the first page of his tax return on the copy machine and hit start. I heard Milly's office door open. I snatched the file out of the copier, slapped it in the folder and flung it on the heap.

"What 'cha doin'?" Milly asked from the doorway.

"Nothing. I was—"

"I'm bored. You busy for lunch?"

"Oh. No. I mean—" My phone rang and startled the guilty hell out of me.

"Hold on," I said to Milly, then grabbed the phone. "It's Tom."

Milly nodded. "Tell him I said, 'Hi.'"

She headed down the hall to her office. I clicked the answer button on my phone.

"What's up, Tom?"

"Just wondering if you can meet me for lunch."

"Oh. Sorry, but Milly just asked me."

"Well, aren't *you* Miss Popular."

I snorted. "Yeah. But I think I can fit you into my schedule. How about drinks after work? My place around 5:30 or 6?"

"Even better. Okay."

"It's a date then." I hung up and went back to Milly's office.

"What did Tom want?"

"To go to lunch. But I told him I had plans with you."

Milly grinned, then scrunched her nose. "He wasn't mad?"

"No. Why should he be?"

Milly sighed. "You know, there ought to be a law against boyfriends like Tom. He's smart, reasonable, says he loves you, and he's got a firm butt. He sets the bar pretty high compared to the lowlifes left loitering around for the rest of us to haggle over. There's not many like him. In fact, you might have landed yourself the last decent bachelor out there, Val. Yes. You've quite probably doomed me to spinsterhood."

"I just can't picture you as a spinster, Milly. You've got way too much to offer."

Milly sighed again and smiled weakly. "Flattery will get you nowhere, sister. It's your turn to pay for lunch."

*WHY HADN'T I GIVEN myself more time to prepare?*

Before I'd begun working, I'd had all day to get ready for a sexy rendezvous with Tom. Thanks to a clot of slow-moving tourists on Gulf Boulevard, I now I had less than ten minutes. I jumped in the shower and shaved my armpits and legs. I toweled off quickly, then slapped on skin lotion and tugged on a pair of sexy panties. I didn't wear perfume. The light, rose scent of my moisturizer was enough. I hated colognes. *All of them.* They burned my eyes and throat, and made my mouth taste like soap. *Sexy? Nope.*

I fastened my push-up bra and studied a scrape on my inner arm. I'd gotten it yesterday when Winky and I'd moved the old couch to the bonfire pit. I slipped on a silky sundress and combed back my damp hair. Thankfully, my makeup had survived the shower pretty much intact.

I was officially ready to rumble. When Tom arrived a moment later, so was he. But not in the way I'd hoped.

"I thought we'd talked about this before," he barked as he marched through the door, his sea-green eyes stormy with anger.

"What are you talking about?"

"You're putting yourself at risk again. With another of your silly stakeouts. Seriously, Val. You could get injured—or worse. People are crazy out there. Don't you know that?"

Tom was dead serious. I joked to ease the tension.

"Of course I do, Tom. I'm friends with Winky and Goober, aren't I?"

"I'm not joking, Val. What is this about? You having Winky on lookout at Garvey's?"

"How did you know that? Did Jorge tell you?"

"What? No. Jerry Muller did. He said he overheard some hot brunette talking to a red-headed pile of freckles about a stakeout at Davie's Donuts. I figured it was you and Winky."

I winked. "Oh. Hot brunette, huh?"

Tom wasn't amused. "So it's true?"

"Yes. But it's not like last time. I'm not trying to catch a criminal, Tom. I'm just trying to find Cold Cuts."

Tom's face contorted in confusion. "Lunch meat?"

"No. The woman who bought the RV. Her nickname is Cold Cuts."

"Wait a minute. You know her nickname, but not her last name? Val, you truly are a lousy detective."

"Look, when she told me her nickname, I didn't even know it was her."

"Her?"

"*Her* her. The one in the RV. It's no big deal, Tom."

"If it's no big deal, why didn't you just tell me what you're up to? Why keep it a secret from me?"

"I dunno. Things can get...*unpredictable* when the guys are involved. I didn't want whatever happens to get traced back to you."

Tom grabbed me by the shoulders and stared into my eyes. I'd never seen him so intense. "Val, we're not going to make it if you keep hiding things from me."

"What? But...I don't mean to keep secrets from you, Tom. I just want to protect you from my stuff. You're a cop. I know you have to tow a different line than me."

"I get it, but I don't agree. Do you have any other secrets you want to tell me? I need to know I can trust you to come clean with me."

"I do have one."

"What?"

"I ran into Hans Jergen yesterday."

Tom's face registered anger and suspicion. "What did he want?"

"Nothing. I ran out of gas. He gave me a lift. I saw his baton. No biggie."

"You saw his *what?*"

I cringed. "Baton?"

Tom looked dumbstruck. "Are you saying what I think you're saying?"

"It was an accident. We were at the gas station and—"

Tom's face flushed with anger. He wasn't listening. "How...I mean...geez, Val. I know that you're a magnet for the bizarre. But *this?* What have you got to say for yourself?"

I tried again to lighten the situation with a joke. "Let's just say, unlike you, Hans has his shortcomings."

Tom shook his head. "Val, this is just too much. I've got to go."

"But Tom!"

He didn't hear me. He was already halfway out the door.

I WAS ON MY SECOND Tanqueray and tonic when I heard a knock at the door. *Tom!* I raced to the door and flung it open. Laverne was standing there with another hideous lump of wasted ceramic in her hands. This one showed a bit more skill. But, I mean, the last one looked like it was rescued from a prison toilet bowl.

"Hi, Laverne."

"Hi, sugar. You okay?"

"Yeah. Why?"

"Well, I saw Tom's car drive away in a hurry. And you look like you just lost your last dollar at the slots."

I shrugged. "Come on in."

Laverne smiled, but her face still registered concern.

"I'm glad you got that couch moved, honey. Neighbors were starting to talk."

"What? Really?"

"Aww, don't worry about them. How do you like my latest sculpture?"

"It's...," I said, then, quite unexpectedly, started bawling.

Laverne looked at the lump of clay in her hand. "Oh, honey! Is it that awful?"

Her misinterpretation of my crying made me laugh through my tears.

"Oh, Laverne. No! I'm just...upset about Tom. We had a fight."

"Well, what about, sugar?"

"He thinks I'm not being honest with him. Not telling the truth. I tried to convince him, but I just mucked it all up."

Laverne put her sculpture on the kitchen counter, grabbed a paper towel and led me to the couch. She sat beside me, and put her long spider arm around me.

"It's gonna be okay, Val. It's just a misunderstanding. That's all."

"Do you think I'm honest, Laverne? That I tell the truth?"

She handed me the paper towel. "Only you know that for sure. But I tell you what. In Vegas, I learned to spot a faker a mile away. You're no phony baloney, sugar."

I sniffed and dabbed my eyes with a paper towel. "No?"

"Listen, Val. I know Mr. Happy Banana looks like a turd. But you were nice enough not to say so. That's not being fake. That's being kind. There's a big difference."

I laughed again, shocked by Laverne's insight and kindness. "It's not that bad."

"Yes it is. And this one's not much better. But hey, it's been fun learning. That's what counts."

"I guess you're right, Laverne. But I don't seem to ever learn. When it comes to guys, I mean. I don't know why Tom would be so angry over our stakeout. It's just—"

"Honey, I guaran-dang-tee you the stakeout's got nothing to do with it. Tom's probably sore over you not saying you loved him back."

I looked at Laverne, stunned. "But he didn't even mention that."

Laverne winked at me and smiled. "I know it may sound funny, sugar. But we don't always say what we really mean."

# Chapter Fifteen

I knew it was wrong, but I couldn't help myself. While Mrs. Barnes took a smoke break, I rifled through the battered metal file cabinet labeled "F-G." I just *had* to see if Tom was a customer of Griffith & Maas. I'd almost convinced myself it was research—a simple salary comparison between Tom and Hans Jergen. But what I truly wanted was to know was if Tom was broke. More specifically, if he was fiscally irresponsible.

*I can't afford to get swindled again.*

The thought surprised me, and kicked off a fierce internal debate.

*But Val, the only way you could get swindled by Tom was if you married him. Are you thinking of marrying him?*

*No. Not really. But I don't have to be married for him to go through my things...forge my signature.*

*He wouldn't do that!*

*Crap! He's already has! With the RV!*

My sticky fingers were on a file labeled D. Formack when a voice rang out behind me. I jumped like a cat waking up next to a cobra.

"What are you doing?"

I dropped the file and shoved the drawer closed. I whipped around to find old lady Barnes leaning on the doorframe, one ankle crossed over the other. She tapped her finger on a pack of filter-less Camels.

"Well?" Mrs. Barnes' eyes danced with the pleasure of watching me squirm.

"Uh...."

"Our business was built on discretion, Ms. Fremden. You'd best come clean with it."

I cringed and spilled my guts. "I was looking to see if my boyfriend's files were in here."

The skunk-haired woman's face morphed from a scowl to a grin. "Oh. Why didn't you say so?"

She walked over to the cabinet. "Any luck?"

Relief perked me to attention. "No. The closest I got to was Thomas Format."

"Too bad. It always pays to know your enemies. He might still be in that pile you're working on. Want a donut?"

I didn't, but I took one anyway. I figured this was one woman I didn't want to piss off.

MILLY WAS OUT OF THE office most of the day. I skipped lunch and begged off early so I could prepare for the stakeout. When I got home, I wasted the extra hour taking a nap. The doorbell woke me up. It was Milly.

"You look like hell."

"Thanks."

"Were you sleeping?"

"Yeah. Just a catnap. This job is kicking my butt."

Milly laughed and closed the door behind her. "Mrs. Barnes can be pretty demanding sometimes."

I flexed my tired shoulders. "*Sometimes?* You know, she caught me going through the filing cabinets today."

"Isn't that your job?"

"Yeah. But I was snooping. She nailed me."

"Oh my word! What happened?"

"When I told her I was looking for my boyfriend's file, she laughed. Then she offered me a donut."

Milly shook her head. "I told you! Step *awaaay* from the donuts."

"I know. I hid it in my purse and tossed it in the dumpster."

"Why were you looking for Tom's file?"

"I dunno. Why do you work for Mrs. Barnes? She kind of gives me the creeps."

Milly smirked. "Only kind of?"

"So, I don't get it, Milly. Why *do* you work for her?"

"Why does anybody work for anybody? The money. Griffith & Maas pays better than a lot of other firms. Believe me, I've looked. And now that I'm getting older, it's hard to get someone to take a chance on me."

"You're not old."

"I said *older*, not *old*. And fatter. And look! I'm starting to get wrinkles on the bridge of my nose!"

"What? Where?"

"At the top. Between my eyes." Milly pointed at her nose and drew her face close to mine.

"They're nothing."

"Nothing? I'll probably look like a crypt keeper in another six months."

I shook my head. "Quit it. You're scaring me."

Milly's face registered mock shock. "See?"

I punched her on the arm. "Oh, shut up! How about a drink?"

"Geez. I thought you'd never ask."

"TNT?"

"Works for me. So what are we gonna do for disguises, Val? I'm not wearing my good suit to this showdown at the not-okay corral."

"Very funny. Hmmm. Wait a minute. I've got an idea."

I went to my bedroom and returned with the two bags of used clothes I'd bought at Laverne's bidding. Milly rifled through them while I made the gin and tonics.

"These are hideous, Val! Where did you get them?"

"Laverne."

Milly tugged a yellow polka-dot dress on over her slim skirt and silk camisole. She held her blonde hair in a bun and struck a pose with her index finger to her cheek. "How do I look?"

"Ravishing, darling Daisy. Donald is gonna eat you up."

The doorbell rang. Milly stopped smirking at me and stuck an eye in the peephole. "Speak of the devil." Milly turned her nose up. "Should I let Laverne in?"

"Yes, of course, Milly."

"All right." Milly rolled her eyes, pouted and opened the door.

"Well hi there, Milly! I just dropped by to see if I could help you girls out. Oh! Look at you! You look sweeter'n a set of triple sevens in that outfit."

I smirked. "It's one of the dresses you picked out, Laverne," I said in a syrupy tone, then dead-eyed Milly. "Milly's going to wear it tonight."

Milly smiled sweetly at Laverne, then shot me a death stare. "I'm ready for that cocktail anytime now, Val." Milly grabbed something out of the clothing bag. "Oh, and here's what Val's wearing."

"Why that's the perfect choice," Laverne said. She beamed, clasped her hands together and looked us both up and down. "Now all we need is hair and makeup."

# Chapter Sixteen

I was wishing for dusk...to hide my shame. My "outfit by Laverne" made my trashy interview outfit look like a bashful Southern belle.

Milly glanced over at me from the passenger seat and giggled. I scowled and mashed Maggie's gas pedal to the floorboard. The faster we got to Garvey's, the fewer the people I could be accused of causing to die from laughter.

"Oh, let's stop here," Milly said. She pointed toward an approaching convenience store. "I need some gum."

"No way. I'm not being seen anywhere in this getup."

"Aw, come on. You don't look *that* bad."

I shot Milly a sideways glance, my eyelids heavy with mascara and iridescent purple eyeshadow. Laverne had really done a number on me this time. The old woman had explained her strategy as she'd applied false eyelashes to my upper lids. It was simple, actually. The plan was to offer two kinds of bait. One of us was to be a lady and the other a tramp. Well, Daisy Duck was no tramp.

I tugged on the inseam of my red hot-pants in a futile attempt to release their camel toe grip. As I did, my right boob nearly fell out of my black tube top. *Classy.*

"Oops a daisy!" Milly remarked at my close call, then laughed at her unintentional joke.

"Ha ha." I said sarcastically, then looked at my ridiculous face in the rearview mirror. "I think KISS wore less makeup than this."

"Which one?"

"The whole band. *Combined*."

Milly studied me for a moment. "You know. You may be right."

Milly glanced down at my silver knee boots. They delivered the finishing touch for my call-girl cabaret outfit Laverne had fished from her own private stash.

"I think their boot heels were lower, too," Milly remarked. "How can you drive in those? They look like you took them off a disco tranny."

I shot her some side eye. "Well, while we're hurling insults, if your pumps were white, you could get into Disneyworld for free. Quack quack."

Milly punched me on my arm. "Oh yeah? Well, there ought to be a law against pants that tight. I can see your religion!'

I snarled and yanked at the inseam again. "At least we've got one thing going for us. In these getups, no one will ever recognize us."

"Thank goodness for that," Milly agreed. "What about the guys? What are they wearing?"

"I dunno. Goober promised not to wear overalls with no shirt again. Jorge's usually dressed within normal human parameters."

We pulled into the lot at Garvey's and waited for the guys to show. I blew out a breath and made a wish. "Here's hoping the third time's the charm."

Milly glanced over at me and shook her head. "Val, charming's not your style."

MY MASCARA WAS ABOUT to drip when the grey-blue Dodge finally rambled into the parking lot fifteen minutes late. Winky waved through the open passenger window and yanked open the door from the outside.

"Ain't y'all a sight for sore eyes," he laughed. "Where's my salve?"

Winnie stared at us, wide eyed. Her mouth slacked opened and formed a tiny "O" but she didn't say a word.

The side door slid open and Goober ambled out like a brown wolf spider. He was clad in a dark-tan tweed suit that would have looked quite presentable if the pant legs weren't six inches too short. The flood-water hem left exposed a pair of dull, black-and-white spats and orange ankle socks that perfectly matched the T-shirt under his jacket. A sickly-sweet, burning odor filled the air. I punched Milly on the arm.

"You take Goober. Please!"

Milly shot me a suspicious pout. "Why?"

"His aftershave is already damaging my olfactory receptors."

Milly sighed. "Okay."

Jorge was the last to emerge from the van. Dressed completely in black, he nearly disappeared under the shadow cast by the oak tree above. Whether he looked fashionably cool or like a mafia drug dealer, I couldn't decide.

"Hola, amigas," he said, and tipped his black fedora.

Jorge's dark eyes shone brightly, even in the shade. For some reason, they unsettled me. I was used to them being dull and glassy. Then a realization shook me. Jorge just might be...*sober*.

I wobbled hastily in my space boots over to Jorge and grabbed him by the arm before Milly could change her mind about Goober. "You're with me, Jorge."

Winky wolf-whistled in my direction. "Hoochie coochie mama!"

His remark broke Winnie's silence. She hollered out the van window.

"Get back in here, Winky!" He flinched and ducked his head as if Winnie's words were flying objects, then obeyed like a scolded pup.

Goober watched Winky cower into the van. He sniffed and stuck his chin out. "And that, my dear ladies, is why I prefer bachelorhood." He took Milly's arm. "Shall we?"

Milly shot me a look that said I owed her big time. She smiled up at Goober. "Yes, lets." She daintily took his arm.

"Okay, here we go," I said. "And remember, we don't know each other."

Behind me I heard Daisy quack, "I wish."

WHEN WE STEPPED INSIDE Garvey's, I was surprised. The old lady with the orange-whip hairdo wasn't around. Instead, a relatively normal-looking, red-haired girl stared at us blankly.

"How many?"

Jorge looked at me uncertainly. "Uh...two," I answered.

The girl led us to a booth and carelessly flung two menus on the table. She returned a moment later and seated Goober and Milly at a table for two just a few feet away from me and Jorge. Unfortunately, that put me back in range of Peanut Head's noxious cloud of cologne. My eyes began to water.

Jorge reached across the table and patted my hand. "Don't cry, Val. We'll find her."

I was going to say something snarky, but Jorge wasn't joking. His dark, serious eyes burned with compassion, not comedy. I settled for a simple, "Thanks."

A few seconds later, the waitress reappeared with glasses of Garvey's signature tainted water. Even though I hadn't seen the girl in Garvey's before, she had to have been a regular employee. She hadn't so much as batted an eye at the four of us. I glanced around at the other clientele and suddenly didn't feel so conspicuous anymore.

"Where's the regular lady?" I asked.

The girl's left eyebrow ticked up a notch. "At Garvey's, *we* don't ask questions, and *customers* don't either."

Given her red hair and bad attitude, she and the old lady had to have been related. Or maybe it was something in the water....

"So? What'll it be?" The girl tapped a pencil impatiently on a pad.

Before I could answer, Jorge piped up. "We'll have the cheese fondue."

*Great. I may never poop again.* "I'll have the biggest glass of chardonnay you've got."

The waitress scribbled on her pad and looked over at Jorge.

"Just water for me," he said softly. He started to pick up his glass. I grabbed his hand.

"Do you have Coco Rico?" I asked the girl. "It's a coconut soft drink. It's Jorge's favorite."

"I don't think so. But I'll see what I can do."

She left. I let go of Jorge's hand like it was a rattlesnake. "Don't drink that water," I whispered.

"Why not?"

"I dunno. Just don't."

The waitress returned with a wineglass the size of a grapefruit. It was filled to the brim with urine-colored liquid. For some reason, just the sight of it made me need to pee. I smiled tentatively at the waitress. Her expression dared me to take a sip. When I didn't, she shrugged and turned to Jorge.

"And for the gentleman." She sat a glass of clear, bubbly liquid on the table with a proud flourish. "Sprite and coconut syrup. Give it a go."

Jorge took a sip. His eyes lit up. He nodded to the waitress, then me. "Gracias. It's good."

I looked over at Milly. She was sniffing at a glass of red wine as big as my dodgy chardonnay. Goober was sucking down a beer like a baby goat with a milk bottle. *What have I done?*

THE CHEESE FONDUE TURNED out to be a bad choice, but not just because of its potential to permanently clog my colon. Jorge's hands shook so badly during dinner that he got more cheese on the tablecloth than in his mouth. By the time he'd finished, the trail of cheese from the pot to his plate made it appear as if the entire cauldron of greasy, yellowish goo had been dumped in his lap.

Even worse, Cold Cuts hadn't shown.

I looked over at Milly and shrugged. The evening was a bust. I flagged down the waitress.

"Could we get our check, please?"

"Separate or together?"

"Oh. Together. And I'll get their check, too."

I pointed over at Milly and Goober. The girl didn't bat an eyelash.

"A foursome. Huh. Never saw that one coming."

The waitress scooted off before I could defend myself. I waved over at Milly and Goober. "You guys ready to go?"

"Absolutely," Goober said, and yanked the paper napkin from his T-shirt collar.

"Did you enjoy your meal?" I asked Goober. Milly had stuck to wine. Smart girl.

"Negatory," Goober replied. He nodded at a plate empty except for a few crusts of bread. "They call this a tuna-fish sandwich? I've had better tasting cat food."

I didn't doubt it. I started to say so, but one of my fake eyelashes fell off and landed in the fondue pot. My nose was stuffy from inhaling Goober's radioactive aftershave, and my stomach was starting to boil. I felt like Cinderella after midnight. I was falling apart at the seams.

"I'm going to the toilet," I said, and yanked on the hem of my cherry-red hot pants.

As I hobbled along Garvey's human gauntlet of shame back toward the restroom, I held my head high. My mind focused on one thought; *No one here knows who I am.* I shoved open the bathroom door and got a gander at myself in the mirror straight ahead. I was so mortified I barely noticed the waitress standing beside me, applying mascara.

"You know, Val, you could do better."

The hair on the back of my neck curled in horror. "What?"

"The guy's obviously a drunk. He's got the DTs. Still, not the worst I've seen in here. Great costume, by the way."

I stared at the red-haired hash slinger. "Excuse me, but who *are* you?"

She stopped applying mascara and grinned at me. "All right! You didn't recognize me! *Yes!*"

Then I did.

"Oh my word! Cold Cuts?"

Cold Cuts' victory face disappeared. "Yeah."

"I.... Look. It's a long story. I've been trying to find you. I need to ask you something."

"What?"

"Did you buy an RV from Lefty's scrapyard last Saturday?"

Cold Cuts frowned. "Well, yeah. Maybe."

"Cold Cuts, that was *my* RV! I need to get it back."

The girl crinkled her nose defensively. "Why?"

"That's another long story. It belonged to my mother."

"So *she* wants it back?"

"Well, no. She's...dead."

"Look, Val. I *like* the old RV. And I've already got her all fixed up."

"But my mother *loved* it."

"Even so, she's *gone*," Cold Cuts said. "She can't use it."

I frowned. "I know. But I want to keep it...for the memories."

"Memories don't exist in *things*. They exist in your heart."

"But...." I didn't know what to say. Why was she being so...*rational?* "I don't want to argue with you, but this is personal."

Cold Cuts cocked her head and studied me. "I get it. But the RV was a mess. You weren't actually using it. *Or* taking care of it."

"I was going to," I whined. "Then my boyfriend sold it without asking me."

"Looks to me like he did you a favor, Val. It was time to let it go."

I slumped my butt onto the bathroom counter. Maybe she had a point. "Did you happen to find a Mr. Peanut piggybank in the RV?"

"What? No. But you're missing the point, Val. Memories don't exist in—"

"My mother's ashes were inside that bank."

Cold Cuts' face softened, along with her tone. "Oh. I see. There wasn't any piggybank."

My heart sank. "Are you sure?"

Cold Cuts dropped the rest of her tough-waitress persona. "Look, Val. My cousin scoured that thing from top to bottom. Like I said, it was a mess, you know."

"I'm sure it was. But...do you think your cousin might have found it?"

"Huh. There's an idea. He *is* a bit of a black sheep. Always looking for easy cash, you know? I made him work for it with *that* job. Probably the only honest, hard work he's done in a decade. He *could've* found the bank and not told me. I wouldn't put it past him. He's a scrounger. Digs through dumpsters and stuff. Anything good he finds he sells on eBay. I could see if he has it."

My body involuntarily straightened with hope. "Cold Cuts, that would be...*wonderful*. Could you call him *right now?* It's really important."

"Look, I would, but he doesn't have a phone. And I've got to get back to work. I'll try and reach him and get back to you."

I told Cold Cuts my number. She punched it into her cellphone.

"Please. Call me as soon as you find out *anything*."

She nodded. "Okay. But it could take a while. Capone isn't the easiest person to get a hold of."

My next thought was interrupted by a loud crash. "What was that?" I gasped.

Cold Cuts and I dashed out into the dining room. My mouth dropped open like a busted glovebox. The clown-haired old lady was straddling Goober in his chair, throttling the life out of him. As Jorge and Milly looked on in horror, Goober's brown-tweed monkey arms and legs flailed and his face turned from pink to red. Glass from broken wine glasses and beer bottles littered the floor.

My eyes scanned the room. The regular patrons were watching with glee, apparently delighted with the free, after-dinner show. I blinked and focused on Milly. She stood rigid, her back to a booth, frozen in dread. Jorge's eyes met mine for a second, then he sprang into action and tried to pry the old lady's fingers from around Goober's throat. Dressed all in black, he was a poor-man's imitation of Zorro. *Zerro, perhaps?*

I started to scream, but Cold Cuts beat me to it. "Selma! Grandma! Quit!"

The geriatric strangler looked up, spied her granddaughter and loosened her grip. Goober hacked and sucked a giant breath into his beet-red face. Jorge pulled the old woman off Goober and helped her to stand. She smoothed her orange hair, brushed off her rumpled brown dress and pulled up her knee-high stockings. The room had gone church-mouse quiet. The old woman cleared her throat and raised her nose two inches.

"I'll have you know Garvey's used to be the height of cuisine," she announced to the captive crowd.

Goober stood up, cleared his throat and rasped. "Yeah. And my granny used to look good naked."

The crowd burst out laughing. The old woman lost her temper and dignity and lunged at Goober again. He bolted for the door, Jorge hot on his heels. I slapped a hundred dollar bill in Cold Cuts' hand and grabbed Milly by the arm. Cold Cuts held her grandmother at bay while I led poor, stunned Milly out the door of Garvey's fine dining establishment as fast as my camel toe permitted.

A quiet, dignified getaway wasn't in the cards. But at least I'd found Cold Cuts. Good thing, too. Returning to Garvey's was now out of the question.

# Chapter Seventeen

On the drive home from Garvey's, my remaining false eyelash gave up the ghost and flew away in the damp night air. When we reached Central Avenue, Winnie's Dodge honked behind me and turned the opposite way. I looked over at Milly in the passenger seat. She hadn't said a word since she'd witnessed Goober's near strangulation.

"I wonder if they called the cops," Milly muttered.

I tried to make light of the situation. "I hope not. They'd never believe I wasn't a prostitute."

Milly shook her head in disbelief. "You know, sometimes I feel like you couldn't make this crap up. Our lives, I mean."

I tried to unzip my silver platform boots. "Yeah. The thrill of victory. The agony of the feet."

"So, how'd you leave it with Cold Cuts?"

"Besides quickly, you mean?"

"Ha ha. Are you two getting together? Is she supposed to call you or what?"

"I gave her my number. But I don't think I'll be getting the RV back. She wants to keep it."

"That's not very nice."

I sighed. "Yeah. According to Cold Cuts, memories don't live in objects. They live in our hearts."

"Huh. And in our thighs," Milly said dryly. "Mine remember every ice cream sandwich I ever ate."

"Don't get me started." I smiled over at my best friend. She'd rallied back quickly from the shock.

Milly smirked, then her face went serious again. "What about the piggybank, Val? Does she have it?"

My gut slumped. "No. She said she never saw it. Her cousin cleaned out the RV. She's going to check with him."

"Well, at least there's still a chance, then. Right?"

I shrugged. "I sure hope so."

"Speaking of hope, any word from Tom?"

I shook my head. "No. And I haven't had time to call him, either. It was such a stupid misunderstanding."

Milly laughed. "That seems to happen a lot between men and women."

"Yeah, but it doesn't usually involve seeing another man's junk."

Milly gasped. *"What?"*

I WOKE WITH A VAGUE memory niggling at my brain like a tiny, parasitic worm. I couldn't decide if it was part of a dream or one of those words that won't come to you no matter how hard you try, but then pop up randomly out of nowhere when you least expect them.

Capone.

I shot up in bed. *Capone!* Cold Cuts' cousin.

*No. It couldn't be.*

I'd met Capone not long after my birthday last month, when I'd been searching for the owner of a finger that had mysteriously ended up in my couch. Capone had tried to swindle me out of five dollars by introducing me to an imposter—a guy with a rag over his hand and all ten fingers. But in the end, Capone had come through with the real guy. And he'd done it all for fifty bucks and a slice of pepperoni pizza.

What were the odds that the Capone I knew was Cold Cuts' cousin? But, on the other hand, it had to be him. I mean, how many dumpster-diving, scar-faced Capones were running around St. Pete? What's more, I knew the general area where he typically hung out.

I climbed out of bed, brewed a cappuccino and checked my phone. No word from Cold Cuts. I slipped into a pair of shorts and a tank top. I was about to jump in Maggie and head in the vicinity of Old Northeast Pizza when I realized it was Friday.

*I had to go to work. Dang it!*

I went back to the bedroom to change. I'd have to wait until after work to find Capone. Then I remembered I'd told everyone to come over for a bonfire party tonight. I hadn't done squat to prepare.

*Double dang it!*

I DROVE UP IN THE LOT at Griffith & Maas just as Milly was climbing out of her Beemer.

"I see you survived the night, tramp," she joked.

"Quack, quack," I shot back. "It took me half an hour to get all that crap off my face."

Milly made a dramatic swoop with her arm and touched her forehead with the back of her hand. "Alas! Poor me! I gave myself to Donald...and then he never called."

I snorted with laughter and hauled myself out of the car.

"Geez, am I glad that stakeout crap is over with, Val. Any word from Cold Cuts yet?"

"No. But if she calls, I'm going to invite her to the bonfire tonight. Maybe she'll change her mind about giving me back the RV when she sees how nice I am."

Milly snorted, then touched her fingers to her lip. "The bonfire! Val, I forgot. I can't come."

"Why not?" I whined. "I need you to help me play nice with her."

"I would...but I've got a date."

"A *real* date?"

"Yes."

"MatchMate?"

"No."

"Don't tell me you met him at *Garvey's*."

Milly grimaced apologetically but didn't say a word.

I stuck out my lower lip. "Well, bring him along."

"I can't. I want to see if he lights *my* fire, not yours. I tell you what, though. Let's go to breakfast in the morning. We can fill each other in on all the gory details."

Milly opened the front door to the office and held it for me.

"I'm not happy about this, Millicent."

"You'll get over it, Valliant."

I WAS AT PUBLIX DELI, grabbing boxes of potato salad, Cuban sandwiches and marshmallow treats when Cold Cuts called. I tried to sound breezy.

"Hi there!" *Hi there? I sounded like a telemarketer.*

"Hi, Val. Listen. I put the word out for Capone. He usually gets back to me within a week or so."

*A week or so? He could have sold Glad's cremains to someone in China by then.* I debated whether to tell Cold Cuts that I knew Capone. I decided to save it for bonfire talk.

"Why don't you come over tonight? I'm having a bonfire in the backyard."

"Bonfire? What's the occasion?"

"A couple of things. I got a job. My friends found a place to stay. I found you." *I found you? Over the top, Val.*

"Sounds like things are going your way. Okay. What time?"

*Yes!* "I figure we'll throw the couch on the fire after dark, so be there before eight?"

"What?"

"The...uh...around seven?"

"Okay. Text me your address."

Cold Cuts clicked off before I could say goodbye.

I WAS UNLOADING A BACKSEAT full of deli boxes and beer when Laverne spotted me. She waved and walked over.

"Whoa nelly! Looks like a party's going on!"

"Yes. And there's some big news to celebrate, Laverne. We found Cold Cuts!"

"I see that. And chocolate chip cookies, too."

"What? No. I mean, *yes*. We found her, Laverne. The lady who has my RV." *And a really dumb nickname.*

"Oh. That's fantastic, sugar! Did my cabaret outfit do the trick?"

I squirmed at the thought of camel toe. "Yes, Laverne. That's what did it."

"I'm so glad! Anything else I can do to help?"

"You can help me bring in this stuff. I didn't have time to cook anything. But I *am* going to make my famous tortilla dip."

"Sounds yummy." Laverne grabbed a handful of bags and followed me into the house. "Who all's coming?"

"The usual. You, me, Winky, Winnie, Jorge and Goober. Oh! And the woman who has the RV."

"I can't wait to meet her. But wait. No Milly? Or Tom?"

"Milly's got a date. And Tom's iffy. We had another...misunderstanding."

Laverne's eyes went soft. "Oh. Want to talk about it?"

"Not really. You know, it was Tom's fault I lost the RV in the first place."

"But you found it, right?"

"Yes. Exactly. *I* found it. He didn't help at all. I mean, he had a friend run some plates. Or at least he said he did. Then he goes running off yesterday in a huff over a stupid misunderstanding. I don't know if all this drama is worth it."

"Did you tell him you loved him?"

"No."

"Think about it, Val. If *you* had told *him* that you loved him and he didn't say it back, how would you feel?"

*Like the biggest jerk on the planet.*

SOMETHING WAS MISSING. My famous tortilla dip didn't taste right. I stuck a finger in the concoction and then in my mouth. *What was it?*

I hadn't made the dip in let's see...*nine years!* I never made it once the whole seven years I was in Germany. I'd been back two years and, to be honest, I hadn't made the dip or cooked a dang thing the entire time. But to be fair, it wasn't my fault. I'd grown up cooking Southern food. No respectable Southern recipe could be made for just one person. Not even two. No, I figured the minimum serving for anything I'd learned how to make was six. And those were generous portions. What was the point in all that fuss for just me?

I stuck my finger in the half-gallon of light-green glop and tasted it again. *Cumin?* I hoped not. All I had in the spice cabinet was salt, pepper and, strangely, tarragon. I put a lid on the dip and shoved it in the fridge. There was no time to go to the store. Folks should be arriving any minute. I dried my hands on a dishtowel and stared at my cellphone. I'd already picked it up a dozen times, but I still hadn't managed to call Tom.

I grabbed the phone, took a breath, closed my eyes and punched his number.

"Hello?"

*Crap*. I'd dialed Laverne by mistake.

"Hi Laverne. Uh...do you have cumin?"

"I don't think so. I went to the doctor's last week."

"No. Cumin is...never mind. You coming over soon?"

"On my way, honey, with bells on!"

The doorbell rang. I set the phone down. The doorknob twisted and Winky peeked his freckled face through the crack.

"Anybody home?"

"Yeah. Come on in."

# Chapter Eighteen

In the backyard, the party was in full swing. I hesitated at the sliding door, the bowl of tortilla dip in one hand, a beer in the other. While the fireside festivities looked nice from afar, everything was far from nice.

As I watched the flames in the fire pit dance, I realized the whole party had lost its meaning. I should have been celebrating my new job. But Milly wasn't there. I should have been celebrating that my boyfriend loved me. But Tom wasn't there. I should have been over the moon that Winky wasn't here anymore. But he *was*. So, I made do. I settled for one simple reason to celebrate...

"Is it time, yet?" Goober yelled.

...the imminent demise of my former nemesis. Goober waved at me with a crap-brown cushion filched from the old finger-infested sofa.

"Let it burn!" I yelled back.

I put the dip on a folding table next to the tiki hut and set my beer next to a chair by the fire pit. I wondered if the fire's glow made my face look as goofy and maniacal as the three cave men who were busy poking the flames with spears fashioned from palm fronds. At my instruction to 'let it burn,' they hooted, abandoned their spears and disappeared behind the tiki hut.

"What's that?" Winnie asked, then tucked a chocolate chip cookie in her mouth. I wasn't sure if she was asking about the dip or the couch, so I gave an answer applicable to both. "It's the grand finale."

"Oh!" she said, garbling the syllable. She wiped her hands on her jeans, then rubbed them together in anticipation.

The guys emerged from behind the tiki hut, tugging and wrestling with the old couch like an unwilling captive. Once they reached the pit, they stood it on one end.

"Ready?" Goober asked.

"Ready!" I yelled.

"Stand back, everybody," Jorge commanded.

"Let's get this show on the road!" Winky hollered.

"Here goes!" Goober said.

At Goober's command, Winky and Jorge grabbed the couch at the bottom and heaved. The sofa gained altitude sluggishly, like a flying pig, then crashed with a spectacular belly flop into the middle of the blaze. A cloud of sparks danced like fireflies in the pinkish-grey twilight.

"Wait for me!" Laverne called from her side of the fence. She straddled the low pickets and worked her way through the bushes over to the pit. I hadn't realized she'd gone home for a moment to retrieve Mr. Happy Banana. She beamed and lifted the sculpture up for Winky's inspection.

"Lemme help you with that, young lady," he said.

Winky grabbed the ceramic figure from Laverne's proud clutches and flung it into the fire. Blue flames shot up, illuminating Laverne's shocked face. A sudden volley of firecracker-like pops rang out, startling me and flushing a mallard from the cattails by the water.

Immobilized by surprise, I watched as the duck zigzagged across the yard like a stray bullet, flapping its wings and honking hysterically. It got airborne, but barely cleared Jorge's head before crash-landing in the bowl of tortilla dip. A moment later, it took off again, its yellow webbed feet plastered with green goo.

Goober dove for the tiki hut. Winnie and Winky took refuge behind the lounge chairs. With everyone scrambling for cover like a drug raid, the poor duck, weighed down with dip, made an emergency landing on the highest stable point it could find. Laverne's head. Rendered catatonic at the demise of Mr. Happy Banana, she hadn't even tried to get out of the way.

The duck roosted on her noggin and quacked up a storm until Jorge got brave enough to shoo it off with a spear. We all watched from our battle stations as it flew low, like a B-1 bomber, across the yard and splashed down in the waterway, complaining indignantly the entire way.

"Waaahooo!" Winky yelled. "If that ain't the funniest dang thing I ever did see! Looks like you just got yourself dipped, Laverne!"

Laverne blinked and closed her gaping mouth. She scowled, picked up the last unburned sofa cushion and whacked Winky in the face with it. He fell over backward, hit the buffet table and ended up with coleslaw in his lap. Laverne marched past me into the house, her pride in shambles. I glared at Winky then followed her to the kitchen. Her face was hidden behind a cabinet door as she rifled through the shelves.

"Laverne, Winky didn't realize it was art."

Laverne slammed a cabinet door, revealing the sorry state of her affairs. Her usually carefully coiffed strawberry curls looked like a rancid bowl of pesto linguine. I bit my lip to keep from laughing.

Laverne pouted. "I know he didn't. But *nobody* does. You got any scotch?"

"Scotch? Gross! No. But I can make you a TNT."

Laverne sighed. "Okay."

I handed her a dishcloth. Here. You might want to wipe your...uh...."

I bit my lip harder. Laverne smirked and snatched the cloth from my hand.

"That bad, huh? Ever since I've met you Val, my luck has changed."

I grimaced. "I'm sorry."

Laverne's face registered surprise. Then she laughed. "No. I mean for the *better*, honey. Tell me, how many women my age can say they spent the evening burning crime evidence and providing a landing strip for a lunatic duck? I feel...*alive* again. Thanks to you."

I sniffed back a sudden hotness in my nose and handed Laverne the TNT. "I gotta say, Laverne, you never cease to surprise me."

Laverne took the glass and raised a toast. "Or you, me."

My cellphone buzzed. I glanced down at it on the kitchen counter, then looked back at Laverne. She wiped her hair with the dishtowel and eyed me curiously.

"It's a text from Cold Cuts," I explained. "She can't make it. Has to work. I was really hoping to talk to her."

"Oh. Well, then. Don't take no for an answer. Set something else up with her."

I shrugged. "Yeah."

Laverne fashioned the dishtowel into a turban and stared at me. "I mean *now*."

"I...I'm meeting Milly for breakfast...I guess I could invite her along."

"Well, there you go."

I SAT ALONE, WATCHING the last embers in the fire pit glow like chunks of molten lava. I'd just witnessed an era go up in flames. The guys and me. None of us were homeless anymore. And against all odds, I'd found a job. Laverne felt alive again. Milly had a date good enough to warrant keeping clear of tonight's festival of fools. And I had my house all to myself again. I guess we were all making progress.

I sat back in the chair and swirled my third TNT, then drew the glass to my mouth to take a sip. A huge, brown moth chose that exact moment to do a cannon ball in my alcohol. I was so startled I flung the drink into the grass. *Really?* I sighed and muttered to myself.

"Could something *normal* happen to me just *once?*"

"What would be the fun in that?" a deep voice said behind me.

I nearly came out of my skin. I whirled around to find Tom standing under the moon, his blond hair glowing like a Greek god.

"Am I too late?" he asked.

"No. Am I?"

Tom took my hand and pulled me out of the chair.

"You know why it's illegal to burn a chest of drawers?" he asked, then pulled me to him.

I showed him a crooked smile. "No. Why?"

Tom took my hand and swayed me to his own, unique rhythm, then whispered in my ear. "Because that would be a bonfire of the vanity."

I rolled my eyes, then snickered despite myself. Tom swirled me around in the moonlight, then dipped me. When he brought me up, he kissed me lightly on the nose, a little *less* lightly on the lips.

It would have been the perfect time to tell Tom that I loved him. I mean, how could I *not* love a guy with the balls to tell such horrifically bad jokes with a straight face?

But even though our actions spoke louder, those three little words went unsaid.

# Chapter Nineteen

I woke up Saturday morning with a cop in my bed and thoughts of Capone in my head. Tom was sprawled out on his stomach beside me. I nudged him on the shoulder.

"You've gotta get out of here."

"What?" Tom groused. He squinted his sleepy eyes and stuck out his lower lip. "Was I that lousy a lay?"

I laughed out loud and playfully kissed him on the cheek. "No. I've got breakfast plans with Milly."

"Oh. You didn't mention it."

"I just did."

Tom sat up on one elbow, revealing his smooth, tanned chest. "I thought we said no secrets."

"*You* said no secrets. Besides, that's not a secret. It's a...it's *breakfast*."

Tom shot me a sexy grin. "In that case, can I have mine first? I *like* to eat and run."

He tugged on my gown strap. I pulled it back up.

"You are full of one-liners this morning."

Tom smirked. "Thanks."

I shifted my legs and climbed out of bed. "I didn't say they were good."

"MILLICENT!"

"Valiant!"

I walked over to the table where my best friend was busy drinking coffee and checking her cellphone. Milly tore her eyes away from the screen to greet me. Her shining green eyes darted around the restaurant, then back to me.

"How do you like the place, Val?"

I glanced around. The place couldn't have been more generic if it had been called Restaurant X. "Not bad. But I don't see what's so special about this place that you come here every Saturday morning."

Milly gave me a knowing nod. "Wait until you try the omelet. You'll be hooked."

"Well, the place *is* called The Omulette. I hope the chef can cook better than he can spell."

"Ha ha. What's your favorite breakfast place, Miss Smarty Pants?"

"My bed."

Milly rolled her eyes. "I wish."

"No dice last night?"

"Not even a roll."

"Bummer. But I still want juicy details. Who, what, where and when."

"Okay, but don't laugh."

"Why would I laugh?"

"The guy's name was Hardy."

I stifled a smirk and pushed back the urge to ask how hardy he was. "Okay."

"Hardy Peacheater."

I bit my lip for ten seconds. "Go on."

"He took me out dancing."

I willed my face to stone. "Was it a ball?"

Milly eyed me suspiciously. "No. Country music."

I crinkled my nose. "Milly! I thought you *hated* country music."

"I *did*, but—"

"I see you two travel in pairs."

Milly and I froze, then looked up toward the voice. Standing before us was a woman in a dowdy brown dress. She wore a pair of tortoise-shell bifocals on her plain, unmade face. Her mousy red hair was pulled up in a careless, frizzy bun. At first, I thought it was our waitress. Then I realized it wasn't.

"Hi, Cold Cuts," I said.

The woman frowned. "Shoot."

Milly's mouth fell open. "Is that really *you?*"

Cold Cuts shrugged. "Guilty as charged. Val, how did you know it was me?"

"The ring. I've seen you wear it before."

"Oh."

I turned to face Milly. "I meant to mention it. I invited Cold Cuts to join us."

Milly looked a bit put out. She didn't like to share the stage. Especially when she had a juicy role to act out. She scooted over begrudgingly.

"Oh. Sure. Have a seat."

Cold Cuts slid into the booth beside her. Milly smiled thinly. "So tell us, Cold Cuts. How did you get that name? Let me guess. Because you cut men off cold?"

Cold Cuts smirked good-naturedly. "That, and I adore salami."

"Well, they don't *have* salami here."

I shot Milly a look. She sighed and softened her tone. "But they do make a nice cheese omelet."

"Oh yeah?" Cold Cuts asked. "You've been here before?"

Milly beamed proudly. "Every Saturday for the last...I dunno...five years or so."

A wormy-looking waiter in his late thirties with a soul patch and a 20-inch waist dragged himself over to our table. He pulled an order pad from the back pocket of his size-zero pants and stared at it blankly as he spoke.

"What'll it be?"

"I'll have the Saturday-morning special," Milly said politely.

"What's that?" Cold Cuts asked.

The waiter sighed heavily. "Cheese omelet, toast, orange juice and coffee."

"Sounds good. Make it two," Cold Cuts said and closed her menu.

"Make it three," I said.

The waiter gave a quick nod of his head and ambled away. I would have killed for a butt his size.

"I get the same thing every time," Milly said. "It's *so* good."

Cold Cuts studied Milly for a moment, then looked back at the waiter. "So, is that guy new?"

"Jackson? No. He's been here for years. Why?"

"He didn't seem to recognize you at all. And he didn't know your order, either."

"Oh, *that*. That's the 'woman of a certain age' curse, Cold Cuts. Val and I call it 'The Cloak of Invisibility.' You're too young, but you'll get yours one day."

Cold Cuts crinkled her nose. "What are you talking about?"

Milly shot me a knowing smirk. "I'm impervious to attention. Nobody notices me. At least, nobody I *want* to notice."

Cold Cuts looked over at me. "You, too?"

"Yeah. It happens all the time."

The waiter returned with two more coffees and a stack of paper napkins big enough to thwart an oncoming tsunami. Cold Cuts studied him as he unceremoniously dumped the items from his tray.

"Hey buddy. See my friends here?"

Jackson glanced dully at me and Milly, then over to Cold Cuts. We were as interesting to him as drying paint.

"Listen to me," Cold Cuts said. "These two are *not*—"

I kicked Cold Cuts under the table. She glanced at me, then at Milly. She picked up on Milly's look of dread and switched her attitude in the blink of an eye.

"—ones to waste napkins." Cold Cuts grabbed half the napkins and handed them back to the waiter. "Take these back with you."

"Your wish is my command," Jackson replied robotically. With the speed of a paralytic sloth, he placed the napkins on his tray and headed to the kitchen. When he was out of earshot, I scolded Cold Cuts.

"What are you doing? Drop it!"

"Are you serious? You guys don't care?"

"It's not exactly something you can fight."

Cold Cuts bared her teeth in disgust. "When did you know you had this...cloak of...?"

"Invisibility," I said dryly.

"I remember exactly," Milly said. "It was like, ten months ago. I was leaving a restaurant after a horrible MatchMate date."

"Of course," I interjected. Milly smirked and continued.

"I couldn't find my phone. So I talked to the maître de about it. You know, I described my phone, left my name and address. Anyway, I went to my car and my phone was ringing. It had fallen under the seat."

Cold Cuts folded her arms. "Yeah, so?"

"So I went back inside the restaurant to tell the guy. You know what he said?"

"What?"

"Good evening, ma'am. May I help you?"

Cold Cuts' mouth fell open. "Oh no he didn't! Ouch!"

"Yes. Me, Ms. Milly Halbert. Gone less than a minute and completely erased from his memory banks. That's the day I knew I'd gotten my cloak."

Cold Cuts turned to me. "And you?"

I shrugged. "I dunno when it started, exactly. But like I said, it happens all the time."

Cold Cuts shook her head. "Unbelievable!"

The thoughtless waiter returned. He slapped an omelet in front of Cold Cuts and me, then placed a plate of fried eggs and grits on the table in front of Milly. Cold Cuts nearly lost it.

"Uh, dude, that is *not* what she ordered."

Milly shrugged. "It's okay. It's close enough."

"Are you kidding me?" Cold Cuts objected.

The waiter turned to leave. Cold Cuts lost it for real. She stood up, grabbed the waiter by his choker-sized belt, and hauled him back to the table.

"Dude, see what's on my plate? We ordered three of the same thing!"

"Excuse me," he replied, in a tone that was anything but apologetic. We watched with piss in our eyes as Jackson picked up Milly's plate and headed to the kitchen. Halfway there, he turned around and dropped the plate in front of an old, grey-haired woman sitting alone.

Cold Cuts stared at us, dumbfounded. She flopped back down into the booth as if she'd just finished a marathon. "Geez! I hope you two aren't contagious!"

I blew out a jaded breath. "Like we said, it's—"

Cold Cuts bolted upright and slapped her hand on the table. "This is ridiculous! You two are...*gorgeous!* You know what? I think it's time you two put your powers to work. Against this...*evil!*"

"What are you talking about?" I asked.

"I think it's time we get the hell out of this stupid place."

"The restaurant?" Milly asked.

"Yeah."

"Now?"

"Hell yeah! Before Captain Oblivious returns."

I looked over my shoulder. The waiter was heading into the kitchen. He paused a moment to pull his pants out of his tiny little butt crack.

"Okay. I'm in," I said.

Milly gave me a shocked look. "Really?"

Cold Cuts and I jumped up. She grabbed Milly's hand and tugged her out of the booth. We made a run for the door, me trailing behind. As Milly and Cold Cuts made it out the door, I looked back just in time to see the waiter delivering Milly's omelet to our empty booth. He looked up as if in slow motion. I could almost see the scales fall off his dull eyes. He focused in on me. I panicked, shot him a bird and ran out the door.

Milly and Cold Cuts were waiting for me just outside.

"Woooo hoooo! That was killer, ladies!" Cold Cuts yelled.

"What have we done?" Milly cried out, then laughed nervously.

"Let's get the hell out of here!" I said, and ran past them.

We hooted and hollered and screamed with laughter as we ran to our prospective getaway cars. You'd have thought we'd just robbed the place.

"You know, I can never go back there," Milly yelled as she climbed into her Beemer.

"Why the hell would you want to?" Cold Cuts yelled back.

*Yeah. Why the hell, indeed.*

# Chapter Twenty

I squealed into my driveway and slammed on the brakes. Milly's Beemer pulled in behind me a second later. She climbed out of her car and wobbled, weak in the knees, to my driver's side door. We both stared at each other, speechless. A moment later, we heard a vehicle backfire. Milly flinched as if it was a gunshot aimed at her head. We looked back at the road and the old RV came into view, Cold Cuts at the wheel. Milly and I both exhaled loudly. Hopefully, her safe arrival meant we'd made a clean getaway.

Cold Cuts waved an arm out the window and touched her thumb and index finger together to form an okay sign. She pulled up behind Milly and shut off the RV. It shuttered and coughed and finally cut out.

"Wow! That was fantastic!" Cold Cuts yelled. She jumped out and sprinted to join us.

Milly chewed off her last fingernail and looked over at me, her face marred with guilt and fear. "Do you think they'll call the cops on us?"

"Who?" Cold Cuts asked.

"The restaurant!" Milly cried, exasperated. "Jackson!"

Cold Cuts shook her head confidently. "No way."

"How can you be so sure?" I asked.

"Think about it. Your cloaks of invisibility. He could never pick you guys out in a lineup."

Milly's fear gave way to relief, then a grin. "You know Val, she's probably right."

Cold Cuts cocked her head and pointed a thumb at her own chest. "I *know* I'm right."

"Yeah, I agreed," I said. "But please, both of you, not a word to Tom."

"Who's Tom?" Cold Cuts asked.

I shot Milly a "keep quiet" look. "Even better," I said.

I MADE MY PARTNERS in crime a consolation breakfast of strawberry Pop Tarts and coffee. We munched them while Cold Cuts gave us a tour of the RV.

It was unrecognizable inside. All the dragonfly stickers on the walls were gone, as far as I could tell. They'd been replaced by clothes, scarves, belts, hats and bags full of wigs and shoes. They covered every wall, hung from sturdy hooks screwed into the paneling. I noticed one dry-cleaning bag had a name on it. Sherry Perry. Inside was the blonde wig and purple rhinestone shirt that had saved me from the oaf in Publix.

"What do you do with all this stuff?" Milly asked, beating me to it. She picked up a small hairpiece and studied it.

"I'm a freelance makeup artist, slash wardrobe consultant, slash whatever I have to be to get hired. I work on local TV commercials and low-budget indie films."

"That's so cool!" Milly said. She played with the little wig and giggled. "Mind if I use your mirror? After that run for it, I might need a disguise for a while."

Cold Cuts raised her eyebrows, then shrugged. "Knock yourself out. There's one in the bathroom."

"Are all of these costumes for your movie clients?" I asked.

"Well...sort of."

"Where do you get the ideas?"

"Some from client requests. Most, though, from my imagination. This one's Scary Kerry." Cold Cuts held up a clear plastic bag containing a rainbow-colored Mohawk, tattoo sleeves, a pair of ripped jeans and a piece of cardboard poked through with piercing jewelry.

Milly peeked out from around the bathroom door. "Yes! She's the one who saved me from Dexter!"

"Dexter the *dweeb*," Cold Cuts corrected.

"How do you remember all these characters?" I asked. "I mean, how do you keep them straight in your mind? What they would say?"

Cold Cuts shrugged nonchalantly. "Back stories."

"Back stories?"

"Yeah. You know. Little quirks to make them more real. Odds and ends to give them depth. *Motivation*."

"Motivation?" Milly came out of the bathroom wearing the little wig on her chin.

"Yeah. A reason to act."

Milly giggled and lowered her voice. "So, what's my motivation?"

Cold Cuts grinned. "You tell me. By the way, that's a merkin, not a beard."

Milly scrunched her brow. "A merkin?"

"Yeah. For nude scenes. Everybody's shaved nowadays."

Milly cocked her head like a puzzled gnome. "Huh?"

"It's a pubic wig."

"Aaargh!" Milly ripped the curly wig from her chin and tried to fling it away, but it stuck to her finger like a piranha on a tube steak. "Eeeww! Get it off me! Val! Help!"

But alas, I couldn't help Milly. I was too busy trying not to pee my pants.

Milly screeched like a bat and flailed her fingers back and forth in the air like a miniature helicopter. The little wig finally flew off, but it landed on top of Milly's head. She screamed and tore at her hair like it was on fire. The merkin finally let go and fell to the floor like a dead tarantula.

"I think she just invented a new dance," Cold Cuts sniggered. "The Merkin Jerk!"

I crumpled over and grabbed my gut. Cold Cuts and I nearly choked to death on Pop Tart crumbs and our imaginations.

"Quit laughing! This thing is disgusting!" Milly shrieked. She ran a hand through her hair to smooth it down, then looked down at her fingers as if they might have picked up an STD. "Why didn't you tell me?"

"I thought you knew," Cold Cuts sniggered. "Hell, I didn't know you were going to *sixty-nine* the poor little thing."

Cold Cuts stuck out her tongue and waggled it. She and I grabbed onto each other to keep from falling over laughing.

"Ha ha. Very funny." Milly stomped the three feet to the kitchen and turned on the tap. "Do you have any bleach?"

"No," Cold Cuts managed to choke out. "But there's wig sanitizer under the counter."

Milly shot us both a look that could have curdled milk. I turned my back and tried to regain my composure before Mount Halbert blew her top.

I bit my lip between words. "So...what's...Scary Kerry's...back story?"

Cold Cuts eyed Milly once more, smirked, then gave me her full attention.

"Mohawk Kerry? Let's see. She's a rebel without a clue. She wants to right the wrongs of the world, but all she's got to work with is a warped sense of humor and a rusty old hammer."

"Reminds me of someone I know," Milly quipped. She'd come up behind me. She eyed me with a mixture of hurt pride and embarrassment. I returned her volley with a scowl.

"What about the one you did with me? Sherry Perry?"

Cold Cuts' eyes looked upward, as if she could see into her brain better that way. "She's an ex cheerleader. Now an aging beauty-pageant has-been. Lives for gossip and glamour magazines. And she always seems to get the crap-end of the stick when it comes to relationships."

"Hmmm. Reminds me of someone *I* know," I deadpanned.

It was Milly's time to scowl.

WE LEFT THE RV AND moved into my kitchen, so Milly could give her hands a "proper washing." As she used up the rest of my bleach and Ty D Bol, I realized from her surreptitious angry glares at Cold Cuts that the two had gotten off on the wrong foot. *Big time*. I needed to fix this situation, pronto. I liked Cold Cuts. I wanted Milly to like her, too. The last thing I needed was to tick this strange girl off. Besides, if I did, I might never find Glad's ashes.

I offered my most potent olive branch. Wine.

"Wow, Cold Cuts. How do you stay so thin?" I asked, and handed her a glass of pinot grigio.

She shrugged. "Poverty helps."

Milly's hard glare softened a notch. I handed her a glass. She slurped down half of it in one gulp.

"Your work sounds exciting," I said, like the ultimate hostess. Or, perhaps, peace negotiator.

"It can be," Cold Cuts admitted. "I got to see Channing Tatum once when he was here filming *Magic Mike*. But mostly, it's just grunt work. And I never know when my next gig is coming."

"My job is mind-numbingly steady," Milly said unexpectedly. "I've done the same thing for twenty years. Monday through Friday, rain or shine. Boring, boring, boring." She drained her glass. I sprinted back to the fridge to grab the bottle.

"What do you do?"

"I work in an accounting office."

"Oh," Cold Cuts said without judgment. "Did you always want to be an accountant?"

Milly was taken aback by the question. I refilled her glass as she thought about how to answer it. "No. I mean, it was a process of elimination, I guess."

"What were your other choices?" Cold Cuts asked with genuine interest.

The wine seemed to be working its magic. Milly sat up and made a joke.

"Well, princess and mermaid didn't seem like valid options once I hit junior high."

Cold Cuts laughed. "Hey, it's never too late to change careers."

Milly shook her head as if it weighed 80 lbs. "Oh, I don't know about that. I mean, who would hire me at *my age?*"

"Who says you have to find someone to *hire* you?" asked Cold Cuts. "You could be your own boss."

The reply stumped Milly. She scrunched her eyebrows and uttered one syllable. "Huh."

"Listen, I'm going out to the RV," Cold Cuts said. She set her glass of wine on the counter. "I need to change my clothes and head out. Mind if I change them in your place, Val? You've got a little more elbow room."

"Oh. No. Not at all. Take a shower, if you want. Save your water."

Cold Cuts grinned appreciatively. "Great! Thanks, I will."

When Cold Cuts left, I turned to Milly. She was busy downing the last of her wine. "What's your problem with Cold Cuts anyway?"

Milly shrugged and looked confused. "She took your mom's RV, Val. And won't give it back."

"Not yet. She still might. Maybe. And she *did* say she's going to help me find the piggybank. I'm okay with it. Why can't you be?"

Milly pouted. "Val, she's just so...*young*. And *perky*."

"There's no law against perkiness."

"Well, there ought to be."

My best friend and I grinned at each other with the soft comfort of knowing we had each other's backs. The front door cracked open. We watched Cold Cuts reenter with a bag of clothes.

"Bathroom's that way," I said and pointed down the hall.

"Thanks!" Cold Cuts smiled and headed in that direction. Milly eyed her with a sad, envious look.

"Val, who would you be if you could be anybody?"

"I dunno. I like my life fine."

"Even the schlepping files part?"

"Well, maybe not *that* part."

"You know, I wouldn't mind working for myself, like Cold Cuts said. Mrs. Barnes is a pain in the neck. And poor Mr. Maas. He's so old he could go any day. They *both* could. Maybe I should work on a plan B."

"Oh crap! Speaking of plan B, I should call Tom. I was supposed to meet him for dinner tonight. But I'd kind of like to invite Cold Cuts to stay the afternoon. Are you up for a girl's day? I could order pizza or something. Watch a movie?"

Milly nodded. "How about that *Magic Mike* movie. I heard it was pretty sexy."

"It was," said Cold Cuts. She appeared, fresh from the shower. She dried her hair with one of my towels. "I've got the DVD in the RV."

"Can you stay?" I asked. "Watch it with us? I'm ordering takeout. Pizza or Chinese?"

Cold Cuts grinned. "Sure. Why not? Chinese for me. Chop suey? I'll be back in a minute." She sprinted out the door.

"Give her a chance?" I asked Milly.

"Okay. For you."

Cold Cuts returned with the DVD in one hand, a plate of brownies in the other. She beamed at me and Milly.

"All right, ladies. Take off your cloaks. Let's get this party started!"

# Chapter Twenty-One

I woke up Sunday morning sprawled out on the couch like a drunken harlot. Milly's bare foot was in my face. I shoved it away, waking Milly in the process. She cracked open an eye.

"Where am I?"

"My place."

"What the hell?"

"Yeah."

Memories like snippets of confetti fell into place in my mind. "Geez, Milly. The brownies. I think they had pot in them."

"What?" Milly pulled an oven mitt off her hand and stared at it. "Crap, Val. I knew we shouldn't have trusted her. Is she gone? Did she take your wallet?"

"Come on. She wouldn't do that."

But I had my nagging doubts. I crawled off the couch on my hands and knees and peeked inside my purse. It was hanging on the front-door knob. Everything appeared to be intact. I pulled myself to standing using the door handle. Something odd in the backyard caught my eye. I slapped on some sunshades and peered through the sliding glass door. A foot was hanging out of the swaying hammock. Its nails were painted, so unless Winky had suddenly decided to become a transvestite, it was probably Cold Cuts.

"She's out there. In the hammock."

Milly stood up and rubbed her neck. "Geez. What time is it?"

"Nine fifteen. You want some coffee?"

Milly's eyes flew open like a doll in a horror movie. "Oh, crap! Val! My Ladies' Leadership Brunch! It starts at 10 a.m.!"

"Ughh. Just skip it."

"I *can't*. I'm *leading* it!"

"Crap on a cracker." My brain kicked into action as much as it could without caffeine. "You go take a shower. I'll make coffee, then go rouse Cold Cuts."

Milly ambled crookedly down the hallway. "If I were you, I'd let sleeping dogs lie."

I got the pot brewing. When I turned around, Cold Cuts was coming through the sliding door. She looked way too chipper if you asked me.

"Morning, Val! I tell you, it was beautiful sleeping under the stars."

"Huh. Well, I'm glad you enjoyed it. Look, Cold Cuts. I've gotta warn you, Milly's on the warpath again. We've got to be across town at Tyrone Square Mall to make her leadership meeting in like...half an hour."

Cold Cuts twisted her lip. "I guess I'm back on her naughty list."

"The brownies didn't help."

Cold Cuts smirked, then her face lit up. She snapped her fingers and pointed the index one at me like a gun. "I know what. I've got a plan."

"I've had enough of your plans," Milly jeered. She'd emerged from the bathroom with a towel wrapped around her. Her hair was sopping wet.

"Come on, Milly, we can do this!" Cold Cuts said cheerily. "I can dress you and do your makeup in the RV. You'll get there in plenty of time."

Milly eyed her angrily. "Are you crazy?"

"No. I do it all the time. It's literally *what I do*."

I gave my best friend a pleading look. "Milly, it's probably the only chance in hell we have of making it on time."

Milly scowled. "All right, already. But no wigs this time."

I PULLED UP IN THE lot at Tyrone Square Mall with five minutes to spare. I'd gotten dressed while Cold Cuts drove, then taken over the wheel while she performed her magic on Milly. I shut off the ignition. Above the cough and sputter of the engine, I heard Cold Cuts clear her throat.

"Introducing the dashing business tycoon, Milly Halbert!"

Cold Cuts stepped aside and Milly sauntered into view. My eyes nearly dropped out of my skull. Milly was dressed to kill in a stunning red skirt and matching jacket. A cream-colored silk blouse made her skin look like peaches and cream. And her hair? *Fabulous!* Her shoulder-length blonde locks had been swept up into an amazing bun that tucked into the back. A single, long curl swept down the side of her face. Cinderella herself might have punched a dwarf in envy.

"Un-freaking-believable," I muttered.

Milly held up a hand mirror and admired her reflection. "Val, if I actually looked like this in real life, I'd never speak to you—*or me*—ever again!"

I slapped on a worried pout. "What about me?" I asked Cold Cuts.

"We've still got three minutes. Let me see what I can do."

MILLY AND I LEFT COLD Cuts in the RV and traipsed into Fandango's restaurant. The hostess led us to a small banquet room set up for a dozen people. By the door, a Hispanic woman was busily filling out name-tag stickers and ticking off names on a list. Milly marched confidently over to the woman.

"Hi Carla."

"Hello. May I help you?"

"It's me. Milly."

"Milly who?"

"Milly *Halbert*. I'm leading the brunch today."

Carla eyed Milly dubiously. "Huh? No. Is that *really you?*"

"Yes!" Milly beamed.

"Wow! It's about time you got a makeover!"

Milly's smile ticked down a notch. "Thanks."

Carla glanced my way. "Who's the lady with you?"

"That's my friend, Val Fremden."

I waved. "Hi."

"No. I mean the other one."

Carla pointed to a woman walking in the door. She was blonde, busty, and clad in an immaculate, royal-blue business dress. As she passed by a table, her zebra-striped go-go boots came into view. Milly's face flushed crimson to match her suit.

"Oh. I don't know."

The woman strode up and took Carla's hand. "Name's Cold Cuts."

Carla shook her hand enthusiastically. "I love your boots!"

Cold Cuts grinned and looked down. "Yeah. Aren't they great? No animals were harmed in their making, either. Unless you count naugahydes."

Carla laughed, scribbled our names on stickers and handed them to us. Milly ushered us along like naughty children. I half expected her to grab us by the ears. When we got to the table, she shot us a stern face and warned us with a whisper.

"Look, this is a business networking meeting, so I'd appreciate it if you two could keep things on a professional level. Don't mention...you know...*last night*. And no weird stuff, please!"

"What do you mean by weird stuff?" Cold Cuts asked.

Milly opened her mouth to say something, but never got the chance. Carla approached her with a final head count.

"Everyone's present and accounted for, Milly. Ready when you are."

Milly straightened from her hovering position over us. She cleared her throat and plastered on a smiley face. "Good morning, ladies!"

The women around the table gasped. A plus-sized gal with the nametag Terri, spoke without thinking, spoiling Milly's game face.

"Is that *you*, Milly?"

"Huh? Oh! Yes, Terri, it's me." Milly beamed her best fake smile over the crowd. "So, today we'll be talking about synergizing our business strengths. We all—"

"Wait a minute," Terri continued. "You sound like Milly, but you sure don't look like her. Are you *sure* that's who you are?"

Several of the women laughed, and voices began to buzz around the table. Milly's plaster started to crack.

"Look. It's really me, okay? Now, let's get to business. When we all work together, our total skills and talents are greater than the sum of our—"

"Dang, Milly! You look amazing!" said a sharp-dressed black woman with the nametag Sharon. "Where can I get a makeover like that?"

Milly's jaw grew taught. "Could we please just stick to the program, Sharon?"

Cold Cuts stood up suddenly, causing her chair legs to scrape loudly. "I don't know about you ladies, but if this is the program, somebody stick an ice pick through my eardrums. I don't think I can stand to hear another word. *Synergy? Please!*"

The women's faces formed a silent choir of O's. You could have heard a roach fart. Milly turned to Cold Cuts.

"*Why are you doing this?*"

"You haven't seen anything yet!" Cold Cuts bent her elbow in a tight V and pointed an index finger toward the ceiling. "Excuse me, ladies. But who wants to talk about *synergy* when we could be talking about *sexergy?* When's the last time any of you got what you *really wanted* in bed?"

I heard a cockroach fart. The room broke into hoots and hollers and cheers. Milly looked as if she'd been hit in the face with an invisible cream pie.

"Now *that's* what I'm talking about!" Cold Cuts encouraged. "Forget all this boring business crap. I think it's time to get back to the *real* world. Sex!"

A woman in a pair of librarian's glasses spoke up. "Excuse me, but who *are* you?"

"*I'm* the woman who did Milly's makeover."

The women cheered. The mousy lady cracked a grin. "Well, why didn't you *say* so?"

"And I'll do a makeover for one of *you*, too. The winner of the 'Ladies Leadership Worst Date Ever Competition.' Come on. I bet we've got some contenders up in here!"

Milly crumpled into her chair. The ladies went wild.

Sharon stood up and yelled, "I've got one!"

"All right, then. Tell us, Sharon!"

"I went out with this fine-looking guy from Our Time. Yeah, I said it. Over-fifty. *Our Time*. I'm owning it."

The women around the table banged their coffee cups and cheered like knights at the round table.

"So what happened?" Cold Cuts asked.

"Oh. So, I met him at this park. For a picnic. You know, that man didn't bring anything with him but a six-pack of beer and his dusty, worn-out old game."

Commiserative grumbles erupted around the table.

"I thought, okay. The guy doesn't cook. And he's got no game. But I'm fair. I'm still willing to give him a chance. So, to make conversation, I ask him how he ended up on Our Time. You know what he said?"

"What?" the ladies shouted.

"He said he liked *the name*. 'You know, it's like, I've done my time. Now it's *Our* Time. Get it?' I said, 'Oh hell yeah, I get it. Then I got my butt up on out of there!"

The women cheered and roared with laughter.

"Very nice, Sharon," Cold Cuts commentated. "Good story. Who's next?"

Carla stood up and waved her finger in the air like she didn't care. "I can beat that! I met this guy on MatchMate."

At the mention of Milly's online dating nemesis, I glanced over at her. She was pallid, but still breathing.

"We met up at a restaurant," Carla continued. "The guy was like, 10 or 50 years older than he said he was online. I mean, he could'a been the *father* of the guy in his profile picture. Anyway, he wasn't completely hideous, so I thought, what the hell. You know what I mean?"

The women nodded and hummed.

"So I sit and talk to him for like, two hours. Not great, but better than another night of Netflunks, you know? Anyway, by the end of the meal, he says he likes me and wants to see me again. I thought, man, he's way too old for me. But he was nice. I'll give him a chance. I was about to say, 'okay' when he leans over the table and says he wants to tell me something."

Someone yelled, "Uh-oh!"

"So, I got close to his wrinkly old face. You know what he says to me?"

"What?" someone cried.

"He says, 'I just want you to know I've got GH—genital herpes. But it's okay because I've discovered *flavored condoms!*'"

"What the hell!" Sharon yelled. "What did he think you were gonna do? Suck his banana-flavored wiener?"

The crowd roared and cheered and hooted with laughter. Finally, Cold Cuts had to beat a spoon on the table to regain control. "That was pretty darn good, Carla. Anybody think they can top that?"

The meek, mousy woman in the librarian glasses raised her hand timidly.

"Okay. What's your name?"

"Nora."

"Let's hear it for Nora!"

The women cheered. "Nora! Nora! Nora!" Cold Cuts brought them back to attention with a wave of her hand. Nora began tentatively, her voice wavering like bad cellphone reception.

"I had an affair once. With a married man." Nora looked around nervously, but pressed on. She must have been desperate for that makeover.

"I didn't know he was married. Or that men lied about stuff like that all the time."

The women grumbled in agreement.

"Anyway, we were out one night at a motel, you know, *doing it*, when his phone beeps, for a text. Well, he ignores it the first time. But it keeps beeping. So finally he stops, you know, *doing it*, and checks his messages. He seems shocked, so I ask him if something's wrong. He says, 'It's my wife. She must have found out about you.' Then he just stood there, his red flagpole sticking in the air, and scratched his head like a flea-ridden ape."

Nora mimicked an ape scratching its head. The women laughed.

"So, all of a sudden, ape-man smiles, all relieved and everything. He looks over at me and says, 'All right! Whew! I thought my wife's message meant she knew I was with a girl. But it's okay. I just figured it out. "It's a girl" doesn't mean you. It means *the baby* is a girl.'"

"What!" voices screamed out.

"That's what *I* said! I looked at that creep and said, 'Are you telling me your wife just had a baby?' He says, 'Yeah. *Sweet!*' But not sweet like it's a baby girl. No. Sweet like he didn't *get caught*. Then he tries to get back in bed with me. Can you believe that?"

The crowd of women went wild. Cold Cuts smiled and pointed toward Nora.

"I think we have a winner!"

RIDING HOME IN THE RV, I thought the radiator might boil over. Not the one in the RV. The one in my best friend. Cold Cuts seemed oblivious to Milly's nuclear-level rage.

"That was awesome!" Cold Cuts said as she pulled onto Gulf Boulevard.

I smiled weakly at Cold Cuts. "Yeah."

Cold Cuts nodded toward Milly in the back. She'd stripped off the red suit and donned my rumpled clothes from yesterday. She'd also torn down her golden hair. It hung in clumpy ringlets around her still made-up face. From the rearview mirror, she looked like a spoiled child pageant loser sent to her room without supper. Little Miss Piss Pants.

"What's wrong with her?"

I opened my mouth, but Milly's voice came out.

"You know, I was really feeling it," she yelled from her seat at the banquette. "With the fancy clothes and all. I felt *different*. *Powerful*. I thought, 'I can do this. I can be a business tycoon.' Then *you* go and take over and *you ruin everything!*"

"Take it easy!" Cold Cuts said.

"*Me* take it easy? *You* take it easy. That was *my* meet-up, Cold Cuts! I was trying to make *business connections*. You turned the whole thing into a freak show with your *Sheena the Destroyer* getup or whoever you were today. Now I can never go back."

"What are you talking about?" Cold Cuts asked. "Why not?"

"They'll never see me as the old Milly again."

"And that's bad?"

I ducked involuntarily, but the only thing Milly hurled was more words.

"You don't *get it*. You're too young. You haven't *worked* and *scraped* to make a name for yourself. No. You just go off on your crazy rants and escapades. You don't care who you hurt!"

Cold Cuts lifted an eyebrow like Spock and turned into my driveway. Milly bolted out the RV's side door. She made a run for my backyard, but tripped and fell over a newspaper in the grass. She picked it up and flung it at the RV.

"Looks like someone needs a Valium."

"Take it easy on Milly. It's hard for someone our age to change horses midstream. We have a lot more to lose than you."

Cold Cuts looked confused. "But what are you losing when you give up things you *hate?*"

"We don't all hate the same things, Cold Cuts."

Cold Cuts conceded with a nod. "Point taken. What do *you* hate, Val?"

"I dunno." I noticed a picture of Cold Cuts and an older woman clipped to her visor. "Who's that?"

"My mother. I should call her. It's Mother's Day, after all."

*Oh, crap!*

# Chapter Twenty-Two

The craziness of the last week had caught me up short. I'd completely blanked about it being Mother's Day. It was nearly 1 p.m. and I hadn't called Lucille Jolly-Short yet. I was doomed.

Even so, I first had to deal with another crazed woman on a tear. Milly Halbert.

I'd sent Cold Cuts away to avoid a catfight. Milly was still red-hot piping mad when I found her sitting at the tiki bar. But I didn't have time for her whining. I took her by the arm and yanked her into the house so she could gather her things.

"Look Milly, I know you're mad. But I don't have time to talk right now. Tom will be over any minute to take me to lunch. I've got to get ready."

Milly scoffed as she changed into her crumpled clothes from yesterday's girls' night. "Excuse me, Miss Perfect. I forgot. You have a fairytale life."

"What? *My* life? A *fairytale?*"

Milly wriggled into her yoga pants and spit her words. "Better than mine."

"Come on. I can trump your sorry life with two words."

Milly sneered at me. "Oh yeah? What?"

"Lucille Jolly."

Milly's scowl faded to a pout. "Okay. You win."

She hugged me reluctantly, then sighed and slipped on her sandals. As she grabbed her purse and headed for the door, her goodbye sounded like an apology. "Have a nice time with Tom, Val. And good luck."

Through the living room window, I watched her drive off. I padded to the bathroom and turned the tap on for a bath. I scrounged around under the sink for a box of bath salts. I dumped the crumbly blue dregs into the water and watched it foam.

*Halcyon, take me away.*

WHILE I SOAKED IN THE flamingo-pink tub, a name popped in my mind like a dirty soap bubble. Capone. Cold Cuts told me she still hadn't heard back from him. I was itching to find out what he knew. The longer I waited, the bigger the chance he'd have had to sell the piggybank and I'd have lost Glad for good. I made up my mind. I'd ask Tom to take me out to lunch today at Old Northeast Pizza. I could snoop around for Capone, and Tom would never be the wiser.

*That didn't qualify as a secret, did it?*

I climbed out of the bath, dried off and slipped into a yellow sundress. I was going to need as much sunshine as I could muster to make it through the task ahead. I picked up the phone to call my mother, but my index finger turned to stone. I couldn't mash the button.

*I'll call after I do my hair and makeup.*

After I'd combed my hair and put on lipstick and eyeliner, I picked up the phone. Medusa struck again.

*After I put my shoes on.*

I reached over to set the phone on the bathroom counter. A sudden sneeze overtook me and I dialed accidently. I listened in hopeless panic as the phone rang once and my mother's voice filled the air.

"'Bout time you called, Valiant. I was fixin' to give up on you."

I raised the phone to my ear. "Sorry, Mom."

"Yore sister done called three hours ago. What took you so long?"

*Angela always was a brownnoser.*

"Are you having a nice day, Mom?"

"I've had better."

"Did you get the flowers I sent?"

"Yep. They's right purty for the price you paid. Saw 'em on sale on Amazon for $25.99."

"I didn't know you used Amazon."

"I'm not that backwoods, Valiant. You comin' by today?"

"What? Uh...no. I have to work tomorrow."

"So?"

"It's a six-hour drive, *one way* Mom."

"I see. I'm not worth it."

"Yes you are. I'm coming up to see you during the holidays."

*Why did I say that? Kill me now!*

"Uh-huh. So you went and got yourself a job. Finally."

"Yes, I did."

"How'd you manage that? Don't they know how old you are?"

"What?"

"Well, I have been prayin' for a miracle. I guess that's it."

"I'm not *that* old, Mom."

"Uh-huh. Well, like yore Pa used to say, 'Idle hands are evil's workshop.'"

"Mom, he never said that. And it's *the Devil's*."

"The Devil's? No. I taught Sunday school, you know. That don't sound right."

*Of course not. How could* I *possibly be right?*

"Okay, Mom. Listen, I have to go. Happy Mother's Day!"

"Well, excuse me. Sorry I took up so much of your precious time."

"Bye, Mom."

"See you at Christmas. And Valliant, bring that there man you been livin' in sin with. I need to set him straight."

*Aw, crap!*

I clicked off the phone just as Tom drove up in his 4Runner. The tightness in my chest eased a little as I watched him smooth his bangs from his forehead in the side-view mirror. He grabbed a bunch of daisies from the front seat. I opened the front door before he had a chance to knock.

"Hi there, pretty lady. I'm here to sweep you off your feet. How does Caddy's sound?"

"Caddy's? I haven't been there in ages! Come to think of it, I haven't been to *the beach* in ages. Why *is* that?"

Tom looked skyward and scratched his head. "I think it's called working for a living."

I punched him playfully on the arm. "Ha ha. But why Caddy's? I was thinking we could—"

Tom silenced me with a kiss. "Caddy's is where you met Glad. On Mother's Day a year ago, if memory serves."

"Yes. I hadn't thought about that."

*But he had. Wow.*

Tom handed me the daisies and wrapped his arms around me protectively. "Speaking of moms, did you do the dirty deed yet?"

"Yes."

"Good girl. How was it?"

I pushed away from Tom's embrace and padded into the kitchen in search of a vase.

"The usual. Everything said was between the lines. I tell you, Tom, that woman is missing whatever it is that makes a person...*human*. I don't want to say she's missing a soul. Maybe it's just compassion. But it could be a soul. I'm no scientist."

Tom winced. "That bad, huh?"

I crumpled. "Crap, Tom. *I caved*. I promised I'd come home for Christmas!"

Tom grimaced, then chuckled. "I meant to mention this earlier. I may have to break up with you for a short spell around the holidays. You know, so I don't have to see your mother again. Is that wrong?"

I pursed my lips into a wry grin. "No, Tom. It's one of the most right things about you."

LUNCH AT THE BEACH with Tom turned out to be just what I'd needed. The sunshine and music and Tom's funny charm lifted my spirits and diluted away the poison injected by my mother during our brief phone conversation. The sex didn't hurt anything, either. We'd made love in my bed, then idled half the afternoon away curled up in the hammock together, watching the clouds shapeshift and change colors with the evening's approach. We didn't talk much. The closeness of our bodies had communicated plenty. We hadn't seen the need to spoil it with words.

After Tom left, I went out on the backyard to gather up the pillows we'd carried out to the hammock. I saw Laverne sitting alone on her porch, staring out at the water. I waved, but she didn't respond. It dawned on me that she might not have had anyone to celebrate Mother's Day with. I went inside, grabbed half the daisies Tom had given me, and knocked on her front door.

She didn't answer. I knocked again, louder.

*Oh, lord! I hope nothing's happened to her!*

Relief rushed through me when she cracked open the door. Even the sight of Laverne's skinny, geriatric body in a skimpy pink nightgown didn't dampen the comfort that had washed over me when I'd realized she was okay.

"Well howdy, neighbor!" she beamed.

"Hi Laverne! Here, these are for you." I handed her the flowers.

"That's mighty sweet of you, sugar. Have you had a good day?"

"Yes, thanks."

"Well, come on in." Laverne waddled over to her kitchen. "Did you call your mom, sugar?"

"Yes."

"That's nice. Want some tea?"

"Sure."

I took a seat on a stool at the kitchen counter. Laverne put the flowers in a vase and set them in front of me. She flashed her perfect, denture smile.

"These are gorgeous, honey!"

"I'm glad you like them. Hey, I've never asked, but do you have any kids, Laverne?"

Laverne filled two glasses with ice. "Nope. Never had any kids of my own. A pregnant showgirl was no showgirl at all."

She turned and opened the fridge. I knew what came next. I did a one-eighty on my stool to avoid the oncoming peep show.

"So what did you do today?" I asked, and looked around room.

"Well, I went by the school and picked up my latest sculpture from class. Wanna see it?"

"Sure."

"There it is."

I turned around and followed the line of Laverne's long, manicured finger to the end of the countertop. Sitting in the middle of what appeared to be a red ashtray was a wrinkly little, round-bodied creature that looked like a golden raisin with human-like arms and legs.

"What do you think? I call it Mister E."

"Well, Laverne, you're improving. It almost looks human."

Laverne burst out laughing. "Ha ha! That's wonderful, honey! I'm glad you feel close enough to me to be *that* honest."

The word "honest" stuck in my craw. "That's weird you should say that. Tom told me he wants us to be completely honest with each other. No secrets. I'm not so sure it's a good idea."

"Why not? Have you ever tried it?"

"Honestly?"

Laverne shook her horsey head. "No, *honesty*."

I bit my lip. "No, not *complete* honesty."

"Me either, honey. Maybe that's why we're single."

"Maybe that's why we're still *alive*."

Laverne chuckled and raised her glass of tea in a salute. "You could be right there, sugar."

"But honestly, Laverne, if we told the truth all the time, could any of us stand each other? And honesty in a relationship with a man? With *their* fragile egos? It's just not worth it."

"No man's ever going to be *worthy* of you, Val."

I looked up from my tea glass, surprised by her words. "Thanks."

"I didn't mean it as a compliment. You're not a *prize to be earned*, sugar. Whether a guy's an honest man or a bald-faced liar isn't the point. *Any* man can pretend to be something he's *not* for a good span of time. A *lifetime*, even. If he pretends to be something else to make *you* happy, does that make him a bad guy?"

I had to think about it. "I don't know."

"Honest or dishonest, 'happily ever after' is never guaranteed."

"So what should you look for in a man, Laverne?"

Laverne set down her glass of tea and looked me in the eye.

"Someone you're *drawn to*, sugar. Someone you think about. You want to *be* with him, no matter what. Even after the love flames have died down to embers."

"I get it, Laverne." I looked over at Mister E. "Like they say, find someone you could imagine being as old and wrinkled as that poor little raisin guy over there, and you'd still want to be by his side, laughing together and holding hands."

"Well, not exactly. Reverse it. Find someone you could imagine would stay by your side when *you're* the one old and wrinkled as a raisin and smelling like last night's doggy dinner."

The truth of Laverne's words made me sit up straight on the stool. "Wow. Have you ever found someone like that?"

"Yes, honey. Yes I did. I let go of his hand three years ago. His name was Edgar."

Laverne went over to a bookshelf and returned with a framed photo. She handed it to me. It had to have been taken not long before Edgar passed, because Laverne still looked just the same. Edgar, however, was frail and wrinkly and the spitting image of the little ceramic raisin man, Mister E.

# Chapter Twenty-Three

It was Monday morning, and I was back at work at Griffith & Maas, along with Milly, Mrs. Barnes, and all the other poor working slobs of the world. I finished hauling around a small mountain of files and decided to take a peek in and see how Milly was faring.

"What's up?"

Milly looked up from her computer. "I'm still alive. I guess that's something."

I smiled. Milly sounded more like herself.

"I'm glad you're—"

"Here you go," Mrs. Barnes interrupted. The skunk-haired old lady sashayed into Milly's office and dropped a small plastic cup with a lid onto Milly's desk.

Milly glanced at the cup, then up at Mrs. Barnes' smug face. "What's this?"

"New policy. Random drug test."

"You've got to be kidding! I've been working here twenty-three years and you're going to test *me, today?*"

An evil grin crept across the old woman's pinched face. "There's nothing to worry about if you have nothing to hide."

"Why now?"

Mrs. Barnes folded her arms across her chest and raised her chin as she spoke. "You girls have been acting peculiar. I called Mr. Maas. He thought it was best."

Milly pursed her lips, stood up and grabbed the cup. She blew by me and headed down the hall, Mrs. Barnes two steps behind her. Milly turned on her heels. "You're not going to *watch me* are you?"

Mrs. Barnes' smug face skipped a beat. "Oh. No. Just drop it at my desk." The old woman toddled down the hall. I followed Milly into the restroom and grabbed her by the arm.

"Oh crap, Milly!"

"What?"

"You can't take that test."

"Why?"

"The brownies."

"What?"

"Cold Cuts' *special* brownies."

Milly's eyes doubled in size. "Aw crap!"

She clenched her teeth, brushed by me and disappeared out the bathroom door. I followed, hot on her heels. Milly flung the cup down the hall as she marched back to her office. "I'm not a lousy lab rat! I'm not a freaking animal!" she muttered as she grabbed her purse and stormed out of her office. "I am *not* going down in flames, Val."

Milly stomped past Mrs. Barnes and out the front door. I couldn't see my friend's face, but it must have been bad. It made Mrs. Barnes swallow hard. Twice.

I ran to the file room, grabbed my things and dashed out into the parking lot. Milly was in her Beemer, a second away from bursting into tears. I climbed into the passenger seat beside her.

"Are you okay?"

"No I'm not okay!" Milly screeched. "Thanks to Cold Cuts, I can't go back to my favorite restaurant. I can't go back to my networking group, and now I can't go back to my job! What's that psychopath going to do next? Burn down my apartment?"

Milly rolled down the window and screamed at the world. "I hope you're happy, you witch! You just totally ruined my life!"

I hugged Milly and sat with her until she calmed down enough to breathe normally again.

"Let's get out of here, Milly. I know just where to go. Follow me."

"A PIZZA JOINT? THAT'S supposed to make me forget my life is going down the drain?"

"Hey, you have to start somewhere."

I smiled at Milly. "They have wine."

Milly sighed. "Okay. What the hell. Thanks to Cold Cuts, I have nothing else to do."

I opened the door to Old Northeast Pizza and let Milly in ahead of me. She looked around at the place and eyed me suspiciously. "I don't see any wine. Is this a trap?"

Her words caused a stampede of guilt to trample my heart. In a way, it *was* a trap. And to mix metaphors, I'd selfishly brought her here in the hopes of catching two birds by beating around the same bush. I replied with the only line of truth I had left.

"Oh, crap. I forgot they didn't have wine, Milly. But they've got the best pizza you'll ever eat. Melted cheese is almost as good as wine, right?"

"Hardly."

"Two cheese specials, please," I said to the tattooed pizza baker before Milly could change her mind and bolt. I lowered my voice a notch and asked the young man, "Seen any of those weird guys around here lately?"

"Actually, yeah," he replied and pointed toward the front door. "Over there."

I turned to see Capone fishing through the trash. He crammed a crust in his mouth.

"Pick what you want to drink out of the cooler, Milly!" I said with too much enthusiasm. "I'll be right back. Forgot something in the car."

I bolted outside and grabbed Capone by the shoulder. He wheeled around and gave me a hard look that softened when he realized it was me. He smiled and fished a bottle cap out of his mouth, tossed it, then reached out to shake my hand.

"Hey, Finger Lady."

"Hi, Capone. Look, I need your help again."

"I hat'n found no more body parts, if that's what you mean."

"No. Listen, you cleaned out a woman's RV a couple of weeks ago. Did you find a Mr. Peanut piggybank when you did?"

Capone eyed me. "Is there money in it?"

"No, it's got my mom's ashes in it."

"Huh? No. I mean money *like a reward*. I need ten bucks for the information."

"Last time it was five."

"Inflation."

"Okay. I'll go get my purse."

I ran back inside. Milly was waiting for me. Her diet Coke wasn't cutting it. "Who's that you're talking to?"

"I'll tell you in a minute."

I ran back out and handed Capone a tenner. That got the human vending machine talking.

"Yep," he said. "I found one."

Relief flooded through me. "Awesome! Capone, I need it back. Where is it? Can you go get it?"

"Hold your horses. I done sold it to a guy. That's why can't give it to you today. Come back tomorrow with fifty bucks and it's yours."

My gut flopped. I didn't have much choice. "Okay."

"Shake on it?" he asked, and held out a grubby paw.

"That's okay. I trust you."

I went back inside the pizza place. Milly was chomping on a slice. She wiped her face and spoke with her mouth full.

"So, who was that?"

"Cold Cuts' cousin. Capone."

Milly lost it. "Geez, Val! Can't I escape that woman for one second?"

Before I could stop her, Milly bolted outside. She swung her purse at Capone, but missed. He took off with her in hot pursuit. Fortunately, whatever obscenities she screamed at him were unintelligible through the glass. I ran outside. Milly had Capone cornered against a wall. I grabbed her by the shoulders and pulled her away.

"That woman's crazy!" Capone shouted.

"*I'm* crazy?" Milly screamed.

"Sorry, Capone," I said.

Milly looked at me like I was from Mars. "Sorry, *Capone?*"

Capone took his chance and skittered off with one parting shot. "Crazy old bat!"

Milly jerked her shoulder away of my hand and glared at me.

*Great. Now that she's all buttered up, all I have left to do is convince Milly to meet me and Cold Cuts for coffee tomorrow morning.*

*Easy-peasy.*

I FOUND A PLACE THAT served wine. The pizza guy suggested it. It was right next door. Old Northeast Tavern. Just like the pizza place, the interior of the tavern was spectacularly uninspiring. Kind of like a garage someone had cobbled into a restaurant with spare parts. However, it had one good feature. *It was dark.* That would make it harder for my face to end up on the wrong end of Milly's right hook.

I waited until she was almost through her second chardonnay. I couldn't think of an easy way to lay it on Milly, so I just said it plain and simple.

"Cold Cuts wants to meet with us tomorrow morning."

Milly nearly spewed her wine. "Are you kidding? No way! Even if I could, I wouldn't. I have to work...." Milly caught herself. The tendons in her neck stood out. "Forget it."

"But she wants to help you find a new breakfast place. To make up for your old place, the Omulette."

Milly eyed me with suspicious malevolence. "And you told her yes?"

I shrugged my shoulders together to make myself a smaller target. "Just one cup of coffee, Milly. What's the harm?"

"That's true," Milly quipped sarcastically. "What's the harm? There's nothing else she can steal from me except my car. And I owe more on it than it's worth." Milly drained her glass and shot me an angry, confused look. She shook her head. "What do you see in her, anyway Val?"

It was a valid question. One to which I didn't have a clear answer. "I dunno. She's just got something...some kind of power of persuasion. What do you call it? Charisma?"

"More like *kryptonite*. Val, that woman was able to destroy my life in a single week. She's done a number on yours, too. She doesn't have your mom's ashes, Val. Capone does. You don't need her anymore. Let's cut her loose. Take our losses. I'm not wasting another minute with her. Tomorrow morning, I'll be looking for a new job."

"But what about what Cold Cuts said, Milly. About being your own boss. Haven't you ever thought about it?"

Milly scowled. "Sure, I guess. I know I can't count on Mr. Maas to live forever. But I figured I still had some time to figure things out, you know? Cold Cuts put an end to that, too. Thank goodness you were around when Mrs. Barnes came in my office today. If I'd taken that drug test and failed, Val, not only would I have been *fired*, but no one else would have *ever hired me again*."

"I'm sure you can get a similar job, Milly. And get your life back like it was in no time."

"But that's just it, Val. Cold Cuts made me feel like the life I had *wasn't worth keeping*. She thought I should be glad—*grateful even*—that she'd freed me from my pathetic little existence."

"That's not true!"

"Isn't it? I mean, I'm a freaking accounting clerk. Unmarried. And I'm rapidly approaching my expiration date in the boardroom *and* in the bedroom."

"Milly, the girl lives in an RV and dresses up like other people to escape her boring life. You call that a bright future?"

Milly sighed. "No, I guess not."

"She told me she's doing that mousy woman's makeover today."

Milly sat up straighter. "Nora? The one that won the contest?"

"Yeah."

"*Unbelievable*. I've been trying to get that woman to speak at the Ladies Leadership brunch for *two years*. She owns a law firm, you know.

"So?"

"*It's just not fair!* Cold Cuts walks in with her zebra boots and stupid contest and the woman spills her guts like a cheap piñata!"

"You've got to admit, when it comes to people, that girl's got some kind of special charm."

Milly scowled and turned her nose up. "Most charlatans do."

"Oh, come on, Milly. Let Cold Cuts do something nice for you. Go to breakfast. At this point, what have you got to lose?"

"Only my dignity. No thanks."

"Please?"

"No, Val. You can't make me."

"Sure I can. With just two words."

"Lucille Jolly? I don't think so. Not this time."

"Merkin Jerk."

Milly's eyes did that scary-movie doll impersonation again. "You wouldn't!"

I smiled slyly. "Wouldn't I?"

I DON'T KNOW IF IT was the wine or all the drama with Milly or a combination of both, but I was exhausted. By 7:30 p.m. I'd already had a bath and was ready to crash. There was just one more thing I needed to do before I could pull the shades, click on Netflunks and start sawing some logs. I picked up the phone and punched lucky #7.

"Hi, Tom."

"Hey there. You sound beat."

"Yeah. It's been a crazy day."

"That's nothing new for you. How's it going with that girl? Meat Loaf?"

"Huh? Oh, you mean Cold Cuts. Okay, I guess. I'm meeting her for breakfast. I had to twist Milly's arm, but she's coming along, too."

"What...Milly doesn't like her?"

"Oh, they've just had a few minor disagreements."

"What about Glad? Any more news on finding her ashes?"

"I should know more tomorrow."

"Okay. How was work today?"

My heart skipped a beat. With everything else going on, I'd forgotten all about it.

"I dunno. Same old, same old. How about you, Tom? Work going well?"

"Yeah. Well, not really. That jerk Jergen's always on my butt about something. I don't know what the dirtbag's up to now. Muller overheard him saying something about heads were going to start rolling soon."

"Geez, Tom. That sounds bad."

"Not as bad as your tortilla dip, I hear."

My face flushed. "How'd you find out about that?"

"A little birdie told me."

"Ha ha. A blabbermouth named Jorge, more like it."

"Can't keep any secrets from you."

I felt a stab of guilt. "That's right. Goodnight, Tom."

"Goodnight, Val."

I clicked off the phone, frustrated with myself for not trusting Tom enough to tell him the whole truth. I should have told him about Capone. About work. About the odd papers I'd found in Jergen's tax file. But I knew Tom had held back information, too. In fact, I didn't know who was spinning the truth more, me or Tom.

His voice had been joking, but I could tell Tom was truly worried. Whatever was going on at work must've been vexing him sorely. Tom had told a joke that was actually funny.

# Chapter Twenty-Four

"Kelly's Pub?" Milly said. "This is the same place Cold Cuts 'Kamikaze Kerry-ed' my date with Dexter."

Milly scowled at the name painted on the glass front of the small restaurant. I had my hand on the door. "Come on, Milly. Don't start. And wasn't it Scary Kerry?"

Milly shot me an angry glare. "Who cares?"

I opened the door. She raised her chin and huffed through it. At a table in the back I saw a girl in a Goth outfit. I steered Milly toward her.

"Hi, Cold Cuts," I said.

"Darn. How did you know it was me?"

"I've seen pictures of you in this one. You got my friend Winky in Garvey's parking lot."

"Oh. For a minute there, I thought I was losing my touch. Hi, Milly."

Milly looked away. "Hi."

"Sit down, you two," Cold Cuts offered. "I'm gonna run to the john for a second."

Our butts had just flopped onto the seats when a nice-looking, athletic man dressed in khaki slacks and a crisp white shirt came over with two empty cups and a pot of coffee.

"Hi ladies! Welcome to Kelly's. Coffee?"

"Yes, please," we chimed in unison.

The man glanced around and winked a blue eye. "What happened to the grave robber?"

"She's no grave robber," Milly said sarcastically. "She steals lives from the *living*."

Cold Cuts appeared from behind me. "Oh, boohoo, you two. You can't go back to your crummy jobs."

"Wow. No one will ever mistake *you* for Mother Teresa," Milly said snidely.

"Aren't *you* the funny one," said the guy with the coffee. He grinned, revealing nice teeth and a set of killer dimples. "I like a girl with sass," he said to Milly and walked away.

Milly perked up—until Cold Cuts opened her mouth again. "Don't you see, girls? This is your golden opportunity. You have a blank slate. You can be *anything* you want to be now."

"What are you talking about?" I asked.

"Reinvention. Think about it. Val and Milly, 2.0."

"Give me a break!" Milly said sourly.

"Come on, Milly. Think about it. Is the brand new, Milly 2.0 still a blonde?"

"I think she's a redhead, with a red-hot temper to match," I said.

Milly scowled and shoved me hard on the shoulder.

"What's her motivation?" Cold Cuts asked.

Milly piped up. "To seek her revenge *on you!*"

Cold Cuts cocked her head and sighed. "Still there, are we? Okay, what kind of car is Milly 2.0 gonna run my butt over with?"

"A freakin' red Ferrari, okay?" Milly said, then sat back and pouted.

"Abso-freakin'-lutely!" Cold Cuts said encouragingly. "So, what's her favorite food?"

Milly looked at me, caught off guard. "Can I still like nachos?"

I shook my head in amazement. Somehow, Cold Cuts had worked her magic again. She'd engaged Milly and was already winning her over. *Incredible.*

"Sure you can," Cold Cuts encouraged. "So, what's the new Milly's favorite color?"

Milly's eyes scanned to the left, then straight ahead. "Yellow!"

"Huh," Cold Cuts said, skipping a beat. "I would have guessed red. Oh well. And does the new Milly 2.0 go out with losers?"

Milly's scowl had been replaced by a look of determination. "No way!"

"My point exactly," Cold Cuts said. She folded her arms and sat back in her seat.

"What do you mean?" I asked. "What *is* the point of all this?"

"I have an idea," Cold Cuts confided. She opened her mouth to speak, just as the coffee guy returned.

"Everything all right here?" he asked, and winked at Milly.

"How would you like to be your own boss?" Cold Cuts asked us.

The guy answered. "I'd highly recommend it. The hours suck, but the pay is crummy."

"Excuse me, do I know you?" Cold Cuts asked, a tinge perturbed.

"No. I just own the place. Name is Vance. Nice to meet you all."

"Okay, Vance," Cold Cuts said. "So, if being the boss is so bad, why do you do it?"

He didn't miss a beat. "For the glamour, of course." He grinned again, then he cocked his head and opened his mouth. He pointed a finger at Cold Cuts. "Hey, wait a minute. Aren't you the same woman who was in here a few weeks ago? With this lady?" He pointed at Milly. She blushed.

"Uh...I don't think so."

"Yes. I remember now. Rainbow Mohawk chick, right?"

"Good eye," Cold Cuts conceded.

"Good ear, more likely. The only thing I recognize about you is your voice. And your beautiful friend here, of course." Vance held his hand out and shook my hand.

"I'm Val."

"Nice to meet you." Vance turned to Cold Cuts.

She eyed him warily, then extended her hand and shook his. "I'm Cold Cuts."

Vance eyed her up and down. "Hmm. Let me guess. Ham?"

Milly giggled.

Cold Cuts didn't. "Very original. You can leave now."

Vance mimed a look of devastation. Milly came to his rescue. "Don't take it personally. She's mean to everyone."

"And you are?"

"Milly Halbert."

Vance smiled at Milly and nodded his head gallantly. As he left, I watched Cold Cuts size Milly up as she smiled shyly down at her coffee cup.

"Guess your Cloak of Invisibility has a glitch in it," Cold Cuts said.

Milly looked up. "What? No. I'm sure he wouldn't have recognized me if I wasn't with you."

"From what I heard, it was the other way around," I said.

"So, would you go out with him if he asked?" Cold Cuts teased.

Milly gave a wry smile. "In case you haven't noticed, I'm not too good at the dating thing."

"It's true," I said. "Milly could be featured on Wide World of Dolts."

"I'm not talking about the *old* Milly," Cold Cuts said. "What would the *new* Milly do? Would she go out with Vance?"

"Oh." Milly brightened. "The new me? Yes. Maybe. With the right costume...and the right back story."

"Exactly my point," Cold Cuts said.

I sighed. "You said that earlier. So what *exactly is* your point?"

"A whole new *life*. A whole new *career*. For *all* of us."

"What do you mean?" Milly asked.

"I'm talking about dressing ourselves up and shutting other people down."

"I don't get it," I said.

"Girls, we could be like the *Ghostbusters of bad dates!* We could offer a service doing the same thing I did for you, Milly, with that Preston guy."

"Dexter."

"Dexter, Preston, Poindexter. The name doesn't matter. A bad date is a bad date, right?"

Milly and I shrugged. "True."

"So, how many times would you have *paid good money* to get out of a bad date?"

Milly's eyes grew as wide as boiled eggs. "Oh my gawd! Plenty of times. Like...*a jillion* times!"

"Exactly my point."

"That's genius!" Milly said. "We could help all the women on all those dating sites. We could be *gazillionaires!* I bet I know a hundred women in the Leadership Ladies alone! And we'd be doing a public service...."

Cold Cuts broke in singing a little jingle, "When you're on date, and it's going bad. Who you gonna call?"

We exchanged excited glances and shouted together, "Date Busters!"

"So let me get this straight," I said. "A woman is out on a bad date. She calls us, and then what?"

"We show up in our disguises and shut it down," Cold Cuts said. "Guaranteed he'll never call again. I know you two can do it. Your disguises at Garvey's were phenomenal."

I groaned. "Don't remind me. By the way, Cold Cuts. How is your grandmother doing?"

"She retired."

"Oh."

Cold Cuts shrugged. "It was time. So? What do you girls think?"

"I love it!" Milly said.

I shrugged and grinned. "What the hell. I'm in."

I LEFT MILLY AND COLD Cuts at Kelly's Pub, yammering away like new best friends. I had an appointment with a scar-faced garbage eater. But first I had to pick up a mustachioed peanut head. Lucky me.

Goober was waiting for me at the assigned pick-up point, the corner of 1st Avenue and 4th Street. The post office was a good rendezvous point, he'd explained. Its arched porch, designed to protect post boxes from the rain, gladly did the same for him, free of charge. Thankfully, it wasn't raining, so I had the top down. Goober walked over and hopped in the passenger seat.

"Hey."

"Hey, Val. Feels good to be working with you again."

"Thanks for backing me up in case Capone tries any tricks. Like last time."

"Not a problem."

As I pulled off of 4th Street onto 9th Avenue, I started to worry.

"What if Capone doesn't come, Goober? Milly might have chased him away for good with that rabid dog attack of hers yesterday."

"What's the payout?"

"Huh? Oh, fifty bucks."

Goober whistled and shook his peanut-shaped head. "And I'm working for pizza. Don't worry. He'll show."

Goober was right. Capone was waiting outside Old Northeast Pizza with a plastic bag that looked just about the right size to be containing Mr. Peanut. My heart picked up at the thought that Glad was so close. I parked Maggie. Capone ran over to me before I could get out of the car.

"I got it," he said. "Where's the fifty?"

I reached for my wallet.

"Let's see it first," Goober said.

"Look man, I got it all wrapped up to protect it. I promise it's the Mr. Peanut bank. The real deal."

I pulled out a fifty-dollar bill. Capone handed me the bag, then snatched the fifty out of my hand. Goober started to get out and whack him, but I put a hand on his shoulder. Capone stood beside the driver's door as I removed the package wrapped in newspaper from the plastic bag.

He must have used the whole Sunday paper. I handed Goober page after wadded page. Finally, I reached the last sheet. I pulled the paper away and my heart sank. It was a pink plastic pig with a Planter's Peanuts can crammed onto its head like crown. Capone eyed my expression, laughed and took off. Before I could speak he'd dashed around the corner of the building.

"Dang it! I should have known!"

"I'll get his sorry behind!" Goober climbed out of the car and took off after Capone. He'd just rounded the corner out of sight when I heard a man yell out in pain. *Yes! Goober got him!*

I tossed the pig in the backseat and climbed out. I was almost to the corner where they'd both vanished when Goober came around it, limping on his right foot.

"Goober! Are you okay?"

"Tripped on a blasted beer bottle," he said. "I think I sprained my ankle."

"You want to go to the hospital?"

"Hell no."

"Then I'll take you home."

"Okay."

I wrapped Goober's arm around my shoulder and started leading him to the car.

"Where are you going?" he asked.

"To take you home."

"Not without my pizza first. I earned it."

I smiled at Goober. "Yes, my friend, you certainly did."

Goober straightened his back. "Thanks."

I helped him hobble into the pizza shop and settled him on a stool. "What would you like? Anything. My treat."

"I've been wanting to try the sausage and pepper," Goober said. "Extra cheese?"

"Coming right up."

"And a beer?"

"Sorry, we don't serve beer," said the pizza guy.

"Then you still owe me one," Goober said to me.

"Okay." I placed the order with the tattooed pizza baker, then fished a couple of sodas out of the side fridge and sat next to Goober.

"What are you going to do now, Val? Any more ideas where the piggybank could be?"

"Not a one."

"Too bad. I miss Glad, too, you know."

I looked over at Goober. "Yeah. Thanks. But you know, Goober, I don't feel that bad about it anymore. Someone told me recently that memories don't reside in objects, but in our hearts."

"I totally concur." Goober slugged down half a Sprite. "I prefer to collect experiences, not things."

"How's it going with you guys? At Jorge's place?"

"Well, I've been a solo act for a long time, Val. Cohabitation requires adjustments in one's habitual routine."

"Geez, Goober, sometimes I think you were an English professor in a past life."

"Close. Sociology."

"Get out of here!"

"Yeah. Human behavior fascinates me."

"Well, I suspect you stay pretty fascinated at Jorge's."

Goober smiled and sucked down the rest of his soda. "You have no idea."

# Chapter Twenty-Five

I woke up thirsty and fumbled into the kitchen. The clock on the microwave read 1:34. *Crap!* I poured a glass of water from the kitchen tap and drank it down, then padded back to bed. After tossing and turning in the tangled sheets, I finally gave up on trying to go back to sleep. I reached for my cellphone to check for messages. The display read 6:49 a.m. I got up to make coffee and noticed the microwave clock still read 1:34. *What a dumb jerk I am.* That wasn't the time. It was the leftover minutes from reheating last night's dinner.

I did the math. Suddenly I didn't feel so tired anymore. I'd gotten a good night's sleep, considering I'd passed out around 9:30 last night. I smiled. Not just because of that. I'd also just remembered it was Taco Tuesday. Then I remembered I didn't have to go to work. *Sweeet!*

Yes, the day was shaping up to be a good one, indeed. I finished brewing my cappuccino and went back to bed to enjoy it at my leisure. I didn't have to be dressed until 10 a.m. That's when Milly and Cold Cuts were coming over to discuss our new business plan.

COLD CUTS ARRIVED AS her natural, red-haired self. She carried a laptop in one hand, a folder in the other. She looked eager and determined—definitely her scariest outfit yet. She set the laptop up on my kitchen counter and showed us her handy work. She'd already designed a fabulous website and a couple of pretty cool logo ideas for

Date Busters. In less than an hour, all three of us had agreed on everything and ordered business cards for express delivery. Milly was to hand them out at the next Leadership Ladies meetup on Thursday. *Geez. Maybe this was going to be a lot easier than I thought.*

"Hey Cold Cuts," Milly said. "We're busting *bad* dates. But how do you define a date as bad?"

"When it's not good, you just know," she answered. "But remember, we don't have to decide. If a woman buzzes us, she's already made that call."

"Oh. Yeah," Milly said. "So what's a good date? To you, Cold Cuts?"

"I dunno. Someone who doesn't make me want to castrate them."

Milly chuckled. "And you, Val?"

"Someone who's company is even better than being alone."

That's a good one," Milly said. "Me? I want a date that feels as good as being with you, Val. I want to marry my best friend."

I blew Milly a kiss. "Is that a proposal, Milly?"

"No!" she laughed. "A *man* who's my best friend."

"Ah, the elusive man's best friend," Cold Cuts said. "My suggestion? Come back reincarnated as a golden retriever."

"IT SOUNDS LIKE LUNCH Meat has her act together," Tom said absently. He smiled at me from the doorframe, but his eyes seemed distant. Taco Tuesday wasn't living up to its usual spiciness.

"It's Cold Cuts. And yeah, she may be a lot more organized than I thought. She's been running her other business out of the RV. I guess she has some cross-over skills."

"You ready to roll?" Tom asked.

"Sure. But what about my hello kiss?"

"Oh. Sorry." Tom obliged me.

*Huh. Still no habaneros.*

I shook it off and smiled. "Okay, I'm ready now. Look out, Taco Tuesday! Here we come!"

But things never heated up. The entire drive downtown, Tom was silent. He was focused on something other than me, and I didn't care for it. When we walked along the waterfront and he stared at the boats without even mentioning my new pink blouse, I started to worry. Had he given up on the idea of "us" as a couple?

"Is everything okay between us?" I asked.

Tom flinched, as if coming out of a stupor. "What?"

"You seem...*distant*. Did I do something to tick you off?"

"Oh. No. Your fine. This has nothing to do with you."

"Then what is it, Tom?"

He sighed and hung his head slightly. "Work. Jergen threatened me with an internal investigation today."

I jerked Tom's hand to stop him walking. "What for?"

He gave me a smile designed to hide his worry. It didn't work. "Some expensive items are missing from the evidence room."

"Okay. But why in the world does he suspect *you?*"

"Why do you think?"

"He's still holding a grudge about you and his sister? Tom, you didn't even do anything! You were protecting your best friend John. The baby Jergen thought was yours... it didn't survive...."

"Apparently, he doesn't want *me* to, either."

"What are you going to do?"

"You know, for the first time in my life, I don't know. I mean, normally, I could go to the Chief of Police. But, as you know, that's Jergen's dear old daddy."

"Good grief, Tom. What can I do to help?"

"Nothing. Just keep your faith in me? That would be enough."

It stunned me to see Tom so open and raw and hurting. "Of course."

I held Tom's hand through dinner, but neither one of us had much of an appetite. When he crawled in bed next to me later than night, he couldn't perform. He turned his back to me. I snuggled next to him and spooned him. I didn't know what to else to say or do.

As I lay awake beside Tom, I thought about Hans Jergen. That man had crossed the line. His petty bull crap had just become personal. *Very* personal.

# Chapter Twenty-Six

Today I was on a new manhunt. Not for Glad's ashes, but for Jergen's sorry behind!

I spent the morning trying to think of a ruse to tell Mrs. Barnes so she'd let me back in the file room at Griffith & Maas. I wanted that copy of Jergen's tax return. I'd left it behind in my rush to follow Milly when she'd stomped out of the office to avoid taking that drug test.

I settled on a plan. I'd tell her I was asthmatic and forgot my inhaler.

I practiced wheezing in the mirror until I thought I had it down pat. I ate lunch, got dressed and drove to Griffith & Maas. I arrived a few minutes after 2 p.m. Mrs. Barnes should have been back by now. But when I drove up, her car wasn't in the lot. The office looked closed.

*Dang it!*

I was desperate to get Jergen's phone number or address. Sometimes, when you're on a noble mission, the universe steps up and helps you out. I was parked on the side of the road, googling Hans Jergen's name, when the dirtbag himself walked up beside me.

"Out of gas again?" he taunted. "Some people never learn."

His voice startled me. I hadn't seen him pull up. I flinched and pressed my cellphone screen against my chest.

"No. I was just.... Never mind. Listen, I want you to leave Tom alone."

Jergen snorted. "What are you talking about?"

"I think you know."

"Look, Ms. Fremden. Stay out of this. People get what they deserve."

I wrangled around in the seat to face him. Jergen's hand instinctually went to his gun holster. I backed down.

"Tom doesn't deserve this! He didn't knock up your sister Rita. John did! Tom took the hit so you and your pea-sized—"

I glanced at his crotch, but I didn't sink that low.

"*—brain* would think that John wasn't such a bad guy after all."

Jergen hid his stunned look under false bravado. "You're full of it."

"It's true. Every word! So lay off Tom."

Jergen sneered at me. "It's too late for that."

"I don't think so," I said.

"Seriously? You think you can—"

"Shut up you jerkoff!" I was running out of ideas—and insults. I scowled and yelled, "Stop harassing Tom *or else!*"

Jergen laughed. "Or else *what?*"

"Or else I'll spill the beans on you!"

He shook his head. "You've got nothing on me."

"Oh yeah?" I said. "Well, I've got two words on you, Jergen. *Pet Patrol.*"

Jergen's smug face crumbled like cousin Tammy's fruitcake. He wheezed as if he'd been punched in the gut.

I had no idea what Pet Patrol was, but there was no mistaking Jergen's reaction. I'd definitely struck a nerve. Maybe even an artery. I turned the ignition on Maggie and hit the gas. From the rearview mirror, I saw Lt. Hans Jergen staring at me, slack jawed and speechless, like a fish out of water dumped on the side of the road.

FOUR HOURS LATER, I was holed up in the parking lot of a convenience store with Cold Cuts in the old RV. My stomach flopped. I was still a little shaky over my showdown with Jergen, but a new kind of nervousness was moving in to take its place. Flop sweat. Cold Cuts and I were on call for our first, official Date Busters gig. Both of us were dressed and ready to rescue our client, Sharon, at a moment's notice.

Cold Cuts was incognito in a sad-faced clown outfit. I was dressed like a nurse. We'd already passed an hour throwing stale popcorn into a little basketball hoop suction-cupped to the windshield. Bored and anxious, we'd made a game of placing bets on the two winos loitering outside the store. Whichever bum puked or passed out first would determine the winner. The stakes couldn't have been higher. The future of my recently acquired Mounds candy bar was hanging in the balance.

"Ha!" Cold Cuts said and smacked her clown thigh. "There he goes! Old Shaky Legs gives up the goods first! Hand it over."

I slapped the candy bar in her gloved hand. "Beginner's luck." I glanced out the window at my contender. "Great. There goes Thunder Pants." I rolled down the window. "Couldn't toss your cookies just one minute earlier? Thanks for nothing!"

I sat back and looked at Cold Cuts' sad clown face. My gut wrenched in doubt. "What are we doing here? This was a terrible—"

Suddenly the Date Busters hotline buzzed. Cold Cuts grabbed it and looked at the screen.

"It's Sharon. Things have run afoul at the Chicken Hut."

Panic shot through me. "What do we do now?"

"Take it easy. Follow my lead. Here we go."

Cold Cuts turned the ignition on the old RV. It sputtered to life. She backed out of the parking lot and took a right on Gulf Boulevard, leaving Shaky Legs and Thunder Pants in a cloud of oily smoke.

COLD CUTS AND I BURST into the Chicken Hut. I felt like a psychiatric nurse chasing a psychotic clown. We spotted Sharon and made a beeline toward her. The look on her face told me she was more horrified than I was. Cold Cuts sauntered up to the booth and slapped her oversized, gloved hand on the table.

"Who do you think you are, clowning around with my girl?"

"What's going on here?" Sharon's date asked.

Sharon shrugged apologetically and stood up. "I have no idea. Wait here, Stan."

Sharon grabbed both of us by the collars and marched us to the ladies' room.

"What are you doing here?" she demanded.

"We got your call," Cold Cuts said.

"What? I didn't call."

"Look." Cold Cuts showed her the phone screen. "Isn't this your number?"

Sharon pulled her phone from her back pocket. "Crap! I must have butt-dialed you!"

"You're kidding," I said.

"I'm afraid not. Sorry! Listen, could you two go and apologize to Stan? He seems like an actual nice guy, for once."

We followed Sharon back to the table, dragging our feet and hanging our heads like two naughty children.

"We're sorry, Stan. False alarm."

Stan eyed us as if we'd just landed from planet Kreton. He looked over at Sharon. "What's going on?"

"I'll explain after these ladies go." Sharon turned and waved us away dismissively. "Goodbye."

We made a hasty retreat back to the RV.

"Crap! Our first call was a butt-dial," I sighed. "How appropriate."

"I feel like such a clown," Cold Cuts said pathetically. Then laughed.

I stifled a smirk. "Geez. I hope this *whole idea* isn't a mistake. I wanna go home."

“Me too,” Cold Cuts said. “Oh wait. I already am.” She drummed her fingers on the dash. “Ba-dum-bum.”

# Chapter Twenty-Seven

So far, so good. I'd lain low and vegged all day in the hammock, celebrating my newfound freedom. With no repercussions from Jergen or Sharon falling on my head so far, I knocked wood and hoped tonight's Date Busters patrol would turn out better than yesterday's butt dial. Milly and I were on call together. We'd decided to kill the evening waiting around at Kelly's Pub.

I was a parole officer. It was the ironic and perfect foil for Milly, whose outfit could only be described as a trailer-trash prom queen. It was Milly's first attempt at creating a disguise all on her own. For some reason, she'd dressed herself in a polyester, peach-colored dress with a too-revealing lace bodice. She'd accessorized it with a ton of eye make-up and an 80's style, big-haired red wig crowned with a party-store tiara.

We were on our second glass of wine and had run out of patience and conversation. We took to eavesdropping on the couple in the booth across from us. They looked like an interesting couple. *Miserable*, but interesting nonetheless.

The woman was thin, pale, and elegant looking. She was probably around my age, mid to late forties. She was the kind of woman you figured never farted, but she was so nice you forgave her for it. She sat up straight, prim, dignified and patient as she listened to her partner, a moderately attractive man in his late fifties, drone on about himself. He wore an expensive suit and looked like he'd fit right in at the yacht club. I hoped for her sake he was worth it.

"I don't see why that's so offensive," he said.

"Mentioning a woman's weight is always offensive, Harold. It's not like you're perfect."

The man flashed a capped-tooth smile and cocked his head confidently. "Come on, Annie. In what way am I not perfect?"

Milly's lips and nose scrunched together. That was never a good sign.

"You really think highly of yourself, don't you?" Annie said.

"Why shouldn't I?" Harold responded. "Admit it. I'm pretty easy on the eyes. And hard in the sack. In my age bracket, that makes me Superman. Come on, Annie. Being with me? You should count yourself among the luckiest women on the planet."

Milly's jaw tightened until every last tendon stood out around her lace neckline. She looked just exactly how I pictured E.T. would, if he'd just been called a tramp at the Alien of the Universe pageant. "I'm going in," she growled.

"But Milly," I whispered, "it's not our business!"

"I don't care," she hissed. "That Dodo bird deserves to be extinctified."

Milly started to stand. I grabbed at her arm but missed. I watched, helpless, as my fledgling Date Buster partner flew the coop—then promptly crash-landed.

"Listen here, Mister Wonderful," she said, teetering on her heels in front of their booth. "I've seen better...peckers...on a bird bill...surgery...sanctuary."

The guy eyed Milly up and down and blew out a haughty laugh. "Well, look at you, Miss Honey Boo Boo...*1969*."

"Leave her alone, Harold," the woman said. She looked up at Milly pleadingly, but there was no stopping her now.

"You're a...big meanie!" Milly stuttered.

"Ouch! Did you come up with that zinger all by yourself?" he mocked.

Milly stood her ground. "You should know. You look like a man who's had a lot of practice "coming up" with something "all by yourself."

*Oh, snap!*

Harold's arrogance ticked up a notch to anger. "Excuse me, Miss Touch of Low Class, but do you have any idea who I am?"

Milly put both hands to her cheeks and wagged her head. "Oh! Pardon me! If I'd known you had dementia, I'd have cut you some slack." Milly shaped her hands into a megaphone. "Hey, does anyone in here know who this jerk is?"

The guy lost it. "Why don't you get lost, trailer trash!"

Milly smiled victoriously, then turned to the woman. "Annie, you deserve better than this."

Annie looked embarrassed, but her eyes registered restrained amusement. She shot me a sideways glance as Harold, blustering and red-faced, stood up and glared down at her.

"Annie, do you *know* this woman?"

"No," Annie said, then stifled a giggle.

"You *do*, don't you. That's it! I've had enough of you and your low-brow friends and no-talent family. I'm done here." The man lifted his turkey waddle, tugged on the edges of his dinner jacket and stormed out of the pub.

"You can always tell the jerks by their dinner jackets," said a man's voice. I turned to look. It was Vance, the owner of Kelly's Pub. He turned to Annie. "You all right, sis?"

"Uh, yes. I think so."

Vance spoke to Milly, aka the trailer princess. "Thank you, Miss."

Milly's face twitched. "You're welcome." Milly pinched a bit of fabric on either side of her dress and curtsied. I felt my face grow hot.

Vance turned back to Annie. "Are you sure you're okay?"

"I don't know what I was thinking, giving Harold a second chance. Thank you, Miss. What's your name?"

Annie looked up at Milly. Her face registered deer in the headlights. "Uh...Mill...oh. Marsha. Marsha Mello...ski. Marsha Melloski."

"Thank you, Miss Melloski. If you'll all excuse me, I think I just want to go home."

"I'll walk you out," Vance said.

Vance and Annie left. Milly, aka Miss Melloski, walked over to me. She slapped herself on the forehead. "What have I done?"

"Nice work, Marsha Melloski. Why didn't you just call yourself Tootie Frootie?"

"Aww, crap, Val! I might have just ruined that woman's life!"

"No you didn't. You saved a damsel in distress. You're a natural born Date Buster."

"Cut the crap! Do you think Vance knows it's me?"

"I dunno. Should I tell him?"

"No!"

"Why not?"

"Because—"

Vance came through the door. Milly fell over herself to apologize. "Look, I'm truly sorry about all that!"

"About what?" Vance asked. "You did my sister a big favor. I've been trying to get her to leave that jerk for over a year. Can I buy you two a drink?"

"Uh..."

"It's not a pick-up line. I own the place."

"I know," Milly said. I could almost feel her kick her own self in the butt.

"Oh. How did you...?"

"I told her," I said, in an attempt to distract him. "I've been in a few times."

"Oh yes. With that Mohawk girl. And a cute blonde. Milly, right?"

"Right."

"Where's *she* tonight?"

"She's got a case of the Fluzinsky."

Milly shot me a dirty look. Vance didn't seem to notice.

"Listen," he said. "I'm going to get us some drinks. What would you two like?"

"I'll have a Tanqueray and tonic."

"A Shirley Temple for me," Milly said.

I bit my lip. I swore if she curtsied again, I would have to kick her in the butt myself. Vance left to get the drinks. I elbowed Milly.

"A Shirley Temple? Who *are* you?"

Milly shook her head in dismay. "Geez, Val. At the moment, I don't know. How do I look?"

"Don't ask."

Milly took out a compact and stared at her reflection. "Holy trailer trash, Batman!"

"What was that?" Vance asked. He held out our drinks.

"Uh...*bad* man!" Milly answered too loudly. "He was a bad man."

Vance shrugged. "Harold's not bad. He's just a self-important blowhard. Owns a couple of car dealerships he inherited from his father. Now he thinks he's god's gift to the universe. Anyway, forget him. Cheers!"

"Cheers!"

Vance turned to Milly. "So, Marsha...Melloski, was it?"

Milly choked on her Shirley Temple. "Yes."

"That was a very brave thing you did. I wish more people were like you."

"What do you mean?"

"Real."

"Real?"

"Real enough to say what they really thought."

"Well, that's Marsha Melloski," I chimed in. "Keeping it real!"

Vance grinned at me, then turned back to Milly. "So Marsha, would you have dinner with me tomorrow night?"

Milly nearly dropped her Shirley Temple. "Uh. No. Yeah. I mean. Sure."

MILLY DROPPED ME OFF at my place. I stood at her window for a moment before I headed inside for the night.

"Well, we didn't get a Date Buster call, but you managed to bust a date anyway. Smooth move, Ex-Lax."

"Ha ha. Can it, Val. He didn't ask *me* out. He asked out Marsha, the trailer-park princess."

"Oh. Yeah, that's true. But he did say 'Milly' was cute."

Milly brightened. "Yeah, he did. Hey Val, can I ask you something?"

"Sure."

"Who the hell's Honey Boo Boo?"

I shook my head. "You're just gonna have to google it."

# Chapter Twenty-Eight

It was Friday, midday, and an official meeting of the Date Busters was in full swing at the tiki hut in my backyard. We had two customers lined up for the night. Cold Cuts shook three toothpicks out of the container and broke two in half.

"Ready to draw lots for who's on call tonight?"

"I've got a date with Tom tomorrow, so I'll work tonight," I said. "And Vance asked Milly on date tonight. So there's no need to draw straws. It's you and me, Cold Cuts."

"Huh. Vance asked you out?" Cold Cuts asked. "And on Friday. An official date night."

"What do you mean?" Milly asked.

"Well, if a guy asks you out for Friday or Saturday, he's pretty interested. He's not just looking for a little nibble-nibble, so to speak. Weekends are for the big fish."

Milly raised one side of her lip as if it had a hook in it. "Why do I have to be a fish?"

Cold Cuts answered her question with a question. "What's the venue?"

"I'm supposed to meet him at Crabby Dale's."

"So he's meeting you at a beach dive. And he's not even picking you up. Hmmm. Maybe it's a nibble after all."

"Well, aren't *all* first dates nibbles?" Milly asked.

"You have a point," Cold Cuts conceded.

"What do you think Vance really wants?" Milly asked.

"You'll find out tonight, small fry," I said. "Or should I say, Miss Melloski."

"So who's on the docket tonight?" Milly asked.

"Sharon again. And Nora," Cold Cuts replied.

Milly looked shocked. "*Nora* has *a date*?"

Cold Cuts swaggered. "Don't forget. I pimped her ride."

"I'm confused. I figured Sharon fired us after that butt dial disaster," I said.

"No," Cold Cuts replied. "Just the opposite. She told everyone she knows. We've got three new ones on the line for Saturday night. Looks like there's a lot of nibblers out there."

COLD CUTS WAS A GENIUS. It had taken all afternoon, but it had been worth it. She'd transformed herself into a hip-looking man who didn't even look repulsive. As for me? I couldn't recognize myself in the mirror, either. That was a good thing. Tonight, our disguises had to be perfect. Rather than waste time sitting around in the RV, we'd conspired to kill our free time by spying on Milly and Vance at Crabby Dale's.

As we headed out from my place, Laverne saw us and did a double take. I waved and called her name. The surprise on her face said it all. She waved back and gave us a thumbs up. *Yes!* Our plan was to get to Crabby Dale's early, so Milly wouldn't get suspicious if we walked in. We arrived with twenty minutes to spare. We ordered a couple of drinks and tipped the waiter twenty bucks to reserve the booth across from us for a red-headed woman. He asked for her name, but we promised he wouldn't have any problem recognizing her.

"Just look for a lady with a pile of red hair as big as a kitchen garbage bag," I'd said as he walked away to get our drinks.

"Twenty bucks? There goes our profit for the night," Cold Cuts whined.

I grinned. "You know, I'm having fun in these getups."

"You make a pretty good soccer mom, if I do say so myself."

"Soccer mom? I thought I was a hipster like you."

"I think you just proved you're not."

"That's—"

Cold Cuts hit me on the arm. "Shh. She's coming in."

I sat stiff as a board and watched Milly tumble into the restaurant. Compared to us, Milly's disguise looked rather slapdash. The flaming red hair was back, of course. But there was no tiara this time. She'd opted for a short denim skirt, a slinky silver top and an amazing pair of six-inch silver screw-me heels. She grabbed onto the waiter's arm for support as he led her to the bait booth. He helped her in, then turned and winked at us. Milly looked at us and frowned. We jerked our heads back around to face each other.

Milly tapped her long, fake fingernails on the table for a minute, then got up. *Crap. Maybe she's spotted us.* She was acting odd. She put her purse on the table, took a step forward, then stepped back and picked her purse up again. She repeated the action.

"What's she doing?" Cold Cuts whispered.

"I think she can't make up her mind about going to the ladies' room. If she leaves, she might lose her spot. If she leaves her purse, she might lose, well, her purse."

"Oh. Makes sense."

Milly was still doing the toilet two-step when Vance came up behind her. She took a step backward and her spiked stiletto landed on top of Vance's foot.

"Yow!" he said in a muffled howl. He grabbed his foot and hopped up and down.

Milly turned around. Her overly-made face nearly melted in horror. "Oh my lord! I'm so sorry, Vance! Are you okay? Do you need an ambulance?"

"No. It's not...that bad."

Vance tried to take a step and winced with pain. Milly helped him hobble into the booth.

"I am *so* sorry!"

"Stop apologizing. That's what I get for sneaking up on you."

I couldn't tell if Vance smiled or winced after he said that. But he looked right at me and his eyebrows met. I looked back at Cold Cuts and held my breath. If I kept my mouth shut, maybe he wouldn't recognize us. I touched my lip with my index finger to silence Cold Cuts. She got the message and clammed up. Our silent ploy worked. Vance turned back to face Milly...or should I say, Marsha Melloski.

"So, tell me, Marsha. "Are you Polish?"

"Huh?"

"Mello*ski*?"

"Oh. Yes. *Very* Polish."

Cold Cuts snickered. I felt my face heat up. *Oh, come on, Milly!*

Vance teased her. "So, just how Polish *are* you?"

"Polish enough to eat a kielbasa."

*Oh, no, Milly!* I nearly groaned aloud. Cold Cuts actually *did*.

"So, I take it you're hungry?" Vance asked.

"Like a feral cat." Milly scratched the air with her tigress claw.

"Geez!" I whispered to Cold Cuts. "No wonder she never gets a second date."

"You wouldn't be leading me astray, would you?" Vance said.

Cold Cuts kicked me under the table. "And now we know why *he's* still single."

"I've got something for you," Vance said.

Cold Cuts and I turned our heads toward their table so fast I'm surprised we didn't get whiplash.

"What is it?" Milly asked.

Her eyes looked so sexy and innocent at the same time I almost choked on my TNT.

"Can you believe—" I began, then stopped when I felt something vibrate in my pocket. The Date Buster buzzer. I took it out and showed it to Cold Cuts.

"We have to roll," she said.

*Dang it! Things were just getting good.*

Cold Cuts and I got up and walked normally toward the door. Once we were outside, we made a mad scramble for the RV. We'd parked it a block away down an alley so Milly wouldn't see it. Cold Cuts and I jumped in, breathless. She turned the ignition. The engine sputtered to life, then died. She tried it again. Nothing.

"Crap! What are we going to do?" I asked.

"There's only one thing *to* do. Use Milly's car."

"Are you crazy? She'll know we were spying on her."

"So what?"

Cold Cuts hopped out of the RV and sprinted for Crabby Dale's. There was nothing for me to do but follow along.

When we got to the lot, Milly was standing by her car, fumbling in her purse for the keys.

"What's going on?" I asked.

Milly jumped. "Who are you?"

"It's me, Val. And Cold Cuts. Are you okay?"

"What are you doing here? Were you two spying on me?"

Before I could think of a lie, Cold Cuts answered.

"Yeah."

Milly started crying. She hobbled two steps toward me and fell into my arms. I hugged her as she spoke through tears and sobs.

"Vance wasn't interested in *me*. He thinks I'm a floozy."

"Aw. That's not true," I said.

Milly wailed. "He gave me a business card, Val. For *image consulting*. He said his sister wanted to give me a makeover. Can you believe that?"

I pulled Milly back to look her in the eye. Her face looked like a melted birthday cake. I frowned at her sympathetically.

"What a jerk!" Milly shouted. "I threw the card back in his face. You were right, Cold Cuts. I was just a nibble to him. Not a keeper."

# Chapter Twenty-Nine

Poor Milly. How could Vance have been so cruel to her? He was dog meat, and I wanted to ship him to China.

I was back at Publix, in the produce section—the same place I'd been accosted by that disgusting condom creep. I guess it was buy-one-slime-ball, get-one-free day. I spotted Vance over by the douches. I was *not* in the mood to deal with him. I wasn't sure I could trust myself not to throttle him the way old Orange Whip had gotten to Goober.

I pushed my cart behind the end of an aisle and hoped Vance wouldn't see me. When I thought the coast was clear, I peeked around the corner. He was standing right in front of me, all smiles and dimples and perfect teeth. I wanted to knock them out.

"Val! Hi! I've been hoping I'd run into you."

I made a concerted effort to sound civil. "Me? Why?"

"Well, not *you*, exactly."

"No? Then who?"

"This woman I met the other day. Marsha Melloski? Maybe you know her?"

"Maybe." I clenched my teeth. "*Why?*"

"Could you tell her to come by the pub soon? She forgot something. Uh. That my sister wants to give her."

I smiled icily. "Sure. I'll let her know."

"Thanks."

As soon as he was out of sight, I called Milly with the news. She was livid.

"So he wants to see that floozy Marsha Melloski, does he?" Milly said acidly. "Well, if that's what he wants, then that's what he's gonna darn sure get!"

MILLY WAS AT MY PLACE. She'd thrummed through the bags of clothes Laverne had picked out for me from the thrift store. She'd come up with a redneck doozy. They could have named a show after her. *My Name is Pearl.*

She flounced her tight-skirted behind into the chair by my vanity. "Make me extra trashy, Val. With a side of backlash."

"Are you sure you want to do this, Milly?"

Milly hissed like a punctured blow-up doll. "I've never been more sure of anything in my life."

"Okay. It's your call." I laid the shadow on thick and used up my tube of mascara. I teased her sassy red wig into a mountain of frizz. She turned toward the mirror to inspect my handiwork.

"Oh my word!" She cried out in a country twang. "You're a bona-fide genius, Val! I couldn't be trashier if I lived in a garbage can!"

"I've created a monster."

"Ha ha! Wish me luck!"

Milly jumped up, grabbed her purse and disappeared out the door. I wished her luck, all right. But I think Vance was the one who was going to need it. I snapped the eyeshadow compact shut and heard a rap on the door. I opened it. It was Milly.

"My car won't start. Can you give this monster a lift?"

"Sure."

"WAIT HERE. I'LL BE right back." Milly slammed Maggie's heavy steel passenger door.

"It's too hot to wait outside, Milly," I grumbled.

"You're right. Come on, then. But keep a low profile."

I followed Milly, aka trashy Marsha Melloski, as she wobbled across the parking lot in heels that could, in the wrong hands, be classified as deadly weapons. I snuck inside Kelly's Pub in back of her, then hid behind a fake palm tree by the hostess podium. I peeked out between the fronds. *Funny.* Even though Milly looked like Dolly Parton's psycho-killer cousin, Vance appeared genuinely happy to see her. He hurriedly finished a conversation with a customer and walked up to her.

"Hi. I see Val gave you my message. I wasn't sure she would."

Milly tapped a heel impatiently and cracked her gum. "Why wouldn't she? She knows she can't compete with me."

Vance looked puzzled. "What? Compete?"

"Sure, darlin'. I know what a man *really* wants. Poor Val hasn't got a clue."

Vance eyed Milly cautiously. "Is that so?"

"Yeah. You men just want a pretty woman on your arm and a floozy in the sack. Well, too bad. I'm not playing your game."

A lightbulb went off over Vance's head. He held out a hand in protest. "Oh. No. Hold on a minute. Let me explain."

"I've been listening to men's lame-ass explanations for waaay too long," Milly twanged. "You're kind is never satisfied. You want me to change to please you. I get it. I just came to say, 'No Thanks.'"

"But Milly, I'm not asking you to change a thing."

"Then why slap me in the face with that stupid image consulting card?"

"That was Annie's idea. And it was for your *business*, not for *you personally*."

I think Milly swallowed her gum. She choked.

"What?"

"When you broke up Annie's date with Mr. Wheelin' & Dealin', she was shocked. When she got home, she called me, crying. She said you had done her a favor. She was sad, to be sure. But also grateful for what you'd done. Then I told her I'd seen you gals in here a few times, busting guys chops when they treated women badly. Well, she went from crying to laughing out loud. She *loved* the idea. Milly, my sister is a highly successful business woman. She thinks your idea is a *big deal.* She thinks you are, too."

Vance looked at me through the palm tree. "That includes you, too, Val."

I sighed and stepped out sheepishly.

Milly did a double take. "Wait a minute. You said *Milly*, not *Marsha*."

Vance looked at Milly innocently. "I did?"

"You knew it was *me?* How long?"

"Come on, Milly. How could I *not* know it was you? You're crazy and wonderful and amazing. The incredible changing woman."

Milly blinked hard, giving the appearance a blue butterfly had landed on her eyelids. "Really?

"Yes, really. And I just happen to have a superpower of my own, you know. I can see you through whatever disguise you're wearing."

"Does that include her bullet-proof Spanx?" I asked.

"Shut up," Milly said, then giggled. She hugged me, then lifted her arms and toddled over to hug Vance. Before she could reach him she was thwarted by a guy in a Mariachi outfit.

"Sorry buster, but my friend here's into tacos, not chimichangas."

Vance admired Cold Cuts' cheesy sombrero and moustache. "See? Now *that's* what I'm talking about!"

"DO YOU HAVE A SUNBURN or are you always this hot?" Tom was leaning against the doorframe, looking better than a man his age ought to.

I smiled. Tom was back to telling bad jokes. This was a very good sign.

"Come on in, you," I said.

"These are for you." Tom handed me a bouquet of Gerber daisies and kissed me lightly on the lips.

"More flowers? Someone's in a good mood. What's up?"

"The pressure's off at work. Apparently, Jergen found the missing evidence. It appears I'm to be exonerated rather than annihilated."

"I had a feeling that would happen," I said cheerily. I put the flowers in a vase. "Beer?"

Tom looked at me funny.

"What?" I asked. "It's not *light* beer."

"What do you mean you *had a feeling*, Val? Did you *do* something? *Say* something?"

"Tom...."

"I want the truth, Val. Your honest word. I'm serious."

Tom's sea-green eyes weren't stormy. They were clear as glass. All of a sudden, out of the blue, it was make or break time. All or nothing. Sink or swim. Fess up or lie.

I walked up to Tom and took his hand and held it tight. "What kind of a friend would ask you to take the hit for him, Tom? Then abandon you as part of the deal? I told Jergen the truth."

Tom looked appalled. "What? Why would you *do* that?"

"Tom, I just couldn't stand another minute of watching you suffer for someone else's misdeeds. I love you too much to let your good name be smeared in the mud by that...*pin-prick moron*. I'm sorry."

Tom's dismay vanished. "Wait a minute. Did you just say you love me?"

"What?"

Tom grinned. "Don't deny it. I heard it, fair and square."

"Aw crap. I guess I do."

# Chapter Thirty

Milly, Cold Cuts and I had just arrived in the fancy lobby of Pantski & Pantski, Image Consulting. For the first time ever, the three of us were dressed as our normal selves, all at the same time.

"Your knees are knocking, Milly," I said. "Why are you so nervous?"

"I made such a jerk of myself in front of Vance. I think I'm going to be sick!"

"No you didn't. *Marsha Melloski* did."

Milly's panicked face relaxed a notch. "You're right. Maybe he won't hold it against me."

Thin, elegant Annie Pantski walked up wearing a suit that probably cost more than Milly's Beemer. She greeted Milly and me, and shook our hands. Then she turned to our partner.

"Hi. You must be...Cold Cuts?"

"Yes, I am."

"Do you have a real name?"

Cold Cuts looked around and sighed. "Penelope Piddleton."

I would have laughed out loud if Milly hadn't knocked the air out of my lungs with her elbow. I held my head up and tried to look serious as I bit the inside of my lip nearly clear through.

"I'm Annie Pantski. My brother Vance has told me all about you three."

Vance came out of an office and stood beside Annie. He looked almost debonair in his brown suit, his white shirt unbuttoned at the collar. I saw Milly shoot him a worried look.

"All good, I assure you," Vance said with a smile.

"And pretty impressive, too," Annie added. "Thank you for coming. I've got an idea I want to share with you all. Please, follow me."

We trailed like ducklings behind Annie to an expensive-looking conference room. A large map of the USA hung on a wall next to a dry-erase board. We took seats around the exquisite table made of black onyx. Vance stepped halfway inside the room, but lingered in the doorframe. Annie studied our faces for a moment and motioned toward her brother.

"Do you mind if Vance sits in on the meeting? I thought it would be good to include your biggest fan. But it's totally up to you three."

We exchanged shrugs. Cold Cuts spoke for us. "Sure. Why not."

Vance took a seat next to Milly. Cold Cuts and I grinned at each other.

"So ladies, let's cut to the chase," Annie began. "Vance has already given your business concept a big thumbs up."

Vance nodded and smiled.

"And *I've* already been a customer," Annie continued. "A very *satisfied* customer, I might add. Thank you again, ladies."

"You're welcome," Milly said bashfully.

"Date Busters is a brilliant idea," Annie continued. "So brilliant that I've already floated the concept to some of my colleagues around the US...after having them sign an NDR. Uh...a non-disclosure agreement, of course."

"Why would you do that?" Cold Cuts asked. "We thought you were going to help us build our image."

"Why, *franchising*, my dear! Image is the easy part. It's good *business ideas* that are hard to come by. And like I said, this is a *great* idea. Even better, with your skills and ingenuity, you three could cash in without having to actually *do* the 'busting' part."

"What do you mean?" I asked. "What would we do, then?"

"You three would put together a line of disguises and instructions. And a rough 'rules of the road' handbook, if you will. We could take it from there. I envision an on-line guidebook. An app. A couple of coaching videos. A few legal guidelines. With a good brand image, logo, and some discrete marketing, we could make Date Busters a 'Biz in a Box.' The perfect choice for savvy entrepreneurs almost anywhere. We could franchise it across the country to start, then, who knows?"

"But, would anyone *buy* it?" Milly asked.

Annie stood up and walked over to the map of the US. She picked up a pointer and began stabbing it toward cities as she spoke.

"So far, I've got people in San Francisco, Portland, Atlanta, Orlando and New York City ready and waiting to buy in. Ladies, it seems bad dates are happening everywhere."

Milly raised her eyebrows and nodded. "I could have told you that."

Cold Cuts piped up. "So what are we talking about...money wise?"

"With a prepackaged, buttoned-up product, I'd say thirty thousand, easily," Annie replied.

"For the whole country?"

Annie looked startled. "What? No. For *each franchise*. Ladies, I figure you've got a good shot at the top 100 metropolitan markets, just for starters."

Cold Cuts tried to do the math in her head. "That's like—"

"Three million dollars," Annie said. "I figure we could be up and running in two or three months, if we hustle. After all, this isn't rocket science, and we don't need to manufacture anything. I've already lined up an app developer. I've also researched and negotiated the rights for Date Busters dot com. All I need from you three is a green light. And a few signatures, of course."

The three of us looked at each other but didn't say a word. We were too stunned.

"By the way, I love the name," Annie said. "It's a classic. We were thinking we could kick things off with the three of you taking a road trip across the country. Demonstrating your 'product' first hand to interested investors. What do you think?"

Cold Cuts turned to us and said, "I think we're gonna need a bigger RV."

WE LEFT THE MEETING in a daze. We climbed in the old RV and crossed our fingers it would start. Cold Cuts turned the ignition. The engine sputtered to life. We all three cheered with pent-up excitement.

"Wahoo! Where to?" Cold Cuts asked. "We need to celebrate!"

She fiddled with the knob on the radio. A commercial was playing for Crazy Dazy RV Center. A woman who sounded on the edge of an orgasm pleaded for us to "not miss the greatest sale of the century!"

Cold Cuts grinned. "Shall we? Annie did agree we could use a new RV. It's a business write off."

Milly and I exchanged glances.

"Why the hell not."

ALL DOLLED UP AND ELATED from our meeting with Annie, we must have looked like manna from heaven to the hungry Crazy Daze salesman. We strolled up to the biggest RV I'd ever seen in my life.

"She's a real beaut, isn't she?" the salesman said, then rocked on his heels with pride.

"You talking to me?" Cold Cuts asked.

"Uh, yes," the man said, and put both feet on the ground. "The MegaFab 3800 is our latest model."

Cold Cuts turned her nose up. "I dunno. What's so special about it?"

"Is that your camper out front?"

Cold Cuts looked at me before she answered. "Maybe."

"You know, this is your lucky day. We're running a special. Today only, I can give you ten grand for your trade in."

Cold Cuts eyebrows raised an inch. "For *that* RV?"

"Any RV, any condition. But it's today only. By the way, my name's Ralph."

"How appropriate. He makes me want to hurl," I whispered to Milly. She shoved me on the shoulder.

"How much is *this* RV?" Cold Cuts asked.

"This beauty? She's on sale this week for just a hundred ninety-nine."

Cold Cuts blanched. Hell, we all did. "*Thousand? Dollars?*"

"Well, a hundred eighty-nine, with the trade in," Ralph said.

"That's like the price of a *house*," Milly said. "A *real* house."

Ralph pressed on, undaunted. "Well, ladies, the MegaFab 3800 *is* a real house. Without the property taxes and homeowner's insurance. The world's your oyster in a MegaFab 3800."

"Did he really just say, 'The world's your oyster?'" I asked.

"Yeah," Cold Cuts said. She shot me a wry grin. "If he says MegaFab 3800 one more time, I'm gonna MegaFab *him*."

Ralph showed us his bad dental work and opened the door to the huge RV. "Come on in, ladies. Take a look inside."

THE THREE OF US WERE sitting along the sucker side of a cheap desk in the Crazy Daze sales office. Ralph, our salesman, was on the other side. From a window, through the yellowed, plastic blinds, I could see Glad's RV baking in the parking lot in the glaring, late-afternoon sun. It looked tiny and feral and outcast among the big, shiny new RVs. I felt sorry for it.

"Gee, you girls drive a hard bargain." Ralph turned up the fake charm and pressure, hoping to close a deal. He wiped fake sweat from his brow with a handkerchief and stared at a sheet of paper onto which Cold Cuts had written an offer for the MegaFab 3800.

"I'm not sure I'm allowed to do this. I mean, at this price ladies, my commission won't even buy my wife and kids a bag of groceries."

*As fat as he was, a diet wouldn't hurt.*

I kept my mouth shut. Cold Cuts gave me a sideways look that assured me she wasn't buying his baloney. Milly smiled sappily. Like any good salesman, Ralph zeroed in on the most likely target. He winked at Milly.

"I tell you what. I like you girls, so I'm gonna go talk to my manager. See if he'll give me the go ahead to cut my own throat, so to speak."

Milly looked genuinely concerned as Ralph left. When he shut the door behind him, I suddenly felt as if I were trapped in a bad psycho killer movie.

"I'd like to cut his throat myself," Cold Cuts joked. "I hope that's part of the deal."

"Why?" Milly asked. "He seems nice. Besides, we should be excited. This whole thing should be...*a celebration*. We've hit the big time, remember?"

"But the guy's such a sleaze..."

The door cracked open. We were made privy to the end of a sentence Ralph didn't intend us to overhear.

"...a trio of real cash cows."

Milly's sympathetic expression dropped away like a bug sprayed with Raid.

Ralph strutted back into the office, followed by his manager. They smiled and tutted at us as if we were a trio of toddlers. Ralph's manager didn't recognize us. But Milly and I knew who *he* was in an instant. We elbowed each other discretely. The manager was none other than Annie Pantski's jerk-wad ex-boyfriend, haughty Harold. Milly's hard-nose expression calcified to stone.

The two sleazy salesmen stood and beamed at us—Ralph with his missing molars and Harold with his ridiculous capped teeth. The pair looked like a discount dentist's before-and-after photos.

"See?" Ralph said. "Didn't I tell you they were the most gorgeous customers we've ever had in here?"

"Wow! You're right, Ralph! I just might need to go get my sunglasses. They're dazzling!"

I thought I heard Cold Cuts wretch. But Harold appeared completely impervious to rejection.

"My best salesman here told me how I should hire you three," he chuckled. "You're quite the wheeler-dealers! Now, I can't let you have it at the price you suggested. A man's got to feed his family, after all."

Harold blessed us with another look at his fake teeth. When his smile went unreturned, I thought I saw his braggadocio skip a beat.

"Well, ladies. I do believe you drive a hard bargain," Harold said. "I tell you what. I can give you an extra thousand for your trade-in. I think that's mighty generous, considering its age."

Cold Cuts shrugged. "I guess we could think about it."

Harold smiled at her as if she were a simpleton. "I understand. But this is a one-time, today-only offer. Think of it. You're getting top-of-the-line luxury at a rock-bottom price. Besides, I'm not at all sure that sad little piece of scrap metal you drove in here with will be able to make it off the lot."

I saw Cold Cuts' hackles rise. If she hadn't been on the same page as Milly and me before, she was now.

"So, what do you ladies say? Ready to trade in that worn-out old gal for a brand-new, shiny one with all the latest bells and whistles?" Harold flashed the chicklet caps again and dangled a set of keys at us like we were kittens in a box. We stared at him blankly.

He cocked his head and raised his eyebrows. "Did I mention I'm allergic to the word 'no'?"

Cold Cuts got out her checkbook and a pen. I swear both men began to salivate. She grinned at me and Milly like an evil stepmother. She poised the pen over a check, then suddenly snapped the checkbook closed. She shoved it back in her purse as the two men nearly fell off their tippy-toes.

Cold Cuts stood up "You know, I think we'll pass."

"What?" Harold gasped. "I don't believe it!"

"Oh, come on, now, fellas," Cold Cuts said. "Men of your *obvious* charms have got to be used to getting turned down on a daily basis. Hourly, even."

I could almost see the dollar signs fall off the two men's eyes.

Harold scrambled, his bluff called. "Look. There's no problem here. Tell you what, we'll take your last offer. This is a done deal. I'll just go get the paperwork."

Cold Cuts motioned for us to stand. "I don't think so. Sorry, but you two just don't have *anything* that smart, sensible women like us would be interested in."

*Oh, snap!*

Milly and I got up, pointed our noses in the air and followed Cold Cuts out the office door. The two men followed behind us, prancing around as if they were about to piss their pants.

"Ladies!" Harold called after us. "Look, I'll throw in new floor mats."

Cold Cuts didn't even look back. "No thanks."

Harold's confident voice cracked. "Don't make a rash decision. You won't find a better deal."

Cold Cuts stopped in the middle of the showroom and turned to face Harold and Ralph. "We've seen plenty of better deals."

Harold treated us to the grand finale. He bowed, smiled like Uriah Heep, and said, "Okay, you win. Final offer. Free service for a year."

Cold Cuts marched over to the glass showroom door, opened it and stepped outside. I followed her out, then turned to give Milly a high-five. Milly was standing at the open door. She held her finger up for us to wait.

I tapped Cold Cuts on the shoulder. We both turned to watch as Milly put on her most innocent face and called to Annie's ex from halfway through the open door.

"Harold?" she said with thick Southern charm. He jumped to her side, re-inflated at the renewed possibility of making the sale.

She smiled sweetly and said, "Honey Boo Boo says, 'No-no.' Bye-bye!"

She let go of the door and waved goodbye as it slowly closed. Through the glass I watched Harold's capped teeth disappear behind his hanging, hound-dog lips.

# Chapter Thirty-One

When I got home, I called Tom with the good news.

"Tom! Annie loved our idea! We could be rich!"

"That's great, Val. But we've got each other. We already are."

My heart pinged and my nose grew hot. "Tom, sometimes you're so sappy it hurts."

"Hurts so *good?*"

"Yeah. Hurts so good."

"See you in an hour or so, Val."

"Okay."

"I love you."

"I...I love you, too, Tom."

I hung up the phone. My heart felt so much...*bigger*. I wanted to tell Laverne the news about Date Busters. Then the guys. But a sudden thought had me redial Tom.

"Do you mind if I invite Laverne and the guys over, Tom? I feel like celebrating."

"Sure, why not."

"Thanks. Bye.

"I love you, Val.

"Look, you're not going to make a habit of saying that, are you?"

"Yeah."

"You're such a jerk."

AS USUAL, LAVERNE WAS the first to arrive. She'd probably be the last to leave, as well. She came in carrying a present wrapped up in a big pink bow. She'd used the rest of the ribbon to fashion a hair accessory for herself. Surprisingly, it looked good in her strawberry blonde curls. She handed the box to me.

"What's this?" I asked.

"For you. You said on the phone it's a celebration. What are you celebrating, honey?"

"Lots of things. Laverne, Vance's sister Annie wants to take Date Busters nationally. We could be rich."

"That's nice."

"You don't seem that impressed."

"Well, money can't buy love."

I smiled. "I told him. Tom. That I loved him."

Laverne beamed. "That's wonderful, honey!" She wrapped her spidery arms around me. "What took you so long?"

"I was afraid. I thought I might say it because I was scared of being alone. Of dying in an alley, living in a cardboard box. Eating cat food, you know?

Laverne shook her head. "I've never known a girl as mixed up about her feelings as you, Val. Tell me. What would happen if Tom left you today? Or had a heart attack and died.

"I'd be devastated."

"Forever?"

I thought about it for a moment. "No. Not forever. Life would go on. I'm a realist."

"So there you have it," Laverne said.

"What are you saying? That I don't actually love Tom?"

Laverne laughed and hugged me again. "No, silly girl. You love him all right. But not because you *need* him. Because you *want* him. Big difference."

I hugged Laverne again and wiped the tears from my eyes. She smiled like a mother donkey, then laughed.

"Open your present," she said. "Before the others get here."

As I undid the wrapping, Laverne watched patiently.

"I felt bad you never found Glad's ashes," she said. "But don't forget, you've still got that dragonfly pendant. And this picture."

She held up my favorite picture of Glad. The one I thought was lost forever.

"Where did you find it?" I asked.

"I borrowed it. To make *that*." She nodded toward the box. I lifted the lid.

Inside was a little sculpture of an old woman in a one-piece bathing suit sprawled out on a pink lounge chair. Bug-eyed sunglasses adorned her face, along with a wide red-lipped grin.

"Laverne, this is...*good!*"

Laverne beamed. "My teacher helped."

I wiped more tears from my eyes and set Glad up on the mantle, next to the figurines of me, Laverne, Tom, Winky, Winnie, Jorge and Goober.

I smiled at my little ceramic clan and looked forward to their arrival, one by one.

# Chapter Thirty-Two

Milly was in my bathroom, primping for a date. She studied her reflection and crinkled her nose. "I hope Vance is nearsighted."

"Why?"

Milly pulled a pair of bifocals from her purse. "I used to think I looked good until I got these new glasses. Now I can't un-see what I really look like."

"Tell me about it."

"Enough with this, already!" Cold Cuts said. "You two are fine just the way you are. Now, are you two ready to go out and take on the world?"

The Date Busters line buzzed. Cold Cuts grabbed it.

"Hello? What? Who? You're kidding. Okay. Nothing irreversible. Darn. Okay. Yes, I'll let them know. Bye."

"What happened?" Milly asked.

"Did somebody's date go south?" I asked.

Cold Cuts shook her head. "No. Nothing like that. Well, I mean yes, something like that."

"What are you saying?" I asked.

"I guess, what I'm trying to say is...good thing we didn't buy that RV. That was Annie. Legal just informed her that we're getting sued. Someone's filed a complaint against Date Busters."

"Maybe Nora would help us," Milly said. "She's an attorney."

"I doubt it," Cold Cuts said dryly. "Nora's the one suing us."

Milly's mouth fell open. "What?"

"Apparently, she's dissatisfied with our services."

"Well, isn't that what malpractice insurance is for?" I asked.

"That's just it," Cold Cuts explained. "Annie's legal department shopped Date Busters for liability insurance. No one would touch it. Even Lloyds of London turned us down."

"What are you saying?" Milly asked.

"That we're out of business," Cold Cuts said.

"Geez! So what does that mean for us?" I asked.

"Clarity," Cold Cuts replied. "We've got the information we need to move on with our lives. We won't be millionaires today. But tomorrow is another day."

I WAVED GOODBYE TO Cold Cuts as she drove off in Glad's old RV. She'd offered to give it back to me, but I'd told her to keep it. She'd been right. Glad wasn't in there. I turned the tap on the tub and poured in some bath salts. Tom would be over soon. I smiled at the thought of seeing him—of being with him. I wasn't going to be a billionaire after all. I could use a pair of strong, loving arms to sink into. His would do nicely.

The phone rang. I shut the water off. It was Milly. A stitch of pain stabbed my heart. She'd been devastated at the news of Date Busters' demise, and of losing her job, *yet again*.

"Milly? Are you okay?"

"Yes! Oh my lord, Val, you won't believe it!"

"What? Tell me!"

"I just got off the phone with Mr. Maas. It turns out, Mrs. Barnes was doing crack in the parking lot!"

"Shut up!"

"Ha ha! I know, right? And it gets even crazier! Mr. Maas didn't order any drug test. Mrs. Barnes must have done it to prank us...or blackmail us for drug money or something. The thing is, she hadn't planned on us up and quitting over it! Poor old Mr. Maas called me in a panic. He wants me back, Val. He even offered me a raise, and a possible partnership!"

"That's amazing, Milly! I'm so happy for you!"

"Thanks. I knew you would be. And Val? He asked if I needed an assistant. Not a file flunkey, but a *real* assistant. Want a job?"

"Wow. Can I think about it?"

Milly laughed. "Sure, Miss Commitment. Hey, I've got to go. Vance is waiting. Talk soon!"

I CLIMBED INTO THE tub and thought about what a difference a day could make. And about how we all had our little secrets. Some were worth keeping. Some weren't. I picked up the phone and made one last call before Tom arrived.

Nora picked up the phone on the second ring.

"I want you to drop your suit against Date Busters," I said.

"Val? Why should I?" she said with contempt.

"I've got three words for you, Nora. 'It's a girl.'"

"You wouldn't!"

"I would."

ABOUT A MONTH AFTER Date Busters itself went bust, I was tooling along Gulf Boulevard in Maggie. The top was down and the sky was blue, and everything seemed right with the world. I stopped at a light and glanced over at the cake in the passenger seat beside me. It read: 'Congratulations, Jorge!' I was on my way to his house to meet the gang and celebrate his $40^{th}$ day of sobriety.

"Hey! Thought I recognized your car. How are you, Maggie?"

I looked up at the truck idling to my right. Hanging out the window was the cue-ball head of Lefty, the scrapyard guy. He flashed me a toothless smile.

"I'm doing fine, Lefty. How about you?"

"Never better. Hey, did you ever find that RV you was lookin' for?"

"Yes, thanks. But I never found the piggybank. That's what I was truly after."

Lefty scrunched his tiny eyebrows together. "Huh. It wasn't no Mr. Peanut bank, was it?"

My heart skipped a beat. "Yes, it was. What—"

The light turned green. The car behind me honked.

Lefty hollered out the window. "Hey Maggie, foller me."

My heart revved as I got in the lane behind Lefty's truck and followed him into a gas station.

"You got a minute to spare?" he asked as I drove up beside him. "I got somebody I want you to meet."

"Uh...I'm on my way to a party."

"It's just around the corner. Won't take a minute."

"Okay."

Lefty pulled out of the gas station and turned left at the next block. He took a right and pulled up to a little wooden house with a front yard full of flowers. I pulled in behind him.

The big hulk of a man got out of his truck and waved his huge hand at me. "This way," he said. I followed him as he limped through the grass along the side of the house to a fenced backyard. He opened the wooden gate and a small girl around five years old peeked out. She shot me a shy, impish grin.

"Y'all come on in," she said, and took a step back. She limped along the garden path just like lame-footed Lefty. I thought she was just mimicking him until I realized her left foot was artificial. The two stopped at a tiny, one-room garden cottage decked out with gingerbread trim. Surrounded by flowers, it looked like something from a magic storybook. When the two turned to face me, I couldn't help but think of a soft-hearted ogre and a tiny fairy princess.

"This here's Sarah," Lefty said. "She's a lefty, like me. He wiggled a fat-fingered hand through her light brown hair. "Ain't that right, Sarah." Sarah grinned and hid her face in Lefty's pant leg.

"Sarah, this here lady is the one what lost your friend, Peanut."

"Oh!" The girl's eyes lit up. She ran into the garden house, slowed down not a whit by her missing limb.

"It's congenital," Lefty said while she was away. "Missing her foot."

"Is she your daughter?"

Lefty shook his round, bald head. "Niece."

"Here he is," Sarah said. She held up the bank. Mr. Peanut's holographic monocle shifted to wink at me.

"Sarah found old Peanut here when her daddy Karl fixed the engine on that RV of yours. She's always finding stuff, ain't you?"

"Yessir. Peanut is my best friend," Sarah said.

The tiny girl looked up at me with beautiful, brown doe eyes. I wondered if her ears were pointed under that long, silky hair.

"He is?" I asked. "You know what, Sarah? Peanut is very wise. If you ask for advice, he'll help you see clear through to your own heart."

Sarah looked at the plastic piggybank in wonder. "Wow!"

"Sarah, what did you do with the sand that was inside Peanut?"

She looked confused for a second, then brightened. "You mean the magic fairy dust?"

"Yes. That's what I meant."

"Daddy helped me put it in the garden. We planted seeds in it. They came up real pretty. Wanna see?"

A needle of pain began to stitch in my heart. "Yes, please, show me."

Sarah grabbed Peanut tight and took me by the hand. She squealed with delight and tugged me along the garden path to a patch of brilliant, yellow daisies.

"Right there, where the golden flowers are," she pointed. "That's where we put the fairy dust."

"They're beautiful," I said, as the needle stitched away in my heart. But it was a good pain. As if the stitches were closing an old wound.

A green and purple dragonfly buzzed by me. I turned to Sarah and the insect landed on Peanut's top hat. The little girl giggled like water running over a brook.

"Look, it's an angel!" she laughed.

My throat tightened, forcing me to whisper. "Yes. An angel."

My fingers found the dragonfly pendant around my neck. As I touched it, the tiny iridescent creature flitted away into the clear blue sky.

"Goodbye, Glad" I whispered.

*I'm happy for you. Fly free.*

DEAR READER,

Thanks so much for continuing on with Three Dumb! I hope you enjoyed the book! It's a new take on the age old story of self-love versus romantic love. Where do you draw the line between honesty with yourself and with another?

Val's a middle-aged woman who enjoys her own company—at long last! But now it's suddenly in jeopardy because a man tells her he loves her. I wanted to explore the idea of a woman who finds love, but doesn't trust it. She's been fooled too many times before. Would she be able to let go and trust again? But beyond that, would she be able to stay true to herself? Boy, have I been there, done that!

If you'd like to know when my future novels come out, please subscribe to my newsletter. I won't sell your name or send too many notices to your inbox.

Newletter Link: https://dl.bookfunnel.com/fuw7rbfx21

Thanks again for reading Three Dumb. Sometimes life really can go off the rails! ;)

Sincerely,

Margaret Lashley

P.S. If you'd like to check out the next book in the series, What Four, I've included a sample for you in the back of this book. Or click here:

https://www.amazon.com/dp/B075FS6ZKZ

P.S.S. I live for reviews! The link to leave yours is right here:

https://www.amazon.com/dp/B074W8VBFN#customerReviews

P.S.S.S. (Sounds like something a snake would say!) If you'd like to contact me, you can reach me by:

Website: https://www.margaretlashley.com

Email: contact@margaretlashley.com

Facebook: https://www.facebook.com/valandpalspage/

# What's Next for Val?

*I hope you enjoyed Three Dumb! Click the link below now and leave a review. I read every single one!*

*https://www.amazon.com/dp/B074W8VBFN#customerReviews*

*Thank you so much! You rock!*

DON'T MISS ANOTHER new release! Follow me on Amazon and BookBub and you'll be notified of every new crazy Val adventure.

Follow me on Amazon:

https://www.amazon.com/-/e/B06XKJ3YD8

Follow me on BookBub:

https://www.bookbub.com/search/authors?search=Margaret%20Lashley

**Ready for more Val?**

*Where does Val go from here? Home for the holidays, of course. Ho Ho Oh-No!*

Enjoy the following excerpt from the next Val Fremden Mystery:

**What Four: Family Fruitcake Frenzy!**

# A Sneak Peek inside What Four!

## Chapter One

For folks who called the lower half of Florida home, the winter holidays always arrived without warning. There were no harbingers like frosty mornings or roasted chestnuts. Hell, there wasn't even a chilly breeze. Instead, like a malicious mugger, one day when we least expected it, Saint Nick ran up beside us, kicked us in the gut, and left us reeling with dread.

Or maybe it was just me.

THE LAST DAY OF NOVEMBER was one of those perfect, 80/80 days that made St. Petersburg the envy of every warm-blooded creature north of the state line. The sky was blue, the temperature was just under 80 degrees, and the humidity was below 80%. I couldn't have asked for more, except the time off work to enjoy it. Not one to play the odds, I opted for a sure-fire bet instead. I tugged on a bathing suit, turned off my phone, and played hooky from my job at Griffith & Maas.

I lolled away my AWOL morning at Sunset Beach, wading the shoreline and digging my toes into the sugar-white sand that held the Gulf of Mexico's gentle surf at bay. The shell gods were kind. I found a beautiful left-handed whelk in the surf—a rare oddity, just like my beach-combing days of late. December was less than 24 hours away, yet it took barely an hour for the morning sun to tinge my shoulders pink.

I heeded the warning signs of the lobster-hued tourists around me and decided to pack it in for the day.

I felt smug, like an uncaught thief, as I slipped through the picket fence encircling the sandy parking lot of Caddy's beach bar. When I'd been flat broke last year, I'd found out the lot attendant didn't arrive until 8 a.m. to start collecting the five-dollar daily parking fee. Since then, I'd made a point to get there early, just as I had today. I grinned at the young man guarding the entryway. He tipped his baseball cap at me, then turned to take the money from the outstretched hand of a young woman in a black jeep. I smiled to myself. Five bucks could buy a lot of tonic for my Tanqueray.

The top was down on Maggie, my vintage 1963 Ford Falcon Sprint. I tested the red pleather upholstery with a fingertip. It was hot enough to sizzle my porky thighs. I lay a beach towel over the bucket seat and tugged a sundress over my bathing suit. I climbed in, set my hands on the steering wheel, straightened my shoulders and smiled.

*Ahh! The sun, the sea and a stolen day to myself. What could make this day any better?*

Only one thing came to mind.

I turned the ignition key and mashed the gas until the twin-glass-pack muffler rumbled like thunder. As I rolled slowly out of the parking lot, I waved to the sneering attendant, took a deep breath of salt air, and turned left to make my way toward Gulf Boulevard. The four-lane road saddled a thin split of land that jutted out into the Gulf like a bratty kid's tongue. After passing a string of pastel-hued, low-slung mom-and-pop hotels and junky-looking souvenir shops, I hung a right on Central Avenue and cruised toward downtown and the home of my favorite guilty pleasure, Chocolateers.

Chocolate pusher-man Jack was there to greet me when I walked into the shop.

"The usual?" he asked.

"Yes."

I slid a wilted five-dollar bill across the glass candy counter at him. Jack eyed it skeptically, then handed me a paper napkin containing two dark-brown lumps the size of ping-pong balls. He took a step back and cringed in knowing anticipation of what came next.

I crammed both beautiful, hand-dipped chocolate-covered cherries into my mouth, bit down and grinned like that creepy person in a horror flick that you know is up to no good.

*Yes. All was right in my little world.*

I TURNED MY PHONE BACK on. The clock registered 11 a.m. as I left Chocolateers. I still had some time to kill before lunch, so I decided to take a pleasure drive along the downtown waterfront district. I was idling at the corner of 4th Avenue and Beach Drive when I got nailed. I never saw it coming.

I stared, slack jawed, at about a dozen guys clad in shorts and sweat-stained-shirts. They toiled away like ants on an open stretch of green grass in Straub Park. Working together, they assembled the huge, metal ribcage of a forty-foot-tall artificial Christmas tree.

It may as well have been a forty-foot tall effigy of my mother's disapproving face.

A chill ran down my spine that had nothing to do with the weather. Soon I'd be obliged to keep a promise I'd made months ago in a moment of sniveling weakness. I'd have to go visit my mother for the holidays.

A horn honked behind me. I made a hasty left onto Beach Drive. An old, familiar knot gripped my stomach. Its name was Lucille Jolly. Lucille was my adoptive mother—a fact I'd discovered less than two years ago. Up until then, I thought she'd been the real thing. I had to confess, as shocked as I'd been when I'd found out Lucille wasn't my biological mother, the news had left me feeling somehow *relieved.* It meant I hadn't come from her gene pool.

I supposed everyone had a love-hate relationship with their mother. Since I'd only known Glad Goldrich, my true mother, for six weeks before she'd died, we'd never gotten around to the hate part. But on *that* score, Lucille and I'd had nearly fifty years of dutiful practice.

My brain turned to mush, my arms to lead. I drove slowly and aimlessly along North Shore Boulevard, as if I'd suddenly run out of gas. Tampa Bay was to my left. Sunlight danced a billion bright diamonds on the wide expanse of water. Vinoy Park was to my right. Huge oaks canopied over wooden benches and scattered flowerbeds bursting with red and white blooms. But all I could see was doom. I pulled into a parking spot and sighed.

The mere thought of having to spend time with Lucille Jolly drained me like a used-up battery. The woman knew all my buttons and how to push them. Hell, she should've. She'd pretty much installed every one of them. Like a snowball in Florida, I didn't have a chance in hell against her mysterious ability to instantly vaporize my self-esteem.

My cellphone rang, startling me out of my melancholy malaise. I looked at the screen. It was my cop boyfriend, Tom.

"Hey you!" he said cheerily. "What 'cha doing?"

"Thinking of running away and joining the circus."

He laughed. "Sorry, Val. You're not weird enough."

"Tell that to Lucille."

"Uh-oh. Already getting antsy about the trip?"

"How'd you guess?"

"Val, it's just for a few days. Family is family. You're stuck with them, whether you like it or not."

"Don't remind me."

"Hey. I'm going with you. It'll be fun."

I smiled cynically. Even though Tom had already met my mother, it was a pretty brief encounter. He'd never made the acquaintance of my other relatives. This fact had not been unintentional on my part. My family was a Croker sack full of crazy. At the best of times, they were comically tolerable—in very small doses. But the holidays were different. Christmas was to the Jolly clan what a full moon was to a pack of werewolves. Tom had no idea of the level of lunacy he was getting himself into.

I blew out a jaded puff of air.

"Yeah, sure Tom. It's gonna be a blast."

## Chapter Two

As I crammed my toes into my work heels on Friday morning, I realized I'd fallen back into an old, robotic routine I'd thought was a thing of the past. Ten years ago, I'd had a thriving copy-writing business, aka a steady job. Then I'd freaked out, certain that I'd become nothing more than a cog in a machine. My mid-life crises culminated in me ditching my entire life and running off to Europe. I'd ended up spending seven years in Germany as an ex-pat wife and house renovator. When that fell apart three years ago, I'd returned to St. Pete as an estranged ex-wife in dire need of renovation myself.

I caught a glimpse of myself in the mirror. There I was, methodically preparing for a day at the office just like I used to—as if the entire last decade had never happened. *Maybe getting ready for work was like riding a bicycle. Once you had it down, you never forgot.*

But I didn't want to remember. Not if it meant becoming a mindless, dreary robot again. I shook my head as if to clear away the cobwebs inside it. *I couldn't allow that to happen. If I did... good grief! It would mean I'd wasted my entire forties!*

The fear that I'd once again lose myself to my job was the *real* reason I'd played hooky yesterday. I'd needed to shake myself up before I'd gotten hopelessly mired in that insidious, hypnotic, nine-to-five maze again. *Lord knows I don't have another spare decade to squander!*

I checked my hair in the bathroom mirror and laughed at myself. *Look at you and your little rage against the man. You're such a rebel, Val.*

*Yeah, right.*

I found my car keys and grabbed my purse. *Who was I kidding? I needed this job more than this job needed me.* As I headed out the door, I suddenly remembered something. I walked back into the kitchen, opened the cupboard and grabbed a bottle of rum.

It was amazing what an inheritance could do to ruin a person's ambition....

# About the Author

Like the characters in my novels, I haven't lead a life of wealth or luxury. In fact, as it stands now, I'm set to inherit a half-eaten jar of Cheez Whiz...if my siblings don't beat me to it.

During my illustrious career, I've been a roller-skating waitress, an actuarial assistant, an advertising copy writer, a real estate agent, a house flipper, an organic farmer, and a traveling vagabond/truth seeker. But no matter where I've gone or what I've done, I've always felt like a weirdo.

I've learned a heck of a lot in my life. But getting to know myself has been my greatest journey. Today, I know I'm smart. I'm direct. I'm jaded. I'm hopeful. I'm funny. I'm fierce. I'm a pushover. And I have a laugh that makes strangers come up and want to join in the fun. In other words, I'm a jumble of opposing talents and flaws and emotions. And it's all good.

In some ways, I'm a lot like Val Fremden. My books featuring Val are not autobiographical, but what comes out of her mouth was first formed in my mind, and sometimes the parallels are undeniable. I drink TNTs. I had a car like Shabby Maggie. And I've started my life over four times, driving away with whatever earthly possessions fit in my car. And, perhaps most importantly, I've learned that friends come from unexpected places.

Made in the USA
Columbia, SC
12 February 2024

3b1df4e2-2b67-4a28-ae0a-3144250c6b2fR01